Contents

Wanted: Three Smoldering Western Romances

Three stories of love, loss, and redemption in the American West.

Acknowledgment
To our BFF, Callie Hutton. We love you, girl.
Write on!

RODEO KING

by
CiCi Cordelia

Caleb Johnson, the "King of the Rodeo," is on the fast track to becoming Wyoming's next national champion—until a bull leaves him with a potentially career-ending injury.

Forced to return home to Dustin to recover, Caleb comes face-to-face with Rosemary Carmichael, the woman he left behind when he chased rodeo glory.

But Rosemary isn't the only surprise waiting for him.

Now Caleb must decide what matters most—returning to the rodeo circuit and the championship he's always wanted—or fighting for a future with the woman he loves and the son he never knew existed.

Chapter One

Caleb carefully stood, trying not to put too much pressure on his aching leg. He tipped his well-worn Stetson to the young girl sitting with her grandmother in the seat across from him.

"It's been a pleasure, ma'am," he said solemnly.

The little cutie had talked his ear off the entire way to Dustin, Wyoming; all seven hours. Her sweet chatter helped keep him from dwelling on his potentially career-ending fall as a professional bull rider, and the two months of rehabilitation afterward.

Now the memory pushed to the forefront, and locking his jaw he stepped off the bus and shoved down the anger that still roared hot and bright inside him.

Crawling home with my tail between my legs.

How the mighty had fallen. From King of the Rodeo to washed up cowboy by the age of twenty-eight.

He glanced up and down Main Street, lit only by streetlights and the signs from nearby businesses as night settled in, and wondered if Rosemary still lived here. He hadn't heard that she'd moved or anything. His heart thudded hard against his ribs at the thought of seeing her again.

He'd taken notice of her when she was fourteen and budding into womanhood. She'd been a sweet little thing, with a kind heart and a quick smile. And she'd had a crush on him. But being three years younger, as well as his buddy's baby sister, and knowing Mason would kick his ass if he touched her, Caleb had kept his distance.

Then, as her body filled out, Rosemary Carmichael had every cowboy in town salivating for a taste. Jealousy had eaten at him, but he'd been determined not to give in to his desire for her, already knowing he'd be leaving town for bigger things.

At twenty, so cocksure of himself, he'd headed out of town to find fame as a bull rider. And he'd been doing just fine until three years later, during a break from the rodeo circuit, he'd come home for a visit and ended up taking Rosemary to bed. He knew it wasn't a smart move on his part. But he'd wanted her like a starving man wanted a nice juicy steak.

And like a bastard, he'd seduced her, even knowing she wasn't some buckle bunny he could just screw and walk away from.

At least not with a clear conscience.

Images of Rosemary in his bed, naked and trembling with desire as he'd introduced her to the pleasures of sex, flashed across his mind. Barely nineteen, she'd been the hottest girl in town, with a bold attitude for life and huge amber eyes that turned molten gold when she came.

How in the hell was I supposed to know she was a virgin?

Caleb's body tightened even as guilt filtered through him, like it always did when he thought about Rosemary, and their short time together. He swallowed hard, remembering the way her fiery red hair hung loose around her slender shoulders, the sexy sway of her perfect breasts as she sat astride him. She'd been a quick study, and during the week he'd held her in his arms, Caleb had been tempted to stay, whispering sweet promises in her ear.

Then reality set in, and the fact that he even wanted to stay and give up his dreams scared the mother lovin' shit out of him. And like a thief in the night, he'd left without so much as a kiss goodbye.

Even now, six years later, guilt burned through him with the destruction of a blowtorch.

And he still wanted her. Had wanted her since the day he left, never able to completely shut her out of his mind.

"Caleb Johnson, is that you?" a woman's voice called out.

He turned to see Charlotte MacDonald crossing the dusty street with her husband, Mac. Even in the dim lighting, Caleb spotted the look of disapproval on the older woman's face as she and Mac headed his way.

Damn. He'd just gotten off the bus. What could have her panties in a bunch already?

Caleb set his suitcase down and tipped his hat. "Hello, ma'am. Mac."

"Hi, Caleb." Mac was smiling as they neared. "What's brought you back our way?"

Charlotte waved a finger under his nose before he could answer. "It's about time, young man. You should be ashamed of yourself, running off that way!"

Running off? His brows arched. Had Rosemary told folks what happened between them? Yeah, it'd been a crappy thing to do, but the Rosemary he remembered wasn't the type to blast her personal life to any of Dustin's town gossips.

Before he could respond, Mac cut in. "Now, Charlotte, leave the boy be." He offered an apologetic shrug and took his wife's hand, tugging her away. "Glad you're back, Caleb. I think you'll find some things have changed since you left." Mac's soft chuckle followed in his wake as he swept his wife down the street. Charlotte managed to shoot Caleb one more glare over her shoulder before they disappeared around the corner.

What the hell was that about?

He shook his head, reaching down to rub his throbbing leg. The doctors told him he'd get full mobility back, but it was too soon to tell if he'd ever be able to ride again. Caleb was still mulling that over, wondering what he'd do if the worst happened and his career was over before ever really getting started. He loved bull riding, and eight years wasn't nearly long enough. He wasn't sure he could give it up.

Would I really have a choice?

Caleb flicked a glance toward the Bronco Inn, two blocks down from the bus station. Since his folks had moved away shortly after he'd graduated high school, a temporary place to stay was first on his agenda. He'd grab some food, then get a room for the night and start apartment hunting. He'd managed to save up a considerable nest egg, enough to tide him over for a while.

Even though he was loath to admit it, he knew the reason he'd chosen to come back to Dustin was because of Rosemary. They had unfinished business. She was like a burr under his saddle he couldn't dislodge. Maybe if he had another taste or two of her, he could get her out of his system and move on.

Maybe.

He just hoped she was still here.

As he walked down the mostly deserted streets, everyone inside drinking, having dinner, or shopping, with a few stragglers wandering about, he glanced at his watch. Six-thirty. There'd be time to catch a bite and a beer before grabbing a room. He might look up Mason. Word was his old buddy still lived here, and had the veterinary clinic he'd always dreamed of.

Good for him.

A tight knot curled in Caleb's gut. He should have kept in contact with Mason, but he'd let their friendship fall away after sleeping with the man's sister. He raked his fingers through his hair and blew out a strained breath.

When did I become such a bastard? But he knew. It was the moment he'd slipped from Rosemary's bed and hightailed it out of town.

Now in serious need of a drink, Caleb hoofed it down the street, albeit at a slow pace, toward the local brewpub. It was a warm, muggy evening and his shirt stuck to his back as he approached the pub. He licked his dry lips, eager to taste the cold brew. As he headed up the sidewalk, a door flew open a few buildings from the pub, and a man stepped out, calling his name.

Caleb turned slightly and recognized Mason standing just outside the door under a sign lettered with 'Mason's Veterinary Service.'

He set his suitcase down again. "Damn, Carmichael," he said, grinning, "how the hell are you, man?"

Mason's expression darkened ominously and Caleb lost his smile.

Well, I guess that answers that question.

When Mason came toward him with murder in the tense lines of his body, Caleb didn't even try to defend himself as the man brought his fist back and swung at him. He deserved the beat-down he was about to take. It wasn't a glancing blow and pain radiated through his jaw as he fell onto his ass. His Stetson flew off his head and landed on the sidewalk.

He stared up at his former friend as he fingered his jaw, rotating it to see if it was broken. It wasn't. Not yet, anyway. "Feel better?"

Mason stormed toward him, reaching down to grip the front of his shirt, and jerked him to his feet. The movement sent fire shooting through Caleb's leg and he gritted his teeth against the pain.

"Not by a long shot, you son of a bitch." Mason reared back to punch him again.

Caleb narrowed his eyes, but didn't fight back, although anger bent the edges of his control. He'd let Mason get in a few more punches before he defended himself. It was the least he could do after sleeping with his pal's baby sister.

But Caleb's patience only went so far . . .

"Mason. Stop!" The feminine voice shot across the semi-darkness and both men froze.

Mason glared at him. "You have no goddamn idea what you did, do you, asshole?"

Caleb couldn't help it as images of making love to Rosemary flooded his mind. He chuckled. "I've got a pretty good idea."

Yep. He really did deserve the next punch Mason threw his way, reconnecting with his aching jaw and sending him back a few feet, though he managed to remain standing. The force of the blow made him bite hard on the inside of his cheek.

"Mason, no!" Rosemary rushed toward them.

A different woman's voice called from the same direction. "Hit him harder next time, Mason."

Caleb spat blood. "Are we done?"

"Not even close," Mason growled.

Rosemary grabbed her brother's arm and tugged. "Mason, don't, damn it."

Caleb shifted his gaze to Rosemary, and every muscle in his body seized along with his breath, as she flipped her long, wavy hair over one shoulder. She was even more beautiful than he remembered. He wanted to bury his hands in those thick red locks and take her sweet mouth in a kiss. Her heart-shaped face held a healthy freshness, her full lips rosy, but her figure now fully a woman's, generously curved in all the right places.

Perfection.

His body responded to her lush beauty, just like it always had, and he was thankful for the dim light as he shifted slightly to relieve the pressure under his button fly.

Another woman he recognized from high school had come up behind her, but he couldn't recall her name. A little boy held her hand, his small frame tucked against her leg.

Regret filled him. They were fighting in front of a kid. He turned back to Rosemary, ignoring her brother completely. "Hi," he said softly, his heart pounding fast.

Her mouth tightened. She didn't act happy to see him, and rather than return his greeting, she glanced up at her brother. "Let's just go."

Go? Hell, no! Caleb didn't want her to leave, he just wanted to stare at her a little longer. She was like candy to his soul and he was starving for her. By the hard expression on her face, she didn't want a damn thing to do with him.

And who could blame her?

Dickhead! What had he been thinking, walking away from this woman?

Mason's posture relaxed as he glanced over to the woman and little boy. *His kid?* Caleb hadn't heard about Rosemary's brother getting hitched or anything.

"Mommy, can we go home now?" the boy asked in a soft voice.

"In a moment, sweetheart," Rosemary replied gently.

Caleb's world went black, and for a moment he couldn't breathe as his legs shook beneath him, the implication of what just happened like a crowbar to the kneecaps.

He turned toward the little boy, peeking out from behind the woman who still held his hand. Inhaling sharply, Caleb stared into eyes that mirrored his own, a child wearing his face and shocking red hair like his mother's.

His son.

Chapter Two

With a soft, despairing moan, Rosemary Carmichael
registered pain she'd thought long buried. Those hot green
eyes hadn't changed a bit, and they were focused on
Carson. Her innocent baby, who looked far too much like
his daddy despite the red hair he'd inherited from her.

She'd been young, in love, and stupid as well, to think
Caleb Johnson would ever settle down in a two-bit place
like Dustin. He'd been too talented and already too well-
known, riding bulls like nobody's business and winning
every local and then state championship the Wyoming
rodeo circuit could offer. But God, she'd wanted him. And
she'd had him for one short, soul-destroying week.

Hungrily, she drank him in from the top of his tangled,
dark blond hair to the tarnished tips of his battered Dan
Posts. A pair of faded-out Levi's rode low on lean hips she
could recall gripping in the throes of a passion that could
still break her out in a sweat to think on, all these years
later. His denim shirt was just as faded, creased from travel,
the sleeves rolled up to his elbows. The pale blue fabric
strained against the breadth of his shoulders and whipcord
muscles she knew he'd honed during years on the pro rodeo
circuit. He looked bigger, more powerful, more
intimidating. Sexier than hell.

Yet she wanted to slap the shock right off his darkly
tanned face; wanted to scoop up her child and run a
thousand miles away. Until she couldn't see the way his
full lips had begun to form the question she sure as shit
didn't want to answer—

"Mine?" The rough gravel in his voice made her
swallow nervously, which got her anger cooking at the guilt
trying to rear up and smother her.

I've got nothing to be guilty about. Rosemary jerked
her chin high, her lips pursed in annoyance. "Mine."

Caleb's jaw clenched. One wide, long-fingered hand reached for his stained hat and he slapped it against his leg before dropping it back on his head.

Damn it, nobody in the world had the right to look that sinful in a black, worn-down Stetson. The instant she thought it, Rosemary squelched it. She wasn't nineteen any longer.

"Tell me whose boy this is." Caleb obviously wasn't going to back down, which she knew would piss her brother off.

Sure enough, Mason reacted predictably, stepping close to Caleb and bumping boot-tips with him. The similarities between her brother and the man she'd given everything to almost brought a smile to her face. Both of them handsome, tough, tall, broad. Intimidating. And best friends no longer. *My fault.* The words hovered, fueling fresh heartache.

As Carson huddled closer to Susan Lewis, honorary aunt and Rosemary's best friend since first grade, Mason's lip curled in his customary sneer. "None of your business. You lost those kinds of rights when you took off." He leaned in, lifted a hand and flicked at Caleb's Stetson, deliberately knocking it off. It spun once and landed back on the ground, brim-up.

Caleb's face darkened. "You son of a—"

"Susie-Q, take Carson home, okay?" Rosemary broke in as calmly as possible, certain Susan's temper could blow at any second. Her hair might not be red, but when she went into 'aunty' mode, nobody was more protective.

For a second she thought Susan would explode anyway, because she had that look in her pale blue eyes that usually meant her claws were out and ready to shred skin. But her arm curled closer around Carson's small, sturdy body and she nodded, sending jet-black corkscrew curls sliding over one shoulder.

"Come on, Lil' Tuff." She gently led him away, Carson turning with a gap-toothed grin and one hand waving in Rosemary's direction. Off they skipped, her boy's high, sweet chatter floating on the air along with Susan's deeper chuckle.

Blinking back a sudden sting of tears, Rosemary turned, and met Caleb's piercing stare. A feeling of unease swept over her.

"Carson. You named him after my granddad." It wasn't a question.

She fought the need to slump in defeat, instead stiffening her spine. "Mason, can you take off for a bit? I need—I need to talk to Caleb." She shot her brother a 'don't-say-anything-more' look.

He visibly bristled. "Not smart, Rosie." He folded his arms across his chest and loomed close, overprotective as usual.

"I've got things I need to say, Mason. It'll be all right," she assured him. "Come on. Give me a little breathing room. You can be the big bro tomorrow." Her gaze locked with his, eyes the same deep amber as hers.

Mason huffed in anger and turned to face down Caleb, who'd collected his hat off the ground and was brushing dirt off the crown. "If you make her cry, I'll make you suffer." Both hands fisted, he stomped off to catch up with Susan and Carson.

His expression visibly bleak, Caleb watched as Mason took Carson's other hand and walked away, her son gleefully jumping and swinging between two of his favorite people.

Rosemary swallowed the choking lump of emotion lodged in her throat and gestured toward one of the wooden benches the Chamber of Commerce had installed around Dustin a few years back. "Okay, ask your questions." She perched on the edge, ready to jump and run, uncomfortable at the thought of sharing a seat with him.

But Caleb remained standing, shoving his hands in his back pockets. For a moment he stared off down the street, before turning and pinning her in place with a narrow gaze. "I want to know why you never told me."

She hunched a shoulder in a defensive shrug. "Nobody knew where you were."

"That's bullshit! Uncle Zip knew. I asked him to tell your daddy."

"Zip left town about three days after you did, Caleb." She gestured wearily. "And my daddy told me nothing. After he moved to Cody, Mama lost touch, probably on purpose. You know they only stayed together for Mason and me."

The words coated her tongue with bitterness, forcing her to recall how her folks fought, in public as well as in private. "The day after you left, Daddy punched out Zip and accused him of trying to romance my mama. Zip laughed in his face and took off. Then Daddy and Mama started really fighting, and it never got any better. He skipped town before Carson was born, and ended up in Cody. He's got the John Deere franchise up there. Seems happy, but he's only seen Carson a few times over the years. And that's fine by me."

"You could have found out where I was, easily enough," Caleb began, but she cut him off.

"I woke up and you were gone. For God's sake, you left in the middle of the night like you were ashamed of me! No email address . . . I wrote you several times and sent the letters out General Delivery to the State Rodeo Commission. They came back, 'addressee unknown.' Once you started making it big on the circuit, I searched the internet a few times for whatever I could find on you. But I gave up on that, too. As far as I was concerned, we were done."

Her temples had started to throb with an oncoming headache. The pain made her cranky as hell, and Rosemary found she'd reached the end of her patience. She snapped, "You didn't leave me a thing. Not a note, not a phone number. Nothing. Just a clump of cowshit on the carpet from those damned rands you liked to wear." She jerked a thumb at the scarred-up silver trim on his boot heels. "I see you still wear them."

"Don't change the subject." His voice had risen, attracting attention from a few folks wandering in and out of the brewpub.

She stifled a sigh. The town had been nosy ever since she could remember, and trying to keep a secret was as much a wasted effort now as it'd been years ago when she first peed on a pregnancy stick and burst into tears when two blue lines appeared. Within a few months everyone in Dustin knew she was carrying Caleb Johnson's baby, including her furious daddy and sad-eyed, disappointed mama. Time had made some things better, and other things worse.

"Look," she reasoned, "there isn't a thing I can do about what happened years ago. You screwed me senseless for a week and then you left—"

"Stop talking like that!" he protested. "What we had meant more than a week of screwing around."

"No. It didn't. I stopped kidding myself a long time ago, Caleb. Around the same time I found out how much it cost to raise a baby." She pressed chilled fingers to her temples. "Mama didn't really forgive me for months, and Daddy never got over it. All he could see was the way history repeated itself, that I'd done the same thing as Mama, upped and got myself pregnant. Difference was, Mama made my daddy come home and marry her, so Mason would be legitimate. I found out real fast how hard it is being a single parent." She shook her head. "I don't know what I would have done without Mason to help me get on my feet."

"Damn it, I would never have abandoned my son," Caleb growled, stepping closer to the bench.

Rosemary quaked with fresh anger, but held herself steady. "I'm not saying that, you dumb cowboy. I've got a good job at the credit union and a place of my own, so I'm supporting him just fine. I even make Mama accept a little babysitting money whenever she takes him while I'm at work. I've got a savings account building up and Carson's happy. It's all that matters." She dropped into a low, serious rasp. "*He's* all that matters."

She jumped off the bench before Caleb could react to her words. Rosemary pushed her heavy hair out of her face and took little satisfaction at the way Caleb watched her, as if starved for her. It made no difference, because he wouldn't stay. She'd spotted how he favored his leg, and figured an injury had sidelined him. But he'd be gone again as soon as his leg mended. Rodeo was in his blood. In his soul. There wasn't room for anything else, and she'd been an idiot once to imagine she could change him.

She'd grown up a hell of a lot since then.

"I have to go. It's Carson's bedtime soon and he'll want a story." She turned away, but Caleb grabbed her arm.

"I want to get to know him."

Yanking her arm from his grasp, Rosemary spun and shoved a hard finger in his chest. "He has a name. And you have no rights, other than being a sperm donor. You gave up those rights when you snuck out of my bed after popping my cherry. Hell, Caleb, I didn't even warrant a goodbye. Just 'slam, bam, thank you ma'am,' then you were gone. How do you think that made me feel?"

She darted past him, and this time Caleb made no move to stop her. When she glanced back, he stood there like a chunk of stone, and from the short distance between them she could read stark misery on his handsome face. It would have broken her heart if she'd had anything left to break. But what she'd felt inside for him had been sliced into pieces a long time ago.

"Rosie."

Hearing her childhood nickname on Caleb's lips did an emotional number on her, but she schooled her face to utter calm as she spun back around on a boot heel. "What, Caleb?"

"I'm . . ." He paused and rubbed his hand over his jaw. "Hell. I'm sorry. I really want to get to know my son. Please, Rosemary. I just want to be around him a little."

The tears she'd held back all evening spilled down her cheeks, but she wouldn't wipe them away. Rosemary stood tall and replied hoarsely, "I need to think on it some, all right? Just let me—let me think."

She didn't want to act like a selfish bitch. She sure as hell didn't want to hold anything over Caleb's head the way her mama had done to Daddy. She and Mason had grown up in a shaky, uncertain household, privy to hourly bickering, daily arguments and the kind of knock-down-drag-outs no kid should have to endure. All because their father had felt trapped in a loveless marriage, and their mother had tried to hold on to her husband with guilt and duty. To this day Mason had a strong aversion to a serious commitment, and Rosemary would probably go to her grave unsure of whether her birth had been an attempt at reconciliation or just another accidental pregnancy.

What kind of life was that for a little kid?

No way. She'd never do that. For the sake of her son she'd pulled herself together, mended the broken bits, and given all of them to Carson.

Unable to stand there much longer and not break down completely, she fled.

She had nothing left for the King of the Rodeo.

Chapter Three

Stepping up to the Bronco Inn's registration desk, Caleb dinged the little bell sitting on the counter. After a minute or so, the pocket door separating the lobby from what was the living quarters of the owners slid back as Nash Gardner stepped out, wiping his mouth on a handkerchief.

"Hey, Nash." Caleb nodded to him.

"Johnson." Nash tossed the handkerchief aside. "What can I do you for?"

Nash had been a couple of grades ahead of him in school, raised on state welfare. Caleb was impressed at how the guy had dug himself out from the crap side of town and bought The Bronco Inn.

Caleb leaned his elbows on the glass-covered counter. Nash had made a decent motel out of a mere skeleton, no mean feat. While the rooms wouldn't win any awards, they were clean and reasonable, with comfortable beds and showers that didn't smell like mildew. But after only two days, Caleb was already feeling claustrophobic and needed a bigger place. "That apartment complex over on Dart still up and running?"

Nash scratched at his goatee. "Far as I know." He pondered for a moment, staring at Caleb. "How long you thinkin' of hanging around? I got a bigger room set up as a studio. Full bath. Living room. Even got a kitchenette with a stove and a decent sized fridge. More than enough for one person. I rent it by the week or month. It's empty right now. I can show you."

"Yeah?" Caleb's interest was piqued by a month-to-month agreement. Most apartment leases tried to lock you into six months, minimum. Hell, he didn't have a clue what might happen, between his healing leg and the question of going back on the circuit. Not to mention Rosemary. *And the boy.*

Nash opened a drawer and extracted a key with an oblong room number tag attached. He slid it across the counter. "Tell you what. My food's getting cold and I want to finish eating. Go take a look for yourself. All the way to the end. Number Fourteen. I can give you a weekly deal to start." He named a figure that was only a few bucks higher than what Caleb had paid on Room Five for the last few nights, total.

"Okay, I will. Thanks, buddy." Caleb crossed to the door.

"Wait a sec." Nash called him back. When Caleb turned, Nash was holding up another set of keys. "If you're gonna stay more'n a week or two, I got a truck you can borrow now and then. It's kind of beat up but it runs good. That little red Dodge on the back lot." He jerked his chin toward a side exit. "I don't need it and you know a truck's gotta be driven or else the engine ends up choked. Just keep it filled with gas and we're square." He hung the set of keys in a wall cabinet that had a small press-button lock. "Combo's three-six-ten-five."

"Nash, that's really generous, but I—"

"Use it when you need it, Johnson." Nash regarded him soberly. "You helped me out some, years ago. Loaned me money a couple of times and never asked for nothing back. I'm glad to return the favor." He cocked his head to the side and gestured toward Caleb's face with a sudden grin. "That jaw's lookin' better. Nice and yellow instead of black and blue."

"Kiss my ass, Gardner."

Nash rasped out a guffaw, then nodded sharply. "Got to finish my meal. Let me know if you want the studio." He disappeared behind the pocket door, sliding it shut behind him.

Caleb stood for a few seconds, undecided. He hated being beholden to anyone, but Nash's offer of a vehicle was too good to pass up. Dustin was small enough that he could walk just about anywhere he needed, even on a bum leg. Still, the truck would come in handy once in a while.

Heading out the front door, he sought out Fourteen. The two-room unit wasn't grand, but it was spotlessly clean and functional. He could relax in here and map out his time in Dustin. Figure out what to do about Rosemary. She'd been avoiding him the last couple days and he'd let her, not yet ready to face her.

His plan had been simple when he'd decided to return. A short-term lease, something he could get out of when his leg was healed enough to climb back onto a bucking bull. It was supposed to be easy. Check into town, see if Rosemary was still around, then head back out to the circuit when the time was right. Maybe even taking her along for the ride if things worked out.

Staring into the eyes of his son had thrown that out the window.

Caleb crossed to the door and stepped outside, resigned to taking the studio. The weekly rent sure wouldn't break him, and he'd be able to spread out some. At least enough until he figured out what the hell he was going to do now.

An hour later he'd moved his stuff over from the other room and shoved a few things into the highboy drawers; hung up some shirts. A fast shower and shave made him feel more human, and he relaxed on the loveseat with a cold longneck in one hand and the TV remote in the other, flipping through channels.

The world was still in chaos, the local cops were trying to find the kids who scrawled curse words on the school building, and the weather was cool, but seasonal.

And he was a father. If that didn't just blow his ever-lovin' mind!

"A son." He said the word aloud, trying to wrap his head around it. *Carson.* The same as his grandfather. Even after the way he'd acted, Rosemary had thought about him when she named their son. That had to mean something . . .

A loud growl from his stomach reminded him he hadn't eaten in hours. What he needed now was a burger and another beer. Caleb slapped his hat on his head, pocketed the room key, and headed out.

Five minutes later, he pushed open the door to DeeDee's, the first sense of true welcome to hit him since he'd gotten off the bus two days ago. He hardly counted Mason Carmichael's punch to his face a welcome.

He headed straight to the bar area and grabbed a table, then gestured to the burly bartender, busy polishing glasses. "Hey, Mikey, get me a Bud."

"That you, Johnson?" Mikey offered a huge grin. "'Bout time you decided to drop by. I thought you was knocking 'em dead on the rodeo circuit. What the hell you doin' back here in this shithole?"

"Ain't nothin' like a warm welcome, huh, Caleb?" The deep, sexy voice of Evelyn, Mikey's wife, washed over him like warm water.

Caleb nodded in the woman's direction. Perched on a bar stool, she was still slender, her age slowly catching up with her. But the small wrinkles bracketing her mouth and fine lines softening her eyes just added to her prettiness.

"Good to see you, Evelyn."

"Same here, cowboy." She uncrossed her long legs, clad in faded denim, and stepped over to the table, reaching out to rub his shoulder fondly. "You home for good?"

"Hell, I'm not sure." Caleb offered a smile he knew fell short. "Maybe." He gestured toward the swinging half-door beyond the liquor display. "DeeDee still around?"

"She retired to Florida, oh, maybe two years ago. We bought her out. She gave us a good deal, just asked us to leave the name as DeeDee's, which wasn't a problem for us." Evelyn grinned. "Crotchety old biddy. Then she gave us that fancy sign to hang outside and it was a done deal."

Caleb remembered DeeDee well. Mean, grouchy, and no-nonsense, with a face like a horse and as wide as she was tall. "Well, I hope she hooks up with some hardbody on the beach and gets herself a regular lube job." While Evelyn snorted with laughter, Caleb called over, "Hey, Mikey, where the hell's that beer?"

Mikey slid one over. "Sorry, buddy, here ya go."

Evelyn coughed out a final chuckle, then gave Caleb a steady stare, her eyebrows raised in question.

"What?" But Caleb had a feeling he knew what she wanted to ask.

"Nothing, honey. Glad you're back." With a final pat, this time to his unbruised cheek, she picked up an empty tray and headed toward the billiard room to collect dirty glasses.

"You want a burger plate?" Mikey asked.

"Yeah. Loaded." Caleb rested his booted foot on his thigh to ease the stiffness in his sore leg, and gulped half the bottle of beer.

Mikey shouted the order to the bearded cook working behind the kitchen window, then turned back to Caleb. He wiped the bar with a wet towel. "You seen Rosemary yet?"

Does the whole town know?

"Yeah. I saw her."

"You seen her boy?"

"You mean *my* boy."

"The little guy sure looks like you."

"I noticed." Caleb finished off his beer and motioned for another one.

Just as Mikey set it down, his daughter Adrianne strode from the kitchen and slammed a plate in front of Caleb. "Nice of you to come back, you bastard."

Whoa. This was getting crazy. If things kept up, he'd be run out of town. Did they still tar and feather undesirables?

"Hi, Adrianne, good to see you, too." He flashed the smile that got him plenty of action on the circuit, and quite a bit here in town, too—back in the day.

"Don't try that crap on me, cowboy." Adrianne drew up a chair and sat, her elbow on the table, resting her chin on her palm. "You seen him yet?"

Before he could answer, she reached out and grasped his chin, turning his head one way, then the other. "From the look of that fading shiner, I'd say Mason got hold of you already."

"If you're finished prying into my personal business, I'd like to eat my dinner."

Adrianne shrugged and snapped her gum. "Sure. Have at it, cowboy." She stood and swiped his longneck. Tilting her head back, she downed it in one long, easy gulp. "Thanks for the beer." Holding the now empty bottle, she sauntered away.

Caleb stared after her, marveling at how fast the girl could drink down a full longneck, and then walk without staggering. "More and more like her mama, isn't she?" He glanced at Mikey, who nodded and puffed out his chest proudly.

"That she is. But smart with it. Ev and I never have to worry about Adrianne. She can hold her own."

"She'd have to in this cow town, wouldn't she?" Caleb muttered, digging into his food.

Well, so far his welcome home had pretty much sucked. He hadn't expected a brass band to meet him at the bus stop or the mayor to present him with the golden key to the city, but neither had he figured on getting punched out by his best friend.

And aside from all that, he was faced with a genuine problem. He had a son. Carson.

Fuck me twice.

If his calculations were correct, the kid was about five years old. Did he even know who his father was? Did Rosemary ever talk about him? And if she did, was it to let the boy know his daddy was a loser who ran out on his mother?

A heavy hand landed on his shoulder. "Hiya, Caleb."

Caleb turned to face Dave Jamison, former high school football star, and from the looks of it, current deputy sheriff. Great. Was a jail cell his next stop?

"Hey, Dave. How's it going?"

Dave grabbed a chair and straddled it. "Good. Real good." He rested his arms on the back of the chair, and gave him a steady look. "I heard you've been back a few days."

Caleb laid down his half-eaten burger. "Small towns. Lots of gossip. Folks around here need to get some hobbies. I can't figure why my coming back to the town I was raised in would be such a newsworthy event. Why don't y'all go chase the kids who scribbled on the school building?"

Dave broke into a grin. "Don't see why you're getting yourself all worked up. I just came by to say hello."

"I'm sorry." Caleb ran his palm down his face. "I'm still trying to catch up to myself."

"I understand. So, how's things on the rodeo circuit? I hear you've been winning medals left and right."

Caleb shrugged. "A few. But I'll be out of commission for a while." At Dave's raised eyebrows, he continued, "An ornery bull threw me and decided that wasn't enough, so he landed on my leg. Busted it up in a few places."

"Damn."

"Yeah. It's all fixed up now, but I need a couple more months before I can return to the circuit."

If I can ever return.

"Well, we're happy to see you again. Just keep your nose clean while you're here."

The deputy's chuckle grated on Caleb's nerves. But then he'd been out of sorts since he came face to face with his past. At least Dave wasn't punching his lights out or slamming food down in front of him.

"So, what's new with you?" Caleb eyed the uniform Dave wore. "I see you're one of Laramie County's finest. Been doing it long?"

"Yeah, right after you ran out of town to make a name for yourself. Went through the academy, and been wearing the blues since then. I like it. It suits me."

"Locking up all those kids who damage school buildings?"

"And keeping an eye on newcomers to town with busted up legs."

"Ha. Not a newcomer, Jamison, a returnee." He pushed away his empty plate and signaled for another beer. "Can I buy you a drink?"

"Nah. Thanks. I'm waiting for my girl." He shot Caleb a knowing look. "She's gonna meet me here for dinner." He took a vibrating iPhone out of his pocket and glanced at the screen. "And, she just pulled in."

Dave looked up as the door opened. "Hi, darlin'. Just saying hello to an old friend of yours."

Caleb took a swig of beer and turned to stare directly into Rosemary Carmichael's stormy amber eyes.

Rosemary's stomach fluttered with awareness when she spotted Caleb sitting at the bar with Dave. The memory of their time together still burned bright in her mind. The pain of his desertion was just as fresh today as it'd been all those years ago.

Why couldn't he have just stayed away?

Caleb turned toward her with a hard glare. A fresh wave of anger rolled through her, instantly smothering her hurt and leaving only steam behind. He had no right to be angry with her. He was the jackass.

She was so over Caleb Johnson! Been there. Done that.

Didn't need the heartache again.

She snorted. Hell, her life was a damn country song. Squaring her shoulders, Rosemary marched inside and up to Dave, wrapping her arms around his waist and lifting her face for a kiss.

Dave grinned, his eyes gleaming with amusement, because their relationship so far was more friends than lovers, and he'd only kissed her once. He'd understand her brazen display was for Caleb's benefit. But being the gentleman he was, Dave didn't let her down. He threaded his fingers through her hair and leaned in, giving her a deep kiss.

But just like the other time he'd kissed her, she felt nothing. Not even a tiny sensual quiver. Zilch. Instead, Caleb's image floated behind her eyelids.

God! I'm in serious trouble.

She thought of Carson, her little angel, and was able to rein in her betraying emotions. There was no way she'd allow Caleb to crush her son's tender heart into the dirt on his way back out of town.

The sound of a heavy thud broke the kiss, and she glanced up to see Caleb glowering at them, beer foaming over his longneck bottle and running across his tightly gripped knuckles.

Her feeling of satisfaction was quickly followed by guilt. She'd never been the vindictive sort, and she shouldn't care whether Caleb was jealous or not. They had no future, only a sad history.

Caleb wasn't a keeper. He'd never stay. She needed to protect Carson from the same kind of heartache she'd suffered when she'd awoken alone, abandoned. Pregnant. Every tender promise he'd made, a lie. All damn lies.

"So, Caleb," Dave asked, "how long are you in town for?" He tucked her close to his side.

"Don't know. Depends." Steel threaded his voice as he turned away from them. "Mikey, another Bud."

"Be right there," Mikey called over his shoulder as he served two fruity-looking concoctions to a couple of young women at the end of the bar.

"Well. Um," Rosemary stammered as the air sizzled with awkward, uncomfortable tension. "I guess we should get a table."

"I already have one picked out, darlin'."

With his arm still around her waist and a smirk on his lips, Dave steered her toward the dining area. He led her to a corner table and held out her chair so she could sit, then leaned down and nuzzled her neck, before taking a seat across from her.

She groaned under her breath when she saw she had a direct view of the bar, and Caleb. His brooding gaze rested on her as he picked up his beer and took a long draw. *Not. Good.* She'd known him most of her life, and his body posture indicated he was seriously pissed off.

Irritated, Rosemary turned her attention to Dave.

He stared back with a wide-eyed innocent expression. "What?"

"You were baiting him."

A grin split his face. "Yeah. Isn't that what you wanted?"

Was it?

She shook her head in silent denial. Caleb wasn't worth the emotion it'd take to rile him up. She'd already spent too many years crying over him. He meant nothing to her now.

That's not fair and you know it. She stifled a sigh. No, it wasn't fair.

There'd been times, before she and Caleb ever hooked up, that he'd listened to her woes and offered a shoulder, advice; hell, just an open ear. When her mama was driving her nuts or her daddy got itchy and they all wondered if he'd make it through another weekend without bolting. She'd vent and Caleb would display a lot of patience for a guy willingly dealing with an idiot teenage girl.

She shook herself from the memories when Adrianne stopped by and took their orders. Neither she nor Dave needed a menu; Rosemary had eaten here often enough to know exactly what she wanted. She shot a quick glance toward Caleb, noting the two women from the end of the bar had sidled up next to him. Her mouth tightened, the momentary softening she'd felt toward him fading fast.

He seemed quite content to have those bimbos fawn over him. Something ugly rose up inside her and for a second or two she wanted to rush over and pull out their bottle-blonde hair. Rosemary forced her attention back to Dave, who was watching her now with solemn, knowing eyes.

To his credit, he didn't say anything.

Now it was her turn to ask, "What?"

Dave leaned over the small table and took her hand. "Rosemary, you and Carson mean a lot to me."

Rosemary shifted uncomfortably, reluctant to have this discussion. There'd never be anything more than friendship between them. She thought he understood.

Her brows squeezed together. Damn it. She just wanted to enjoy Dave's company, eat dinner, see a movie . . . and forget Caleb Johnson ever existed.

Dave chuckled, although the sound was devoid of humor. Still holding her fingers loosely, he brought his other hand up and tucked a wayward strand of hair behind her ear. "Relax, darlin'. I know you don't feel the same way. I get that."

Rosemary smiled sadly, not knowing what to say. She didn't deserve his friendship. "I'm sorry, Dave. You're a great guy—"

"Whoa!" He released her hand and sat back in his chair, bringing both his palms up in a 'stop' gesture. "Don't give me the 'you're a great guy, we can be friends' line." The look he gave her held real affection this time. "I know you and Caleb have a history. Hell, everyone knows Carson's his."

She didn't deny it—never had—although she didn't talk about it either. "Ancient history. There's nothing between us now."

The words rolled off her tongue easily enough, and yet they tasted like a lie. She frowned, picking up her dinner napkin and spreading it across her lap.

He clucked his tongue. "That's not exactly true, darlin'. There's Carson. And regardless of how things work out between us, I want you both to be happy."

Her emotions churning, a tear slid down her cheek. Why couldn't she have fallen for someone like Dave? He was handsome, solid, and dependable. Not some footloose cowboy with dreams of being a rodeo star. Even six years ago she knew Caleb could easily end up breaking her heart. "Carson and I are happy."

He brought his thumb to her cheek and swiped at her tears. "Are you? From what I can see, you're so tied up in Caleb you can't move on, can't give another guy a chance."

"That's not true. I've dated plenty," she denied, though she knew he was speaking the truth.

Evelyn dropped off their drinks with a quick smile for them both, and Rosemary reached for her margarita. She needed something to help her relax. Her nerves were strung tight.

Dave lifted his frosty beer mug, his expression pure devilment. "Maybe you need some help working him out of your system."

She choked on her drink, giving him an incredulous look. He was so full of it. Damn, but he was cute, with that golden brown buzz cut and those twinkling hazel eyes. Why couldn't she have fallen for him, instead of the town heartbreaker? Still, her tension eased and she laughed. "Are you offering, cowboy?"

He grinned at her over the top of his mug, and took a swig, then wiped the foam from his mouth with the back of his hand before replying, "Maybe."

Setting his mug down, his expression grew serious. "Or maybe you need to give him another shot, or at least an opportunity to know his son. Then you'll be able to finally move on."

Should he have the right to know his son? No! He abandoned us.

But he hadn't known about Carson. He'd only abandoned *her*.

Rosemary looked back at the bar and her stomach clenched, hurt rushing through her veins. Caleb had his arm around a floozie's waist as she stared up at him like some puppy dog looking for a bone.

But his glittering gaze was solidly locked on Rosemary, even as the woman's hand crawled up his chest. Then the other bimbo leaned over and whispered something in his ear as she pressed up against his back. He glanced around to the voluptuous blonde, and smiled.

A smile he used to turn on her right before he made love to her.

A smile he now gave to two sluts in a bar; one he'd probably been giving to women all across the rodeo circuit, along with his body.

Rosemary's heart hardened and she turned away as Adrianne came up to their table with their meals. No, she didn't want Caleb Johnson.

But did that give her the right to keep him away from his son?

Chapter Five

Right about the same time Rosemary finished her meal and got to her feet, Caleb realized the last thing he wanted was a couple of local barflies hanging all over him. The hurt look she cast him, before glancing quickly away, made him feel like a real jerk.

Busy detaching the blonde's inch-long fingernails from his shirtsleeve, he glanced toward the dining room again, just in time to see Rosemary pause next to Dave, slip her purse strap over her shoulder, then lean in and kiss the bastard's cheek. Dave watched the sway of her jeans-clad hips all the way to the door.

Caleb wanted to rip off Dave's head and stuff it up his ass. And then confront Rosemary. Remove the pain from where it burned a hole in his gut as if he'd eaten acid. Clear the air between them, once and for all.

He'd purposely stayed away from her for two days, reacquainting himself with the slower pace of Dustin, trying to take it easy on his leg. He'd looked up a few old, still-local friends, even reconnected with his Uncle Zip, spending an hour or so the other night yakking to him long distance to Rock Springs, where Zip had landed after leaving Dustin. Most of his meals Caleb had eaten at the diner off Main.

Some needed space. That had been his aim. For Rosemary, and for him.

Pointless.

Easing off the barstool, he fished in his pocket for a twenty, tossing it on the counter. Over the drunken protests of the women he'd pushed away, Caleb took the side 'Bar Only' entrance and slipped out. In those damned sexy high-heeled boots, Rosemary wouldn't have gotten halfway across the parking lot yet.

Sure enough, he spotted her a short distance away, near the floodlight over DeeDee's fancy new sign. Rosemary's head was bent and all that gorgeous red hair sheltered her face from his view. She dug through her purse, probably searching for her keys.

Aside from the need for confrontation, he worried to think she'd walk around Dustin with her head down after evening set in. Not paying attention to anyone who could just step up and grab her arm.

Yeah, like me. His mouth set into a grim line at her careless regard for her own safety.

Not breaking his stride, Caleb reached her in under five seconds, taking her arm in a firm grip. With a feminine squeak of protest, she spun toward him.

He caught a brief flash of her lacy black bra as the deep vee of her sleeveless blouse gapped revealingly. For a second he had a chance to admire the way her skin looked like cream against the lace.

With an irritated huff, she started squirming and pulling at his hand. "Damn it, let go, Caleb. What the hell do you think you're doing?"

"We gotta talk." Wanting some privacy from nosy townsfolks, he maneuvered her away from the floodlight and off the sidewalk, stopping just inside the alley where empty boxes had been stacked for trash pickup.

She tugged harder. "Nothing to talk about. Let go."

"Nope." He'd sucked down enough beer to take the sensible edge off his brain. "I've got some things to say to you." He backed her into the nearest brick wall and slapped his hands on her shoulders to prevent her from bolting. "You're damned well gonna listen."

Rosemary shoved her hair out of her face and gave him one hell of a stink eye. "You're drunk and an asswipe. Want to talk about that?" Under his palms, the set of her shoulders tightened like a cocked bow.

"I want to know what Jamison is to you," Caleb growled.

She stiffened even more. "None of your business. Now get your hands off me!"

Releasing her shoulders, he slammed his palms onto the wall behind her, not touching her, but still blocking her exit. "Better?" he growled.

She stared up at him silently. In the dim alley lighting he could see how anger lit her up, more than likely making her too furious to speak. Well, tough, because they had a thing or two to get straight.

"And it *is* my damned business, Rosie. The man's a skirt chaser and if he's hanging around my son—"

Caleb got no further because Rosemary was suddenly in his face, one slender finger drilling into his chest. "You don't get to say who hangs out with *my* son. You sure as hell don't get a vote in who chases my frigging skirt."

She poked his chest harder. "You don't know a thing about me, or Dave, or what's gone on in this town since you've been goddamned gone."

"Knock it off." Beyond irritated, he grabbed for her hand, yanking her closer. Until every inch of the denim and cotton she wore was plastered against him. Her breath hitched, and the rapid rise and fall of her breasts made Caleb break out in a sudden sweat.

The jealousy and anger roaring through him switched off like a light bulb. All he could concentrate on was Rosemary.

God, he could smell her, some kind of flowery stuff he remembered she always used on her hair. Her lips parted and he caught a tang of the margaritas she'd had. The feel of her body brought back memories of hot nights, damp bedsheets twisted on the floor, long, tangled curls; fingernails digging into his bare shoulders.

He stared down into her beautiful face. She'd been a pretty kid, an adorable teenager. And almost too much woman for him at nineteen, in spite of her innocence. Now she simply knocked him sideways. He wanted her. Hell, he'd never stopped wanting her.

The thought of her dating a guy Caleb used to consider a friend . . . *Damn it all to hell.*

He couldn't take it.

Dave Jamison, kissing her, his fingers twined into those gorgeous, fiery locks. Holding her with arms that didn't belong around her tiny waist, mere inches from the breasts Caleb had been the first to claim. She'd smiled at Dave. *And frowned at me.*

The ten-second kissing scene he'd been forced to watch in DeeDee's bar played over and over in Caleb's brain until he groaned aloud. The flash of desire he'd managed to bank suddenly came back with ferocity. Asswipe that he was, he let it take him over.

Grasping her by the arms, Caleb pressed her back into the wall again, then lowered his face until his lips were an inch from hers. He registered the shock in her eyes, dilating the amber until they were almost black.

"Caleb—" She swallowed and licked her lips. The hint of protest in her voice when she uttered his name should have resulted with him treading softly. But then her fingers curled into his shirt lapels and she tugged. Hard. Toward her.

Against her.

Jesus.

On a groan, he took her mouth hungrily. Her taste exploded on his tongue as he dove deep.

Deeper.

He raked a hand over her blouse, finding an opening between buttons, slipping his fingers inside on a search for silky flesh. The lacy bra she wore barely covered her, and he cupped a firm breast. Six years simply disintegrated into nothing as he relearned her skin, the way she trembled in his arms, how her tongue met his with aggression. Rosie

Carmichael had never been a shrinking violet at nineteen, and she wasn't one now.

Closer, damn it. Caleb didn't realize he'd spoken aloud until she moaned a high, thin, "God, yes," into his mouth and opened her stance, rocking on her high heeled boots. He thrust his free hand under her bottom and hoisted her up so she could wrap a leg around his hips, a sensual anchor. Now her fingers were buried in his hair, gripping it tightly enough to rip out chunks. The pain only added fuel to his overloaded system. He pinned her harder against the old brick wall.

Tearing his lips from hers, he ran them down the side of her slender throat, nipping the hot skin, lingering at the curve of shoulder and neck where he knew she was most sensitive. When he bit down, a shudder passed through her body. She untangled the fingers of one hand from his hair and scraped her nails over his chest, to the edge of his jeans, until she reached his button fly. Her palm caged him there, one eager press against the denim covering his hard-on.

"Christ," he muttered, moving his hips in time with her strokes. He raised his head until he could engulf her mouth in another exploring kiss. Her breath hitched and the tiny sob she loosed against his tongue belied the way she clutched him tighter. "Rosie . . ."

"Rosie, what the hell!"

The words, uttered in an angry male voice, came from behind them and she froze in his arms, pulling her lips from his, uncurling her fingers from his scalp. She snatched her hand from his groin and dropped her face to his shoulder. Through his shirt he could feel the heat of embarrassment that emanated from her cheeks.

Caleb glanced behind him and cursed under his breath as Mason stomped over.

"Get away from her, Johnson," he snarled.

"I'm not holding on." Caleb relaxed his arms and let them hang at his sides. The only connection remaining was Rosemary's leg curled around his hips. Her face was still buried in his neck. "Your sister's where she wants to be. Take a hike, Carmichael, before I forget we're friends."

"We're not friends, you son of a bitch. Not any longer." Mason stepped closer and sent his sister a scathing glare. "Rosie, Carson's running a fever. Susan called me when she couldn't get hold of you. I tried calling too, but your phone must be dead."

"Oh, Lord." She slapped her hands on Caleb's chest and pushed him away. "I forgot to charge it! I'm sorry. How high of a fever? I'm sorry—"

She stepped around him and plucked her purse off the ground where it had fallen when he'd held her against the wall.

In that moment, with all of her attention on their son, Caleb knew whatever bond they'd begun forming had cracked. Like hell he'd let go of that bit of reconnection. He swung to face Mason's ire and stated calmly, "I'll go with you."

"No damn way," Mason bit out, surging toward him.

Rosemary dug her fingers into her brother's arm and held him back. "I can handle this, Mason. Caleb has a right to see his son—"

"Why, because he shoved his tongue down your throat and felt you up in a damned alley? You think that means you're better than any other piece of ass he's planked from here to Casper?"

Caleb had heard enough. "Goddamn it, watch your mouth." He eased Rosemary aside and shot out a hand, fisting Mason's shirt collar and dragging him to his toes, uncaring that he was choking him. If Mason wanted to throw down with him again, he'd oblige.

"Caleb, let him go." Rosemary tugged at his hand.

Caleb tightened his fingers, wringing a grunt from Mason, before abruptly releasing him. Mason stumbled but managed to stay upright. Fury and something else that Caleb hoped might be shame radiated from him.

"Call me anything you like, but never speak to your sister that way again, you got me?" Caleb stared him down, until Mason looked away, muttering under his breath.

Reaching for her hand, Caleb pulled her toward the parking lot. "Let's go." He didn't wait for her acquiescence, but strode to where several cars were parked. "Which one's yours?"

"The blue Honda." She pointed to a little Civic. Now she was the one pulling him. "Hurry, okay? Fevers really scare me."

"We'll take care of him, honey. He'll be all right," Caleb assured her.

As he climbed into the passenger seat and Rosemary gunned the engine, Caleb hoped to hell he wasn't lying.

Chapter Six

Rosemary peeled out of the parking lot like a seasoned Indy 500 driver, which only increased the knots in Caleb's stomach. Little kids got fevers all the time, right? Following on the heels of that thought was how many years Rosemary had done this all on her own while he'd been out there making a name for himself. The only name that applied now was *asshole*.

They tore through town before turning onto Smithy Road, which led to an older section of Dustin. Screeching down Benson Drive, she barely brought the car to a complete stop before she flung her door open and raced toward the front porch of a small, older two-story house.

Caleb steeled himself to meet his kid for real this time. He grabbed the keys she'd left in the ignition and followed Rosemary up the porch stairs and into the house. Despite his worry, he took note of the place where she and her son—no, *their* son—lived. The interior of the house was as tidy as the outside. From what he could sense, Rosemary's presence was in every corner of the cozy rooms.

Is this what our home would have looked like if I'd stuck around long enough to find out I was going to be a father?

There was no doubt in his mind he would have married Rosemary. Even if Mason hadn't been standing behind him with a shotgun. But a little voice in the back of his head told him he'd have grown to resent her. Back in the day, his only focus was the rodeo, and how big a name he could make for himself. Looking back now at his wins and losses, and his resultant injury, it all seemed so childish.

Rosemary's boots beat a cadence as she hurried up the carpeted stairs, then made an abrupt turn into an open bedroom door. Without waiting for an invitation he followed her.

The wail of a crying child and a woman's low, soothing voice greeted him. Carson slumped on the bed, bent over, and from where Caleb stood the kid's breathing was not sounding good. Rosemary sat alongside the boy and touched his forehead. She gasped and looked at Susan, pacing near the window. "He's so hot."

"I gave him some children's fever reducer a little while ago, but it didn't seem to work," Susan stopped pacing and shot Caleb a don't-mess-with-my-best-friend glare. "And his breathing is pretty bad."

Caleb felt like a third wheel here. Rosemary and Susan had probably been through something like this before. Totally clueless on how things worked with kids, fevers, and breathing problems, all he could think of was how they needed to get him to an emergency room. Carson's lips were blue as he struggled to take in air. The worry Caleb felt kicked any residual buzz from his brain, instantly alert as he studied his son's flushed cheeks.

After years of watching medical emergencies from stomped-on cowboys along the circuit, his normal decisive attitude took over. He strode to the bed, scooped Carson up, blankets and all, and headed for the door. "Hang on, buddy," he said, as the boy laid his head on his chest.

"What the hell do you think you're doing?" Rosemary yelled as she ran after him. "Put my son down."

Pausing, he said quietly, "I'm taking *our* son to the emergency room."

Susan flanked his other side, tugging on Caleb's arm. "You have no right."

"Get out of my way. I have every right." He nudged Susan aside and cast a glance over his shoulder to a stunned Rosemary. "Let's go."

Either his growl or her motherly instinct kicked in because she quickly grabbed a furry stuffed animal from the boy's bed, and raced behind him.

"Rosemary, you can't let him do this," Susan shouted from the top of the stairs as Caleb shifted Carson to open the front door.

"He's right, Susan. Carson needs help." Rosemary followed him out into the dark night.

She climbed into the passenger seat and held her arms out to Caleb. He placed Carson on her lap and strode to the other side. "Is the hospital still on Baker and Montrose?"

"Yeah." Her voice had gone thick with emotion.

Caleb glanced briefly at Carson. "Has he had breathing problems before?"

"Not like this. Only the usual colds and some allergies, but this is bad. He started coughing yesterday morning but I thought it was just a summer cold." Rosemary chewed her lips, where only about ten minutes ago he'd been happily nibbling. He shook his head to clear it from those thoughts. Right now they had to get Carson taken care of.

Caleb reached out and touched her hand. "It will be all right. The doctors will fix him right up."

Why did his assurance calm her down? Caleb knew nothing about children, fevers, or anything else that she'd lived with—alone—all these years. But seeing his determined face as he whipped around cars on their race to the hospital did just that. It had always been Mason who'd stepped in to take on the role of daddy when she'd needed him to. Now she had to deal with Carson's actual father. But for how long?

She hugged her son's overly-warm body closer and looked out the window at the stores and houses as they whizzed by. It was best not to get used to Caleb being here. Sure, he was taking charge now, and acted the part of the doting father, but her heart told her he'd up and leave as soon as whatever it was that brought him back here was fixed.

She hadn't missed his slight limp and occasional wince when he moved. He'd obviously decided to take a little time off to recover from an injury. But why here? His parents had left town years ago. *Did he choose Dustin because of me?* She snorted. Even she wasn't stupid enough to believe that.

The car came to a screeching halt outside Emergency. She'd managed to unfasten her seatbelt about a second before Caleb wrenched her door open. He gently took Carson from her arms, then rushed toward the entrance, leaving her gaping after them.

"Wait!" She scrambled to catch up as they all reached the reception desk.

"What have we here?" The night duty nurse looked over the top of her computer monitor as the emergency doors slid closed with a whoosh.

"My son has a high fever and he's having a lot of trouble breathing," Rosemary said.

"All right. Follow me and we'll get him checked out." The nurse led them to an empty bed and pulled up the safety rails. "Please lay him down there," she instructed Caleb.

"Mommy." Carson stretched out his hand. Rosemary placed her palm on his forehead, *Still so hot.* She looked down at his frightened little face and her stomach did a whirl.

"Sir, if you'll come with me, you can give me the boy's insurance information and whatever else we need."

"Rosie," Caleb said, "maybe you should do that."

"No. I'm staying here with Carson." She gripped his little fingers as if to anchor herself from being dragged from the room.

He sighed. "I don't know the information she's going to ask."

"Ma'am." The nurse regarded her with sympathy. "Let his daddy stay with him. It'll only take a few minutes to get the paperwork filled out."

His daddy. Had Carson heard her? She glanced down at her son, who was having trouble taking a breath. *God, I hope not.*

Rosemary had to beat down the desire to lash out at the nurse as she followed her to the reception desk. She and Carson had always done just fine on their own. Fighting off tears, she fished around in her purse for her insurance card. Carson belonged to only her. How could she share him now?

"The little guy sure looks like his daddy."

Gritting her teeth, Rosemary handed the card over. The low-pitched tones of Caleb's soothing voice carried into the hallway. What was he saying to her son?

After signing numerous forms she returned to Carson's bedside just as another nurse entered. "We have a little bit of a breathing problem, young man?" The middle-aged woman smiled at Carson as she took his pulse, then swiped his forehead with a thermometer. She moved to the computer and entered information. The night nurse came back into the room with a plastic bracelet that she fastened to Carson's wrist.

"How bad is his temperature?" Rosemary tried to look over the attending nurse's shoulder at the computer screen, but couldn't see the numbers.

"It's slightly over one hundred and two."

Fear gripped her stomach. "That's dangerous, isn't it?"

The nurse approached the side of Carson's bed and put a blood pressure cuff on him. "Children tend to have higher fevers than adults. It's not unusual."

All this time Caleb had been hovering on the other side of Carson's bed, his face creased with worry. Now he moved to stand beside her, slipping his arm around her shoulders. She allowed herself to relax into his strength, the warmth of his body easing her chills, before remembering where she was at and who she was with.

She glanced sideways at Caleb. "You don't have to stay. Though I do appreciate the help."

A stubborn expression formed on his handsome face. "Aside from the fact I have no car, I plan to stay right here until I know what our boy's problem is."

Rosemary fought to keep her cool. Lord, the man had her twisted in knots and he'd only been back in town for a couple of days.

"Mommy, my chest hurts."

She slid out from under Caleb's arm and stepped to the bed to sit alongside her son. "I know, sweetheart. That's why we're here. The doctor will come in and make you feel all better."

This was certainly not the time or place to resurrect the feelings of abandonment she'd suffered when the doctor confirmed her pregnancy and she had no idea where Caleb was.

Carson nodded as another bout of coughing overtook him. His face turned red and he gagged for a minute before leaning back against the pillow, looking so small and vulnerable in the baggy hospital gown.

"Where the hell is the doctor?" Caleb growled, and began to pace around the bed.

Rosemary pushed the hair back from Carson's forehead, her heart speeding up when she felt the heat coming from his body. Yes, where the hell was the doctor?

After about ten minutes of Carson coughing, Caleb pacing, and Rosemary ready to pull her hair out, the doctor knocked softly on the door and pushed it open.

"Good evening." He stuck his hand out to Caleb. "I'm Dr. Vine." He nodded in Rosemary's direction. "I understand we have a sick little boy here."

"He started coming down with a cold a couple of days ago, but tonight his coughing got much worse and he has a pretty high fever." Rosemary pushed aside her anxiety and strove to respond as calmly as possible.

"Well, let's take a listen." The doctor moved to Carson's side and placed a stethoscope against his chest. From the wince he made, the instrument must have been cold. Dr. Vine frowned and moved the stethoscope to Carson's back.

"Pneumonia," he pronounced, after a few more checks.

"Pneumonia!" She and Caleb said at the same time.

"Yes, sir. This little guy has pneumonia."

Rosemary burst into tears. What kind of a mother was she that her son developed pneumonia and she thought it was only a cold?

Carson coughed, his small body jerking from the strain. Caleb moved to her side and once again slipped his arms around her. "It'll be all right."

"Now, now, mother. These things happen. Kids can go from being fine to very sick in no time. Remember, when we adults are sick, we start to think about taking care of the problem right away. A child usually ignores any symptoms until he's flat on his back."

"So what needs to be done?" Caleb asked, worry evident in his voice.

"Given his fever and his age, I'm going to admit him."

Helpless fear made her tremble. *I hate falling apart like this.* Especially in front of Caleb. She'd handled all of Carson's illnesses and other mishaps on her own, no problem. Now she was acting like a sobbing teenager in a bad movie.

She pulled away and wiped her cheeks. "I want to spend the night here with him."

"That should be no problem. I'll have him transferred to Pediatrics and you can work that out with the nurses."

The doctor looked briefly at Caleb before he turned to the computer and began typing furiously. "It might be a problem if you both want to stay."

"It'll just be me," Rosemary replied.

Dr. Vine merely gave a quick nod and continued entering information. Rosemary raised her chin and regarded Caleb. "I'm going to run home and pick up a few things. I can drop you off wherever you're staying."

Caleb tensed. Rosemary waited for him to disagree with her, but then he gave a curt nod. "All right. I'm at the Bronco Inn. Unit Fourteen."

"That studio Nash rents by the week?"

"Yeah."

"That's a decent room." Feeling more in control of herself now, she sat on the edge of the bed and stroked Carson's cheek. "Mommy's going home to get a few things so I can stay overnight with you."

"Don't leave." Two tears tracked down his sweet face as he gripped her hand.

"I won't be gone long, promise." She leaned in and kissed his forehead.

"No." Carson peeked at Caleb from under lowered lashes. "Can't the man go and get your things?"

"He doesn't know what to get, or where to find things, honey. Suppose I call Aunt Susie to bring what I need?"

After another lengthy bout of coughing, Carson nodded and collapsed against the pillow.

"I'm going to have the nurse give him a breathing treatment before he goes upstairs." Apparently having finished what he needed to do on the computer, Dr. Vine opened the door and was gone in a flash.

"I don't like that doctor." Caleb frowned at the door as it swung shut. "He spent more time on the computer than he did looking at Carson."

"I have to agree with you there." She pulled her phone from her pocket. "Carson, I'm going to step outside and call Aunt Susie to bring my things. But I'll be right back, and I'll only be on the other side of the door, okay?"

She elbowed Caleb. "Would you mind joining me?"

He blinked, but nodded. "Sure."

Once they were far enough away from the door that Carson wouldn't be able to hear them, she came to an abrupt halt and turned. "What did you say to Carson while I was at the reception desk?"

Caleb arched a questioning brow. "Nothing. Just tried to keep him entertained."

"Good . . . good." There was a beat of silence. "If I decide to tell Carson you're his father, it'll be when I feel the time is right."

He rubbed the back of his neck and sighed. "I get that, Rosie."

"Excuse me?" A young candy striper wheeled up a cart with a pitcher of juice and some glasses. "Would you like something to drink?"

Glad for the interruption, Rosemary stepped away from him. "We'll talk about this later."

Chapter Seven

Caleb paced the waiting room of the hospital, where he'd spent most of the past several days wearing a path in the carpeting as he worried about his son.

My son!

His hand clenched at his side, still unable to wrap those words around his brain. The anxiety flooding his body was a new emotion for him. The fear ran so deep, it squeezed the oxygen from his lungs. And he'd left Rosie to deal with this by herself over the last five years.

Which made him a first-class dirtbag, and he wasn't sure how to make it up to her. He'd do everything in his power to gain her forgiveness, because he was determined to be there for Carson from here on out.

"Mr. Johnson," the young, friendly nurse said as she approached him. "Ms. Carmichael would like you to join her in Carson's room."

His heart pounded hard as he rushed down the hall. *Is something wrong?*

Although still upset with him, at least Rosemary hadn't shut him out, allowing him to spend time each day with Carson. Even sick and feverish, his son was sweet and funny, and now owned a huge chunk of Caleb's heart. There wasn't anything he wouldn't do for that little boy.

When he entered the room, Rosemary and the doctor stood next to Carson's bed.

"Caleb." Her face glowed. "Carson's being released today."

The gut-deep relief he felt at that news made the wandering-cowboy part of him cry 'uncle' as a protective instinct he didn't know he had slammed into him. A fist squeezed inside his chest as he watched Rosemary feather slender fingers through Carson's hair, before leaning in to tenderly kiss his rosy cheek, murmuring, "Mommy loves you, little man."

She was an amazing mother, and had done a wonderful job raising their boy. But from here on out, Carson would get the benefit of both his parents.

Caleb closed the distance between him and his son to peer down at him. He winked. "Hey, champ. Ready to get out of here?"

He nodded, smiling shyly, then asked, "Are you my daddy?"

A barely audible gasp fell from Rosemary's lips.

Dr. Vine cleared his throat and headed for the door at a quick pace. "I'll get that paperwork going for you."

Caleb's gaze shot to Rosemary as his heart pounded a staccato beat in his chest. "Thanks, Doc." He nervously rubbed his leg, somewhat sore from all his pacing. He truly did not want to screw this up.

Her hand pressing against her throat, she chewed on her bottom lip as she brought her attention to their son. "Carson—"

Caleb laid his hand on Rosemary's shoulder and gave it a soft squeeze. "Rosie," he said quietly, "let me."

She glanced up at him, then back at Carson. "All right," she agreed hesitantly.

He advanced to the side of the bed, then ruffled Carson's hair, grinning in an attempt to keep it light. "Would that be okay with you, buddy?"

His breath hitched as he waited for his son's answer, not knowing what he'd do if Carson hated the idea. And it'd be Caleb's own damn fault for not being there for his boy.

A huge smile split Carson's cute cherub face. "That's great. Can I call you Daddy? Will you play baseball with me and Uncle Mason? Can we go get pizza? I like pizza!"

Caleb sighed in relief. Taking note of Rosemary's emotional state, giving her a moment to collect herself, he stroked his son's silky head. "You bet you can call me Daddy. And pizza's my favorite, too."

Rosemary laughed. "I'm sure Uncle Mason will love having your daddy play baseball with you."

The teasing tone in her voice was directed at him, and Caleb grinned at her as he felt the shift in their relationship. Although he didn't figure he was completely forgiven, at least Rosie seemed willing to give him a chance with their son. That was a good starting point and a much better place than when he'd first stepped off the bus, days ago.

Now Mason was a different story, and he really wasn't looking forward to that conversation. The few times he'd run into him at the hospital while visiting Carson hadn't been pretty. Caleb knew his old buddy would rather kick his ass than share Carson in a game of baseball. But for the boy's sake, Mason would have to come to grips with the fact that Caleb was here and wasn't leaving any time soon.

If ever.

Rosemary watched Carson and Caleb playing with matchbox cars on the floor of her living room. Seeing the two of them together, looking so much alike warmed her heart even as worry and hope warred inside her.

The past week had been a whirlwind of happenings, and she was emotionally exhausted. After another couple days of bedrest, Carson was almost back to normal. Caleb had brought over the pizza he'd promised, and she had the table all set.

Carson giggled as he ran his car across Caleb's broad chest. "Vroom. Vroom."

The deep rumble of Caleb's answering chuckle, as he rolled onto his back and lifted Carson above his head, slid across her body like a caress. Her center quivered as memories of their passionate embrace in DeeDee's alley filled her mind. If not for her brother showing up the other night, she would have let Caleb take her right there, up against the brick wall.

She shoved the memory aside. "Okay, you two. Come eat."

When she'd informed her brother that Carson knew about, and accepted Caleb as his father, he hadn't been pleased. For his nephew's sake, though, he'd deal. But Mason was a long way from forgiving Caleb for deserting her. As was Susan, who'd told her she'd be a fool to let that 'dirty, rotten cowboy' back into her life. Not that she could blame them, since she hadn't fully forgiven him herself.

Which made the way her body cried out for his touch—every time he was near, damn it—totally pathetic.

Caleb glanced at her from under thick lashes as Carson bounced on his eight-pack abs. His sexy grin and sinfully dark green eyes took her breath away as butterflies swarmed in her belly. She pressed her lips together, ignoring the tingling sensation between her legs, and silently told herself to knock it the hell off. That road would only lead to more heartache. She'd had little choice but to let Caleb into Carson's life, but no way was he getting back into her panties.

"You heard your mama, champ. Let's eat." He tossed Carson into the air one last time, before rolling to his feet and bringing Carson with him.

Her son clung to Caleb's hand, a look of hero-worship on his adorable face. "Pizza!" he yelled, rocking on his feet in excitement.

Rosemary could only stare, with her heart in her throat. Except for the bright red hair, Carson was the spitting image of his father. A tickle of unease rolled through her, worry that her baby's heart would be crushed when Caleb went back on the circuit. That thought hit like a bucket of cold water, bringing her back to her senses, and she frowned.

Studying her, Caleb arched one curious brow. "Everything okay?"

"Fine," she lied, turning and heading into the kitchen. They took their seats around the table, their pizza already cut and waiting, along with breadsticks and a pitcher of ice tea. Carson sat between them, his face beaming with happiness as he munched his slice of pizza.

"I'd like to stop over tomorrow and pick up Carson for the day, if that's all right," Caleb said, dipping a breadstick into the container of marinara sauce.

"I—I don't know," she said, concerned at the way her son lit up at Caleb's request. He was growing way too attached.

"Please, Mommy," Carson pleaded. His face had flushed with excitement.

As if to shut down her refusal, Caleb reached across the table and placed his hand over hers, giving it a light caress. Electricity zinged between them, and Rosemary felt it deep. Her resolve weakened.

"I thought maybe I'd take him to the park over near Hawthorn. I'd love it if you'd come along." His low voice coaxed and seduced. Against her better judgment she found herself agreeing. *Damn it.* She'd never been able to resist Caleb when he laid on the charm.

Turning to her son, Rosemary brushed his bangs off his forehead, leaning in to kiss the spot she'd bared. "Okay, sweetheart. But it's straight to bed tonight, with no squabbles. Agreed?"

He vigorously bobbed his head, wearing an ear-to-ear grin that was just like his father's. And she seemed helpless against both.

After the rest of their meal and yet another viewing of *Finding Nemo*, Carson jumped off Caleb's lap, where he'd sat the entire movie, and gave him a big hug. "'Night, Daddy."

"'Night, champ." Caleb's voice sounded suspiciously husky, his expression tender as he cupped his son's face.

For the first time, instead of only thinking of how his return to town affected her and Carson, she thought about Caleb.

She'd had a crush on him since she was twelve and he'd sauntered through her front door with her brother after a victorious football game. But Caleb had never seen her as anything more than Mason's little sister. Until six years ago when he'd rolled back into town, finally taking notice of her as a woman. She'd all but offered herself up to him on a silver platter.

Even though her heart was broken when he'd left without a word, she knew he *was* a good man. They'd both been young, and their one-week affair had been intense, but still . . . it'd only been a week.

So could she really blame him for following his dreams? Maybe it was time to release her anger so he could have a real relationship with his son.

While Rosemary settled Carson in bed, Caleb thought about what a great kid they'd created together. Their son was a joy to be around, sweet and well behaved but rambunctious enough to keep things interesting. Returning to the rodeo circuit suddenly didn't appeal to him as it had a few weeks ago. This time, unlike six years earlier, the idea of a more settled life didn't send him running for the hills.

And Rosie! Damn. She'd been a teasing temptation at nineteen, with flirty ways and a sassy attitude, but she'd grown into a mature, sexy-as-hell woman who took no shit and knew what she wanted. Given the way her eyes darkened whenever she looked his way . . . she wanted him.

He remembered her as a teenager, how sweet she'd been. Her sense of humor and the silly things she'd say, just to get a laugh from him. He also recalled a few times when he could talk to her, really open up about his dreams of making it big in the rodeo, and she'd listen. Caleb knew her folks fought like a couple of cats tied up in a bag, and Rosie had always been a sensitive kid. Too sensitive to have to deal with that shit, day after day. But she'd gotten past it. He was so proud of her.

And he sure as hell wanted her. Not just for a week, but for something like eternity.

Rising to his feet, he strode down the hall and stood outside Carson's room, listening to her tender words and Carson's sleepy giggles as she tucked him in for the night. The emotions he'd been drowning in over the last week fell away, replaced by an overwhelming need for Rosie. He wanted to make love to her, find a way to bring their relationship back where it'd been before he'd run off. He wanted to drown in their shared memories, then create new ones with her.

He absently rubbed his sore leg. He wasn't stupid; returning to the rodeo circuit was iffy for him. Maybe it was time to make a life for himself in Dustin, with Rosie and his son.

If she'd have him.

Her footsteps made a soft shuffle from the bedroom into the hall. Her breath hitched on a low gasp when she spotted him, then she slowly shut the door. "Hi," she murmured. "Is something the matter?"

Caleb closed the distance between them. He inhaled her heady fragrance, the same flowery perfume she'd worn six years ago when he'd explored every inch of her beautiful body, listening to the needy sounds she made as he'd discovered all her pleasure spots.

Oh, hell yeah. His muscles tight, he reached for her and ran one finger down the silken skin of her cheek as her lips parted on a sigh. Yet the resistance he read in her body language made his jaw clench.

"Caleb," she whispered, shaking her head. "We—we shouldn't."

Knowing he'd been her first lover filled him with such a sense of possessiveness. Though it was his own damned fault he'd lost her, he wanted to wipe away the imprint of any man who'd touched her over the last six years. To have her under him again, show her all the ways that she belonged to him, only him . . .

Gripping her gently by her upper arms, he leaned in and nuzzled her slender neck, flicking his tongue at the rapid pulse above her breasts. *Pleasure spot one.* At the sound of her sharp inhale, he nipped gently on her shoulder and tugged her closer. "Rosie." Her name was a shudder on his lips.

When he ran his tongue along the seam of her mouth she opened for him, allowing him to plunder her moist depths until she relaxed against him. Her arms slid around his neck as that sweet whimper he hadn't heard in six years sounded in her throat.

Victory coursed through him.

Chapter Eight

Bending slightly, Caleb slid one arm under Rosemary's knees and scooped her up. Her room was just down the hall and he strode the short distance quickly, kicking the door shut behind him. Lowering her to the bed, he followed her down, removing her arms from his neck and securing them above her head with one hand as he explored her curves.

Caleb's desire skyrocketed. He bent his head and pressed his mouth to hers, an open, urgent kiss, their tongues entwining in rising passion.

His fingers trembled as he went to work on the buttons of her blouse, managing to free her breasts without ripping the delicate cotton. Her bra fastened in the front and after a second of careful tugging, he filled his palm with silky flesh.

Rosie arched her body and moaned into his mouth.

Pleasure point two . . .

"Oh, God, Caleb." Her voice shook; her pelvis thrust and ground against his more-than-ready erection. "Please . . ."

Caleb didn't need any further prompting. He released her just long enough to strip off his clothes as she yanked at her jeans. In their frenzy to get naked, clothing flew everywhere, until finally—*thank God*—they were skin on skin.

Her curves had filled out in all the right places, and he'd never wanted a woman as badly as he wanted Rosemary. Caleb slid down her body to taste one creamy breast. His tongue laved and his teeth nipped at the sweet pink tip.

With a gasp she thrust her fingers into his hair, tugging him closer as he moved to her other breast and gave it the same loving attention. He trailed his mouth lower and her

flesh quivered as he explored every lovely inch laid out
before him. When he flicked his tongue in the hollow of her
belly button, she sighed his name.

Pleasure spot three.

It might have been six years, but he still knew what
Rosie liked in bed, and he was determined to give her
exactly what she needed. The silky curls between her thighs
enticed him and he slid two fingers inside, locating all
those pleasure spots he'd yet to explore.

Rosemary must have had the same thought, because
she gripped his neck and urged him closer. "Please, Caleb.
I need you."

He fought to clear his desire-fogged brain long enough
to remember protection. Six years ago, his stupidity got
them in trouble, and Rosemary bore the consequences. He
wouldn't do that to her again. *Not until it's completely right
between us. Not until we're ready.*

"Condom," he panted in her ear. "Wait."

She nodded as he fumbled through the pocket of his
jeans, found his wallet, and pulled out a crumpled packet—
thankfully still sealed and intact. A few seconds later, he
was ready.

Caleb rose over her as she parted her legs. Holding her
gaze, he eased inside her slowly, inch by inch. Her breath
caught on a soft gasp as he filled her completely, his fingers
threading through her hair, his eyes never leaving hers.

"I've missed you, Rosie," he rasped, the words
breaking on a groan.

He paused, lifting her hips to meld their flesh
completely, his heart racing wildly at the soft cry she
released.

"Oh, Caleb. I—I've missed you, too." Her legs curved
tightly around his waist and she clung to him, her nails
pressing into his back. For a second she looked dazed, as if
she couldn't quite believe what they were doing together.

Then she gave him a gorgeous smile and wriggled her hips. "Now move."

He dropped his face to her shoulder on a shaky chuckle. "Yes, ma'am."

Maybe she hesitated for one tiny moment. Maybe she was making a big mistake. Rosemary wasn't sure. All she knew was the rightness of Caleb, in her arms, inside her body.

Six long years of loneliness crumbled into dust as she felt him, big and hard, moving with her in a sensual dance she'd never quite forgotten. So familiar, she had to blink back the tears and press her lips together to keep from sobbing out how much she'd truly missed him.

There'd never been anyone but him. How could there be? Caleb Johnson had owned her soul from the very beginning and nobody else ever stood a flicker of a chance.

As he moved faster and deeper, she curled her hands along his shoulder blades and held on tight. His fingers would probably leave bruises on her hips, but she didn't care. Each heated breath he panted into her neck, every broken endearment he huffed in her ear, pushed her need higher, made her skin tighten and prickle. There wasn't room for anything else.

All her frustration over the unbalanced situation between them, any insecurity she felt for her son's sake . . . it simply evaporated into nothing when Caleb covered her mouth in a scalding kiss that rocked her senseless.

"Jesus, Rosie. You feel so damn good." His hair hung in damp disarray around his lean, tanned face. Under her hands, is muscles bunched and released as he drove her higher still.

Tension ramped her body into a fierce arch that made her grip him hard enough to choke off his air supply. In answer, Caleb caught the curve of her neck between his teeth and bit down as his hands jerked her hips tighter against his driving thrusts.

She broke, shattering in a convulsive orgasm, muffling her scream in his shoulder. Clinging frantically, she rode out her climax as Caleb pinned her to the mattress and shuddered through his own release. His chest heaved as he fought for breath; his hands had found hers and their fingers twined together as if they both needed an anchor in a storm that seemed to go on and on.

So much like what they'd had between them years earlier. And she couldn't have stemmed the overflowing tears that dampened the hair at her temples. She didn't even try; she let them fall while her heart finally calmed and her muscles relaxed, her body going limp beneath his.

Seconds later, she felt Caleb slump in her arms, sated; another memory she'd missed like crazy. How he'd simply melt over her when the last tiny shivers worked through his large frame, and their damp skin fused together amongst tangled sheets. The best feeling in the world, and here they were again. She loved it.

She loved him.

As Caleb turned his lips to the curve of her shoulder and kissed the place he'd bitten, she realized it was pointless to fight the inevitable. He was her son's daddy. The connection between them hadn't lessened at all over the years, and it didn't seem to matter what he might have done while on the rodeo circuit or how many women he'd probably slept with.

What mattered was now, this minute, and what they built together as a result. Even as she admitted it to herself, Rosemary had a feeling the toughest, at least for her, would be reestablishing trust. But she was willing to try. She slipped her hands from his loosened grip and twined her arms around his neck, holding him close, and let herself drift.

Emitting a soft protest as he moved away slightly, she quieted when he murmured, "Be right back." A soft rustle of the sheets reminded her Caleb needed to dispose of the protection he'd used.

He returned quickly, gathering her into his arms. With a sigh, Rosemary fell into a light doze.

Later—it might have been minutes or hours—Caleb roused her by scattering heated kisses over her breasts. Then he murmured, "I want to stay the night," against one puckered nipple.

Rosemary turned her head on the pillow as he moved his mouth to hers and nipped briefly, before facing her with sleepy eyes and cheeks already shadowed with dark blond stubble.

So sexy; so very male. Caleb Johnson, in a nutshell. *And he's all mine.* At least for the moment. Still, she tried it out in a whisper, her lips touching his. "Mine."

"Yeah, I am." He deepened the kiss, his tongue stroking hers. The moment spun out in the warm, quiet room, the give and take of their mouths echoing in the resurgence of passion that had him hardening against her belly.

She arched, mindless with desire. "Caleb. Yes."

"Yes, I can stay?"

His attempt at lighthearted banter didn't fool her one bit, because she could all but taste the need pouring from him as he slipped a hand beneath her and held her tightly.

In the midst of overwhelming emotion, it seemed cold and mechanical to ask the obvious question, but she regained enough of her common sense to whisper, "Do you have more . . ." She couldn't finish, burying her heated face in his neck.

His shoulders shook beneath her cheek. He was laughing at her! She wanted to slug him, but his body felt so good, she couldn't bring herself to pull away.

"Baby, I've got plenty of, um, opportunities to rock your world," Caleb assured her solemnly, then slid against her suggestively.

She shivered, moaned, shivered again, before reaching for his cock and palming it firmly. "Then I guess you'd better get that endless supply, cowboy . . . and stay." Her breath snagged on a moan as his flesh seemed to leap and pulse in her hand. "God, Caleb." She coiled herself around him. "Don't go, never go . . ."

"I'm not going anywhere." He covered her lips with a hard, wild kiss.

"Mommy. Daddy. I'm hungry." The childish voice piped up close to his ear, accompanied by a cough and a sneeze. Caleb stirred reluctantly, disoriented for a few moments.

Daylight flooded the room. *Rosemary's bedroom.* In a flash it all came back to him; the loving they'd shared, interspersed with an hour here and there of exhausted sleep. Only to awaken in each other's arms and do it all over again.

Then he remembered how he'd ended up here in the first place. Carson was doing much better but still not completely out of the woods from the pneumonia he'd suffered.

Caleb eased his arm from under Rosemary's sleeping form. She muttered softly and curled herself around her pillow as he sat up in bed and beckoned to his son. "Morning, buddy. Hungry, huh? I can fix that." Belatedly he glanced down to assure the sheet covered his naked ass. *Whew, safe.*

"How?" Carson crawled onto the bed and settled into Caleb's arms. His soft red hair was tangled, wayward ends sticking up all over. With his cheeks rosy from sleep, bright eyed and eager for the day to begin, he looked like an adorable, slightly mischievous cherub.

Caleb snatched him close and mock-growled into his sweet-smelling neck, eliciting a torrent of giggles as Carson squirmed away from the beard stubble Caleb tickled him with. "I happen to be the world-famous blueberry pancake king."

"Nuh-uh! Guys don't make pancakes. Girls do!" Carson curled his little fingers into claws and went right for Caleb's armpits in retaliation.

"Uh-huh. Guys make the best pancakes, just wait and see." Though he'd never been ticklish in his life, Caleb emitted loud, chortling sounds as his son dug in with gusto. "If I promise to cook up some amazing pancakes, will you stop tickling me and help me make your mommy breakfast in bed?"

"You bet!" Carson jumped to the floor and grabbed for Caleb's hand. "Hurry! Before Mommy wakes up."

"I have to get dressed first, champ. Okay? And do some stuff in the bathroom. Meet me in the kitchen." Caleb bent close to his son's ear and whispered, "We'll start on 'Operation Pancake,' post-haste." He cracked a grin as Carson whooped and ran for the door. His bare feet slapped along the hallway and stomped down the stairs. The sound brought a lump of emotion to Caleb's throat that he fought to swallow down.

I want to wake up like this for the rest of my life.

Rubbing at suddenly stinging eyes, he smoothed the sheet away, then jerked in surprise as a warm, slender hand stroked over his arm. Turning, Caleb brought Rosemary close as she wriggled to his side of the bed and climbed into his lap, the same as Carson had done.

"So, surprise pancakes? Really?" She nuzzled his cheek, before closing her mouth over his in a delicious kiss.

They shared nibbles and soft, morning caresses, as more sunlight poured into the room and the sound of little-boy feet clomping down the hall reminded them they weren't alone upstairs. Everything felt right in the world, and he couldn't remember when he'd been so happy.

Caleb eased away first, with a lingering kiss to one sweetly puckered breast. "My pancakes will make your tummy weep."

"For joy? Or with heartburn?" she retorted cheekily.

He gave her bare bottom a cuff. "Let me up, smartass, and you'll see."

The kitchen rang with laughter as Caleb and Carson made a shambles of mixing and cooking pancakes. Rosemary had run out of blueberries a week ago, so her son decided nothing but apples would do as a substitute. Worried her boy might actually try talking Caleb into letting him have a paring knife, Rosemary positioned herself on a kitchen chair and kept an eye on both her men. They balked at her interference but were mollified when she vowed not to lift a finger.

Keeping her promise wasn't easy especially after Carson dropped his third egg on the floor, and the flour canister exploded when Caleb knocked it over. She slapped a hand over her mouth to keep in her protest as well as her chuckles, resigned to spending a good hour cleaning up their mess.

Twenty sloppy minutes later, they sat down to surprisingly delicious, fluffy pancakes packed with apples and cinnamon. Carson crammed them in as fast as his fork could cut them, and Rosemary sighed at the taste.

"Yummy. I'm impressed, Caleb. Where'd you learn to make pancakes like this?"

"It's the beer," he replied casually, swallowing a huge bite.

She almost dropped her juice glass. "You put beer in them? You can't feed beer pancakes to a five-year-old! What were you thinking?"

"I'm thinking you're pretty easy to rile up, Carmichael." He offered a smug snort. "Not only do you not have beer in your fridge, but you sat there and watched us make them. Did you see a beer bottle anywhere?"

"Um—" Rosemary felt her cheeks heat and she rubbed at them. As Carson giggled wildly, she mumbled, "Now who's a smartass?"

After threatening to tie her to the chair if she tried to help clean up, Caleb settled Carson with a sink full of soapy water and what unbreakable utensils they'd used. As Carson stood on his little stepstool and played at washing the dishes, Caleb scooted a chair close to her and nibbled at her mouth. "Let's take him to Hawthorn, let him work off some of that energy. We can stop at Sonic and get some corn dogs and onion rings."

"You just ate. How can you think of food?" But Rosemary tilted her head to give him better access to her neck, loving the feel of his callused fingers trailing along her arms.

"I also just had sex. Well, last night," he teased softly so Carson wouldn't hear. "How can I think of getting you naked and under me? I just can, baby."

"Shh, jeez!" She slapped a hand over his mouth. "You think he's not listening but I promise you, little boys hear everything."

Caleb kissed her palm. "Let's spend the day in Hawthorn."

The persuasive tone in his sexy voice left Rosemary unable to form a single objection. She didn't even try. Instead, she slid her hand from his mouth to the back of his neck and pulled him in for a fast, moist bite to his full bottom lip.

"Okay."

Chapter Nine

It'd been ten years or more since Caleb had hung out at Hawthorn. The park sat about three miles outside of Dustin, a sprawling conglomerate of public swimming pools, several carnival rides including a restored carousel, and a children's museum that was a kid's dream.

He could remember taking Rosemary here once, during the few daylight hours when they had actually climbed out of bed for something other than sex. Even then, he'd found ways to ambush her with caresses and kisses. Behind the main cabana at the adult pool. Under the bleachers on the softball field while the Dustin Lil' Wranglers played their hearts out. Up against one of the mammoth cottonwoods scattered through the park, his lips devouring that sweet spot between her neck and her shoulder, bared by the cute little sundress she'd worn. He'd had her hands pinned to the rough bark over her head, one of her long, shapely legs wound around his waist, when a park official strolled by and busted them.

"You okay, Daddy? You kinda made a noise." Carson's sweet chirp dragged Caleb out of the sexual fog of memories and the groan he'd released under his breath.

He looked over at Rosemary's *cut-that-out* expression and then into his son's concerned face. "Just hungry, buddy. It's been so long since our pancakes, right?"

"It's been two whole hours," Rosemary inserted dryly.

"Yeah, but you know pancakes. Two hours later and you're starving."

She snickered. "That's Chinese food, not pancakes."

"Same difference." Sweeping up his giggling son in one arm, Caleb tugged Rosemary forward with his free hand. "Come on, let's hit the merry-go-round before we eat so we won't get pukey."

"I want the camel! I want the camel!" Carson bounced madly, his fingers twisted into Caleb's shirt collar. "Daddy, the camel, okay?"

"You got it, son. As long as nobody else is riding on it."

A light breeze ruffled the edges of Rosemary's long, loose curls as she walked beside him. She wore faded Levi's that clung to every luscious curve and a thin cotton blouse with no sleeves, the unbuttoned ends tied beneath her perfect breasts. Each time he eyed that expanse of creamy pale midriff she'd left bare, Caleb broke out in a sweat. A pair of dusty, beat-up red leather Dingos with squared off toes peeked from the frayed hem of her jeans. He vaguely remembered them from years ago and couldn't believe she'd kept them all this time. Without a speck of lipstick or anything else on her face, she looked no more than sixteen.

Then she glanced sideways and gave him a smile, lips parted slightly and showing a flash of straight, white teeth.

Unable to look away from her beauty, every muscle in his body tightened and clenched with need. *This woman.* Only Rosemary. There'd never be anyone else for him.

When Carson wriggled to get down, then tugged on his hand, Caleb blinked and shook his head. His cheeks heated like a teenager, and from just a single smoldering glance from the fiery redhead standing so close to him.

He broke the contact between them, squatting next to his son whose excitement had him bouncing in his scuffed hi-top sneakers. "You got a bee up your butt, partner?" he teased gently.

Carson waved his arms in a childish frenzy. "Daddy, the camel!" He squirmed impatiently.

The music from a piping calliope floated on the air, and Caleb turned toward the familiar tune. There sat the carousel, an antique marvel of what modern restoration could accomplish. When Caleb was a kid, the carousel worked but its colors had been faded, with the tips of equine ears broken off and paint missing from saddles and muzzles. Somebody had spent a shitload of money to bring the ride to its former glory. It now sparkled in the sun, packed with joyous children riding their favorite animals with happy abandon, while their parents waved and snapped pictures.

"Can we go? Please?" Carson tugged at both their hands.

Rosemary's laughter floated across the air as she allowed Carson to drag her forward, while Caleb pretended to protest and lag behind. More determined than ever, their son pulled harder until they all stood at the chainlink fence circling the carousel. He would have bolted through the gate if Rosemary hadn't grabbed the back of his shirt.

"Carson, calm down. We have to buy tickets, then wait our turn." She knelt and traced a gentle finger along his pouting lower lip. "That camel isn't going anywhere, honey. You and Daddy get the tickets, and I'll hold your place in line." She lifted his chin. "Okay?"

"Okay," he mumbled, then gave her a hopeful look. "Can I ride as much as I want?"

Caleb couldn't contain his snort of laughter. "What an operator." He ruffled his son's soft curls. "Come on, let's go buy some tickets. Maybe a roll of them." His promise got Carson squealing ecstatically and jumping up and down.

As Caleb grinned at his son's antics, Rosemary leaned over and gave him a lingering kiss, a fast, hot flick of her tongue, and a parting shot.

"Sucker."

Waiting in line at the carousel, Rosemary pressed a hand to her fluttering stomach. The kiss she'd given Caleb had been meant as a silly tease, but even a touch of that mouth on hers made her center clutch. She sucked in a steadying breath just as a hand tapped her shoulder.

"Hey, Rosie! How've you been?" Miranda Benson, nicknamed 'Mimi' since childhood, stood behind her in line, three giggling boys holding onto the conch belt cinching her narrow cowgirl hips.

Mimi had made the women's rodeo circuit in Dustin and Cheyenne during her teen years, whittling the baby fat from her body like only an extreme workout of riding and roping could do. Younger by two years, Mimi's sister Dwana had followed in her footsteps, taking it even further and becoming a professional roper on the circuit. Mimi had dropped out to marry, and her husband Frank moved the family to Cheyenne last year.

Rosemary had lost touch with both Mimi and Dwana, catching up only here and there when Mimi and the boys came to town.

She gave Mimi a quick hug. "Hi, Mimi. I've been good. You?"

"Been good. Busy." She blew honey blonde curls off her forehead.

"Where's Frank?" Rosemary hadn't seen him walk up.

"Trucking as usual." Mimi rolled her eyes. "Big load to Montana. He'll be back tomorrow." Her smile held the weariness as well as the fortitude of a long-haul trucker's wife.

Rosemary stood back and grinned at the trio of chubby-cheeked faces peering at her. "I can't believe how big your boys have grown." She opened her arms to collect the adorable herd, identical triplets with their mother's sky-blue eyes and their dad's black hair. As the boys huddled close in a wriggling snuggle, she glanced up at Mimi. "Are you here for the day?"

"Yep. There's nothing like this in Cheyenne, damn it all. And we promised the boys." Mimi tousled two heads and snickered at their indignant groans. "Little buggers are starved as usual. But they begged to ride first, then we're going to Sonic." She looked around curiously. "Where's that cutie of yours? Are you here all day, too?"

"Well, I—" Rosemary didn't get any farther, because Mimi's jaw unhinged in a gape. Tensing, Rosemary looked over her shoulder as Caleb and Carson strolled along the carousel boundary, hand in hand.

"Is that—oh, my—um . . ." Mimi turned a shocked face to her. "Caleb Johnson." She flicked him another glance. "When did he blow in? Are you two together?"

Rosemary sighed as she released the boys so they could run to the fence and watch the carousel spin. "He got in about ten days ago. It's kind of a long story, Mimi. I guess you could say we're trying it out to see if it fits." She scraped her hair back from her face with fingers that held a tremble. "Carson adores him."

"Does he know who Caleb is?"

"Oh, yes." She gestured helplessly. "What else can I do? I have to give this a chance."

"Yeah." Mimi nodded in empathy. "I get it, believe me. You remember what Frank and I went through. I knew damned well the man didn't want to get married even with three babies on the way. My daddy threatened him with a shotgun." She winked. "It wasn't loaded, thank God. Of course Frank loved me back then but he was an immature ass. He's grown up a lot." She squeezed Rosemary's arm reassuringly. "I always liked Caleb even if he was a wild one. He has steady eyes."

Before Rosemary could respond, Carson spotted them and screeched, "Mimi Moo!" He broke from Caleb's grip and tore up to Mimi, flinging his arms wide. With a laugh, she dropped to her knees and cuddled him tightly.

"Mimi Moo?" Caleb murmured as he stepped to Rosemary's side and slipped an arm around her.

She had to chuckle a bit. "You remember Miranda, right? Carson called her that silly nickname because of the

calf she and the triplets raised for 4-H last year. It kind of
stuck."

Mimi got to her feet, and assessed Caleb appraisingly.
"As I live and breathe, he's back." She gave his cowboy hat
a tug and it fell over his forehead. "Good to see you, Caleb.
Whatcha think of this short stack?" She tickled Carson
under his ear, making him squeal.

Caleb thumbed his hat back into place. His lips
twitched. "He's okay in a pinch."

When Carson launched himself against his legs, Caleb
swung him over his shoulder like a sack of feed. "Kind of
scrawny but we'll take care of that." He swatted his son's
backside and Carson shrieked with laughter, hanging
upside down. He dug ten mischievous fingers in the
vicinity of his daddy's ribs and the two of them tussled
while Rosemary grinned like a star-struck fangirl. She
couldn't help herself.

Caleb pulled Carson right side up and hefted him in
one arm. He turned to study Mimi's boys, who were
shoving each other noisily as they ran up to their mother.
"There's a rowdy bunch. Yours?"

She nodded and reined them in with practiced hands.

"How old are you cowpokes?" he asked the boys.

"Four!" they hollered in unison. Mimi winced, but her
expression held plenty of pride.

"Miranda, I'm impressed. Good on ya." Caleb tipped
his hat to her and she loosed a deep chortle.

"Same goes, Johnson. You've got yourself a terrific
kid. I'm glad to see you back." She leaned in and added in
a not-so-subtle murmur, "Hang smart, y'hear?"

Rosemary groaned, "Mimi, for cripe's sake."

Winking, Mimi touched her arm. "I've got an idea.
Why don't you let us take the little stinker for a while? He
can jump on some rides with the boys and have lunch with
us. Probably Sonic." She nodded toward Caleb and they
both watched him balance Carson on the tops of his boots.

He shuffled his feet, bouncing Carson up and sideways, eliciting a fit of giggles.

Rosemary parted her lips to demur as Mimi raised her voice to catch Carson's attention. "Hey, squirt, wanna hang out with the boys and chow down on some corn dogs over at Sonic?"

"Yeah! Onion rings, too?" Carson jumped off Caleb's feet and ran up to Rosemary. "Can I, Mommy?"

"Oh, I don't know, honey—" As she vacillated, unsure, Carson turned to his father with a child's innate knowledge of how to pit one parent against the other.

"Daddy, can I, please?" The soft plea in their son's voice was lethal, and Caleb wouldn't withstand its appeal any more than she could. Behind her, Mimi coughed rudely.

"Ask Mommy, and what she says, goes. Okay?" Caleb hunkered down to their son's level. "And you can have all the tickets we bought as long as you share with the boys. But you have to be really good and do everything Mimi says. You understand?" At Carson's frantic nod, Caleb squinted up at Rosemary from beneath his hat. "What d'ya think, warden? Should we spring the kid?"

She could no more resist those bedroom eyes of his, any more than the puppy-dog looks Carson bombarded her with. "Oh, all right. But if I hear of one single problem, you're in for it." She braced herself for Carson's whoop of joy and the impact of his sturdy little body against hers.

A few minutes later the Bensons were off, with Carson holding two of the triplets' hands and Mimi clutching the third boy. Probably Kenny, who she recalled was the most rambunctious of the three. Kevin and Keith would willingly stick by Carson.

As Rosemary waved at Mimi, she felt a strong arm slip around her waist. Caleb pulled her into his chest and she shivered at the feel of those hard muscles at her back.

His free hand nudged her hair out of the way, then trailed along her neck. His lips followed, brushing over her skin, the tenor of his breathing accelerating when she relaxed against his body in surrender. Loving the way he nibbled and licked, Rosemary refused to think of who might be around, watching or judging her. It didn't really concern anyone but them.

"Let's take a walk," he whispered unsteadily in her ear.

She could feel the mad thump of her heart. Everywhere their bodies touched, heat was generating, blistering what remained of her common sense.

I don't give a damn at all. She turned in his arms and met his seeking lips. Against them she moaned, "Hell, yeah."

Chapter Ten

His hand warm on the back of her neck, Caleb guided Rosemary along the nature path connecting one side of the park to the other. His thumb stroked gently under her hair, over her ultra-sensitive nape. She could have easily melted in her boots.

When she swayed slightly, Caleb's knowing chuckle stiffened her spine and she flashed him a glance, wavering between irritation and affection. *Overconfident smartass.*

Though she loved being alone with him, a mother's natural worry kicked in and she found she couldn't completely relax. It wasn't so much a safety concern. Miranda would care for Carson as one of her own and Rosemary fully trusted her. It was more than that. Despite their reconnection the night before and a new understanding growing between them, she still couldn't completely trust Caleb to stick around for Carson. That made every hour with him as part of a family unit precious. Lord knew, she wanted to trust him. She wasn't quite there yet.

Then she told herself to stop being an idiot and just enjoy what she could.

They passed the adult pool area with its heated Jacuzzi, the water a comfortable temperature year-round. "We should have brought our swimsuits," she commented idly.

Caleb snagged one of her hands and swung it between them, like he used to do years ago. "We can always come back another day, Rosie." He tugged her closer and brushed a teasing kiss across her nose. "Or sneak in after dark and go skinny-dipping."

"Oh, yes. Great idea especially since last year they upped the security system with about a hundred extra cameras." She gave his shoulder a playful shove. "It'd be all over Youtube."

"Hey, I'd download it. Late at night when I'm lonely." Caleb yanked her up hard against his chest. "Lucky for me, I've got the real thing right here." In the shade of a cottonwood he sucked gently at her throat, and everything went right out of her head, wiped clean by those warm, full lips and tongue stroking fire on her skin.

With a breathy sigh Rosemary tunneled her fingers through his hair, fisting the heavy strands, encouraging him to take anything he dared. On a public path like this, half of Dustin could mosey on by at any time and gawk at them. She couldn't bring herself to care.

She tugged until he lifted his head enough for her to kiss him. The kiss deepened, drawing a low groan from him as he slid a hand beneath her thigh and guided her closer, easing her back against the cottonwood's rough bark.

Tree bark poked her back, but she barely acknowledged its scrape. Her head, her heart— everything—was so full of Caleb and what he did to her that nothing else mattered. And those small remnants of mistrust, that he'd up and leave when it suited him, shattered beneath the hot, vital strength of his body against hers. But she felt the tremor in his fingers where they gripped her, the shiver that moved up his spine when she slid her tongue over the firm flesh along his jaw. And she knew what exploded between them affected him as much as it did her.

"Ah, Rosie . . . I'd give anything to have you naked right now." The words burst from his throat, low and rough.

When Caleb propped her on one brawny arm, snaking his free hand inside her gapping shirt collar, a moan of anticipation slipped from her throat.

He flicked open a few buttons, his fingers shaky, then hissed out a curse when he found bare skin. "God almighty, baby. How could I not know you've been braless all day?" He bent his head and covered her nipple with hungry lips.

Her lids fluttered shut, then snapped wide open as she looked around furtively for others on the walking path. Though she didn't see anyone, the sane and yet-unscrambled portion of her brain told her it was just a matter of time before someone caught them doing illicit, probably illegal acts in public.

Still, she couldn't help but cup his neck and keep him close as the feel of his mouth and tongue sent her into boneless submission.

A beam of sunlight filtered through the cottonwood leaves, setting a fiery glow in Rosemary's tangled hair. Caleb had lost track of how many kisses he'd scattered over her bared skin.

"Grandma, cotton candy!" The childish screech echoed from down the path, heading straight for them.

Breaking their kiss, Caleb lowered her leg. With one last brush of his mouth over her lips, he stepped back and murmured, "Company, baby."

Rosemary's eyes popped open, dazed for half a heartbeat, before an amused smile curved her mouth. "You recall the last time we got rousted from this very park for necking in public?"

She swiftly buttoned up as he angled his body to shield her from the approaching grandparents and their sugar-seeking grandchild. By the time they reached the thicker copse of cottonwoods, Rosemary was smoothed and tucked, leaning against the trunk, every bit the picture of innocence.

Caleb nodded a greeting as the towheaded little girl—about Carson's age—dragged her grandparents toward the shack selling cotton candy.

"She'll wear them out in no time." He snared her wrist and pulled her in for a fast, voracious kiss.

Rosemary came willingly enough but a touch of hesitancy in her response told him, better than words, their bubble of intimacy had probably popped for the day. Even so, he had to ask. "You all right, Rosie?" He brought her hand to his face and held it there, inexplicably relieved when she stroked him gently.

"I'm good. But I think we should head back to the carousel and find Carson. It's getting late and I still have to figure out dinner and scrub about ten pounds of park crud off our son." Rising on tiptoe, she brushed her lips over his cheek.

Caleb cradled her tenderly, thinking that of all the wonderful events of today, all the laughter and kisses, the sweetest had to be the words, 'our son' coming from those gorgeous lips now pressed to his cheek. He wondered if she knew how deeply she'd touched his heart.

He wondered if she knew he'd never let her go.

They collected a very excited boy on the short path between the carousel and the picnic area. Carson's hair stuck up in wild tufts, his plaid shirt half in, half out of his cargo shorts, clutching a stuffed alligator almost bigger than him. Mimi and the triplets trailed behind him, all grinning widely. The boys' faces were smeared with what looked like cotton candy and mustard.

"Look, Daddy!" Carson shoved the silly looking purple gator at Caleb. "Mimi Moo and me won Fred!"

Caleb held the gator up for inspection. It wore a bright yellow cowboy hat and hot pink hi-top sneakers on each foot. "This is quite the stylish lizard, huh?" Then he blinked down at his son. "'Fred?'"

"Don't ask," Mimi snorted. She opened her arms to Carson. "C'mere, short stack, and give me some sugar."

Giggling, Carson took a running leap and hung on Mimi like a little monkey, his arms and legs wound tight. He gave her a smacking kiss. "Thanks, Aunt Mimi. For helping me win Fred."

"And?" Rosemary prodded gently.

"And for feeding me, and letting me ride the camel for like a hundred times." He laid his head on her shoulder trustingly. "Can I come see you sometime? And play with the guys?"

She swung him around a few times and got him squealing. "You betcha, cowboy. Anytime. But make sure it's okay with your folks. Don't just jump a club car and ride those rails to Cheyenne, y'hear?"

As Carson's eyes got big at the mention of stowing away on a train, Rosemary groaned. "Oh, jeez. Don't give him any ideas." She knelt and scooped Mimi's herd into a communal snuggle, laughing as they peppered her cheeks with sticky kisses.

Carson wriggled from Mimi's arms and ran to Caleb. "Can we ride the rails, Daddy? Like a hobo?"

Caleb coughed out a chuckle. "What do you know about hobos?" He grabbed for his adorable boy, deftly flipping him upside down, then shared a knowing look with Rosemary. "You buy the tickets, we'll ride in style all the way to Cheyenne, deal?"

"Okay!" Carson flapped his arms like a bird. "Can you carry me this way?" His voice sounded garbled from the rush of blood to his face.

Caleb swung him right side up and planted him firmly on the ground. "No can do, tough guy. Not upside down. But you can piggy." He knelt and thumbed toward his back. "Hop on."

Carson didn't need to be invited twice. He clambered up and clung. Caleb handed Fred to Rosemary, then slipped his hands under Carson's legs to stabilize him, while Rosemary used Fred's sneaker-covered paw to wave goodbye at Mimi and the boys.

Heading for the parking lot, Caleb bounced Carson with every other stride as Rosemary waltzed in circles with Fred in her arms. Their son giggled all the way to the car, the best sound in the world.

"I'm in the mood to cook," Rosemary announced, as Caleb pulled up to one of a handful of traffic lights in Dustin. "Maybe fried chicken and cheesy mashed potatoes. What do you think? You guys hungry for real food?"

In the back seat, Carson immediately started jumping up and down. "Yeah, yeah! Chicken and po!"

"Sit still, buddy," Caleb warned. "And put your seat belt back on, okay? Don't want you flying out the window."

"Aww, gee." But he did as he was told, sitting quietly. Caleb gave him a commiserating grin toward the rearview mirror, understanding how hard it was for a kid to sit still.

When Rosemary hooked her hand over his thigh, he turned the grin into a comical leer and murmured, "I could go for chicken. Maybe a breast."

"Shh, jeez." She pinched him in a tender spot, then rubbed it in apology. "We'll have to stop by Safeway. My supplies are pathetically low. You remember where it is? On Sprig, near the bakery."

"Yep. Hasn't been a whole lot of changes in Dustin, you know." Caleb made the turn onto Sprig Street, then dropped a hand from the steering wheel to cover her fingers and hike them higher on his thigh. "Only the important stuff changed and for the better," he stressed.

"Whatever do you mean, Mr. Johnson?" She wore a demure expression but her cheeks had flushed.

He slowed down to enter the Safeway parking lot and whipped into a slot next to a cart return. Killing the engine, Caleb leaned in and pressed a kiss to her mouth, warm and soft under his lips. Before Carson could start squirming impatiently, he murmured, "All you've given me, that's the most important change of all." He cupped her chin tenderly. "Carson. A chance to prove myself to you." His voice dropped to a rasp. "Your love."

She swallowed convulsively. "Caleb—"

"Mommy, let's go!" Carson hollered from the rear.

Caleb shuddered out a sigh as he pulled away. "You heard the peanut gallery back there. Let's go chase down a chicken."

Inside, Rosemary consulted the shopping list she'd slapped together before they left Hawthorn. Caleb tossed Carson in a cart and wheeled him up and down the aisles, making silly engine noises to the delight of their son. Each item on the list was passed off to Carson who carefully laid them in the cart, then did his best to keep his feet from squashing anything. In between grocery placement, Carson kept up a chattering commentary ranging from multiple corn dogs at Sonic to how many times he rode the carousel without throwing up.

Caleb made appropriate noises of approval while Rosemary muttered, "If he doesn't puke in the middle of the night we'll all be lucky."

"Well, if he does, I'll clean it up." Caleb ran caressing fingers under her hair and enjoyed the shiver that swept over her from his touch.

Her eyes met his, soft amber, tinged with a promise. "Let's get the rest and go home. I'm hungry."

"So am I, baby." But he wasn't talking about food.

At the checkout counter, Carson stood in the cart and craned his neck like a bird dog. "Where's Daddy?"

"Sit down before you fall down," Rosemary scolded gently, then handed him a can of baking powder to keep him occupied. "Here, help me unload. And your daddy got a phone call."

Actually, that call worried her a bit, not to mention the look on Caleb's face when he checked the display. But he'd flashed her a quick smile before swiping the screen, then put it to his ear and stepped away to take the call. She and Carson had continued shopping.

Now she dug bills from her wallet, relieved she carried enough money. Usually she only used a credit card if she absolutely had to. As she tucked her change into her purse she heard Carson screech, "Uncle Mason!"

Oh, just great. Rosemary loved her brother a lot, but lately he'd been pissing her off with his poor attitude toward Caleb and refusal to believe his once-best friend could change for the better. She didn't have time to deal with Mason's crap, especially in public. And by his determined expression as he strode in her direction, she just knew the idiot would say something to make her mad.

"Hey there, Lil' Tuff." Mason yanked on a lock of her son's hair. "Where've you been all day?" He directed the question at Carson but his focus remained on her as she loaded the bags in the cart.

She bit back on her impatience and pinned a smile in place as Carson chirped, "We went to the park! I ate five corn dogs at Sonic, and saw Mimi Moo, and we won Fred, and Daddy let me ride the camel a hundred times—"

Mason interrupted abruptly with the only thing he'd heard in that whole mess of chatter. "Daddy?" He turned to Rosemary with a thundering frown. "You've been with *him* all day?" His voice lowered to a snarl. "What the hell, Rosie!"

She hastened forward, edging him away from Carson's curiosity as he knelt in the cart and stared at them. "Mason, you can just shut up right now." She stabbed his chest with two fingers, unwilling to back down. "None of this is your business. What I do or where I go with Caleb isn't anything to you."

Turning to Carson, she said brightly, "Hang on to the cart, sweetheart. Let's get this stuff out to the car and wait for Daddy." Without another word, Rosemary shoved the cart through the exit doors toward the parking lot.

She hoped her brother would stay in the store, but Mason predictably followed her outside, blocking her path as she moved to unload the bags. "I got news for you, Rosie. This *is* my business. Who took you to your doctor appointments and loaned you money when you had to quit working? Who listened to you cry at night and lent you a shoulder? Huh?"

Rosemary dashed impatiently at wet cheeks, angry her blasted brother could get her riled enough to tear up. Thank God Carson was already in the car and didn't see. "Don't you dare throw that up to me. I paid you back the money. I thanked you over and over for everything you did for me, Mason. I'm a grown woman now. I make my own choices and right now I choose to see how Caleb does as a father. I choose to give my son the chance to know his daddy."

"He'll stomp on your heart, Rosemary. After he gets what he wants, he'll leave as soon as his leg's steady enough to jump on the next rodeo stupid enough to take the entry money." Mason scraped one hand down his face, then waved it toward the car where Carson sat. "What about him? How hurt do you think that boy'll feel when Mr. Rodeo King takes off? Because he will. It's what he does."

"I don't want to hear any more." She pushed by her brother, dragging the cart to the nearest return slot and slamming it in. For a few seconds she stood with her back to the car, striving to regain some sort of composure. If she didn't, she'd likely kill him. At the very least she'd say things she'd someday regret.

With a deep breath she turned and stared at Mason. His face was still flushed with anger, yet she could read concern, the kind you'd expect from a big, overprotective brother. He couldn't help it, any more than she could help resenting his attitude.

She probably owed him some kind of apology. "Mason, look—"

Caleb's sudden appearance interrupted her. "What's going on?" He stepped to her side, cell phone in hand, looking from her to Mason, who was visibly bristling. "Everything okay?"

Mason surged forward with a growl. "Johnson, you son of—"

"*Mason!* Enough." She felt like ripping her hair out by the roots and grinding it under her boot heel. Trying even harder for patience, Rosemary turned to Caleb. "My brother is being a jackass. He thinks you're going to break Carson's heart and leave." She cast a fulminating glare toward Mason. "I told him that would never happen."

"Oh." Caleb slowly pocketed his cell, removed his hat, and slapped it against his thigh before dropping it back on his head.

"So, who was the call from? Sounded important." Rosemary hated the tiny smidge of insecurity that had her questioning the man she knew she'd never stopped loving.

"Yeah, old *buddy*." Mason's lip curled in a faint sneer. "Who was on the phone?"

Caleb edged Rosemary away from her brother with a hand to her arm. "We should really get Carson home."

She didn't like what she saw in his eyes. "Caleb . . ." She grasped his fingers and held tightly. "Who was the call from?"

He released a short sigh and shuffled his feet, before raising worried eyes to hers. "The State Rodeo Commission."

Chapter Eleven

Caleb swallowed hard when Rosemary's eyes narrowed, her expression looking a helluva lot like her brother's. *Not good.* He needed to handle his next words very carefully if he wanted to salvage his relationship with her and Carson.

"O-okay," she said slowly, the hard look in her eyes reminding him of an ornery bull right before he climbed on for their eight-second dance. "The Rodeo Commission. And they wanted . . . what, exactly?"

Mason snorted, but otherwise remained silent. The fury in his expression said it all.

"Let's get home first, Rosie, then we can discuss the phone call." Caleb took a step forward as she pulled from his grasp.

Her hands flew up in a defensive gesture, warding him off. "No," she retorted. "Tell me now."

Caleb knew her well enough to figure she wouldn't get into the car until he'd answered her question. She was stubborn. Just one of the many things he loved about her. And yeah, damn it, he *did* love her. Had loved her from their very first kiss six years earlier, but he'd been too big of a jackass to admit it. Instead, he'd skipped town and did everything he could to put her out of his mind. *Hell.* If she left him now, it'd be his own damn fault.

Tension filled his body. He chanced losing her forever if he lied to her. It was a small miracle she'd allowed him back into her life—into her bed—as it was. He licked his suddenly dry lips. "They offered me a job as Rodeo Announcer."

Rosemary inhaled sharply. "In Cheyenne? Or on the statewide circuit?"

"Rosie—"

"Which, Caleb? Local or circuit?"

Caleb's heart beat frantically against his chest, warning him things were about to go south if he didn't do something fast. Trouble was, the offer he'd been presented had been a bit vague. He started to speak, hesitated, caught the fierce frown on Mason's face, and finally replied, "Circuit."

"And what did you tell them?" Her voice shook. She leaned against the side of the car, as if her legs weren't steady enough to hold her.

Caleb glanced past her to see Carson strapped into the back seat, playing games on Rosemary's cell phone, oblivious to the tension outside the car. Thank God, because he didn't want his son to think for one instant that he didn't rank as number one in his daddy's priorities.

The phone call had come out of left field and thrown him for a loop. His mind was still struggling with how he could have both his family *and* his career. No way was he leaving Rosie or Carson behind. But he couldn't pull his son out of school to drag him around the circuit.

Damn it! I need time to think. Time to negotiate.

Only when Rosemary made a strangling sound and spun to open the car door did he realize he'd been standing there saying nothing as he'd contemplated his options. Which completely gave her the wrong impression, like he'd really desert her again. *Hell, no.* He moved forward, intent on begging her to listen.

Mason stepped in the way, and they bumped chests. His old buddy had murder in his eyes. "Let her go, Johnson."

"Out of my way, Mason." His hands curled into fists at his sides, a rush of adrenaline coursing through him, ramping up a feeling of desperation as Rosemary slid behind the wheel of the car.

"Rosie, come on. We need to talk about this." He made a move to dart around her brother, but Mason shoved him hard in the chest with one hand, sending him back on his heels. His bad leg twinged hard, but Caleb determinately ignored it. "Rosie," he pleaded as he righted his footing, their gazes meeting for a split second.

The pain he saw reflected on her face gutted him. Pain he'd once again caused her. She slammed the door shut, starting the car.

"Wait, damn it. Rosie!"

Panic stabbed him straight through the heart as the car drove away with everything that mattered to him inside. He'd really screwed up this time.

"Just go, Johnson," Mason snapped. "Take the damn job and get the hell out of town. That's what you do best, remember? Leave."

Caleb tensed as a surge of fury tore through him. If her brother hadn't gotten in the way, maybe he would have had a chance to explain. Forgetting for a moment they were in the parking lot of Safeway, he took a threatening stride toward Mason with every intention of kicking some ass.

Mason's posture and clenched fists indicated he was more than ready to have it out.

"Mommy," a young girl's voice carried over to them, halting Caleb in his tracks and making him look around. "Can we stop and get ice cream on the way home?"

Hell, the parking lot was full of women and children. He needed to tamp it down.

"Rosemary was devastated when you left, Caleb." Mason's tone now sounded more tired than angry.

Caleb lowered his head in defeat.

That didn't stop Mason from digging the knife in deeper. "You took her innocence, and I'm not just talking about her virginity, asshole."

So he knew that, too? Damn it, no wonder the guy hated him. He kind of hated himself right now. Caleb swiped a hand down his face. Yeah, he made a huge mistake when he'd walked away from Rosemary. Now it was time to make things right.

First, he had to figure out what the hell he was going to do about the job offer, and his career. Then he needed to find Rosie. He'd worry about making amends with his ex-best friend later. Only Rosie mattered right now.

Without another glance at Mason, he turned and strode from the parking lot.

As he walked away, Mason called out, "It took her years to put her life back together. If you care anything about her, you'll leave her the hell alone."

Caleb stopped, and for one heart-wrenching moment, he wondered if Mason was right. Maybe he should just keep on walking until he hit the bus stop, and continue out of town.

Then images of Rosemary's contented smile after he'd thoroughly made love to her, and the hero-worship shining from his son's eyes, filled his mind.

No, he didn't believe they'd be better off without him. He'd made the mistake of walking away from her once, and he wasn't going to do it again.

Slowly he reached for his Stetson and adjusted it before facing his ex-best pal. "I love her. Rosie and Carson are my world now, and I'm not walking away."

Mason's brows drew into a deep vee. "You say that now, Caleb, but we all know the rodeo's in your blood. How long will it be once your leg heals, before you take off again? Just cut your losses now and go, before Carson takes a worse hit than he's already going to. I remember what Rosemary went through when you put your career above her and Carson."

"That's not what—"

"Save it, Johnson. She's done with you. And once Rosie makes up her mind, there's no changing it."

Caleb's mouth set in a hard line. Mason's words held a ring of truth. Rosie'd always had a mile long stubborn streak. But now wasn't the time for either of them to get stubborn. He was more than ready to meet her halfway or better.

He only hoped she could be persuaded to do the same.

"That no good, dirty, low-down, stinkin' cowboy," Susan hissed between gritted teeth. She stomped around her kitchen, throwing her hands up angrily, then shot a glance into the living room to make sure Carson couldn't hear them.

Rosemary snorted as she dabbed away tears. "Tell us how you really feel, Susie-Q."

Instead of driving home, where Caleb could easily find her, Rosemary had gone to her friend's house to hide out. Sitting at the kitchen table, she crumpled the damp tissue in her hand. Maybe by the time she decided to go home, he'd be gone. But as angry as she was, that thought still cut through her heart with the force of a chainsaw, leaving pain and destruction in its wake. Just like Caleb Johnson.

God. How could I let myself fall for him again? What a fool I am!

She'd never meant enough to Caleb for him to settle down. His career as a rodeo star meant more to him than she or his son ever would. Well, if he thought he could just waltz into town between rodeo gigs for a booty call, he was highly mistaken.

Rosemary glanced at her son, who was happily playing an Xbox game, with his headphones on. Fresh tears slid down her cheeks when she thought of how his daddy's absence would hurt him. *Damn you, Caleb Johnson!*

Susan stopped her angry pacing and came over to give her a hug. "You want me to send your brother over to break his other leg? He'd do it too, you know that."

Rosemary actually gave the idea a moment of thought, then released a humorless laugh. "No. I'm not wasting any more energy on him. It's my own fault, I should have learned my lesson the first time."

Her best friend pulled up a chair to plop down in front of her. "Honey, none of this is your fault. Caleb Johnson is one fine specimen of a man, and any woman would be hard-pressed to resist his considerable charms. So, give yourself a break. It's just too bad underneath that handsome exterior lies a slithering snake. You know, one of those venomous horned rattlers that can't be trusted near women or children."

At the apt description, amusement bubbled up inside Rosemary, helping to get her emotions under control. Susan was exactly right. She'd wasted enough tears her first time around with the Rodeo King, and she wouldn't shed one more damn drop. She had Carson to think about now. Her baby was going to need her when he learned Caleb was gone.

Yet she couldn't help but worry. "You're right, Susie. But how am I going to tell Carson his daddy left us?" That chainsaw took another swipe inside her chest.

"Lil' Tuff's resilient. And he loves you. He hasn't known Caleb all that long. He'll survive. He still has his uncle. You know Mason loves him like his own son. Why do you think he's been so crazy since Caleb came back into town? Your brother's scared shitless you and Carson were going to be hurt." Susan smiled sadly. "And unfortunately, he was right."

Rosemary swallowed against the fresh grief welling in her throat. *No more tears, damn it.* "Yeah. Unfortunately." She blew her nose a final time.

Susan stood, placing her hands on her slender hips. "Hey, you know what? I think we all need a vacation. How about we head over to the lake? We could rent a cottage for the weekend. Carson would love it."

Thankful to have such a wonderful friend to help soften the pain of losing Caleb, Rosemary nodded. "I think that's a great idea. But I'll need to stop by my place and pack a bag first."

Chapter Twelve

After downing half his beer, Caleb reached for the phone, got within a few inches of the damned thing, then clenched his hand into a fist and pulled back, letting it fall with a thud to the table in the kitchenette of his studio unit.

Damn it to hell and back. He stood and moved to the window, staring out blindly at the sun-dappled parking lot.

Three times he'd tried calling Rosemary's cell. The first call had gone to voicemail. So had the second. On the third she'd picked up, and he'd gotten out a fast, "Don't hang up, Rosie," before the disconnect beep clicked in his ear.

Stubborn, pigheaded woman.

Caleb raked his fingers through his hair, blowing out a harsh breath. He loved her so much he ached with it. He also knew damned well if she didn't want to take his calls, she wouldn't, regardless of how many times he hit the redial. His stomach knotted. He'd really messed up this time. After earning back her trust, he'd destroyed it with one small hesitation, instead of giving her the answer she'd deserved immediately. That he loved her and Carson, and there was no way in hell he was leaving them. Ever.

But you didn't do that, dumbass.

Yesterday, knowing he risked having the door slammed in his face, he'd borrowed Nash's truck and drove to her house, hoping to talk to her. She hadn't been there. One of the neighbors, a busybody he remembered from his pre-rodeo days, informed him Rosemary and 'that wild gal-pal of hers' had left for who-knew-where.

Since it was the peak of summer, and knowing Rosie, he figured they'd gone to the lake. So he'd spent several hours trolling up and down the road along Cruller Lake, a retired gravel pit the nearby town of Raymond had filled with water. No luck finding her car.

He'd finally given up and driven back to the Bronco Inn, stopping by the liquor store on the way. Damned if he'd eat his heart out any longer. Rosemary Carmichael more than lived up to her flaming red hair.

Memories of those silken strands tangled in his fingers as he kissed her, held her, made his body go tight with desire and his heart ache with longing.

Jesus, he missed her. Every tiny thing about her, including her temper.

Caleb limped back to the table and dropped into his chair. Hanging his head, he rested his forearms on the edge of the table, his half-empty beer no longer holding any appeal. Getting shit-faced on suds wasn't the answer, although a few days ago it'd seemed like a good idea. Which was why only eleven longneck bottles of amber remained in the fridge. He'd started with a case.

He rubbed at both eyes, then winced. "Son of a bitch!" Cupping his hand over his right eye, Caleb probed carefully. He didn't have to look in a mirror to know the damned thing was still swollen and probably colored a nice shade of purple. It throbbed like a mother, too. Mason Carmichael had a mean left hook. At least he hadn't socked the same side of Caleb's face, from the night he'd first hit town.

They'd gotten into it last night outside of DeeDee's, when Caleb stumbled through the doors just drunk enough to not give a damn, and demanded Mason tell him where Rosemary had gone. Two sore ribs and a black eye later, Caleb had staggered back to the motel and stocked up on ice, digging in his shaving kit for the ace bandage he'd used off and on as extra support for his ankle. After a shitty job of wrapping it around his ribs, he'd passed out half on and half off the bed.

Today he felt every ache, each fist-pound Mason had delivered, not to mention residual pain on his bruised knuckles from the punches he'd somehow managed to land on his hardheaded ex-buddy. Mason might have done more damage, but Caleb had left him with plenty to think about, including a nose that was most likely broken.

"Bastard deserved it," he said aloud, studying his ruined knuckles. He rose and grabbed the longneck, dumping the rest of it down the sink in the kitchenette. *No more beer.* He'd take a shower and go out for a burger, maybe hit that diner outside of Hawthorn and clear his head.

Except thinking about Hawthorn made him relive the hours leading up to the moment his life went to total shit. Groaning, Caleb sank back onto his chair and pushed his face in his palms, uncaring of the pain in his eye.

What was he going to do?

As if in response, his cell trilled. Thinking it might be Rosemary, Caleb grabbed for it.

"Yeah, hello!"

"Caleb Johnson? This is Lenny Folsom with the State Rodeo Commission. You spoke to one of my associates the other day. Bill Knowles."

He'd never felt less like talking rodeo in his entire life. "Yeah, that's right. Nice to hear from you, Mr. Folsom—"

"Oh, just call me Lenny. Listen, I understand you never gave Bill an answer about the job offer. It's a choice one, for sure. And something my team thinks you'd be great at, what with your knowledge and experience. Pays great, too. Did Bill mention the salary?"

Caleb rubbed his free hand over the back of his neck and tried to concentrate on something other than his mounting melancholy and images of Rosemary, naked and warm in his arms three mornings ago, before he lost everything that mattered to him. Which, he suddenly realized, did not encompass goddamn bull riding.

"I must be nuts," he mused softly.

"Beg pardon?" The voice in his ear—Lenny something-or-other—sounded perplexed and a bit irritated.

"Mr. Johnson, have you made a decision? We need your answer. The current announcer is leaving next week. Retiring to Las Vegas with the wife and a thirty-foot fifth wheel. We'd need you in Cheyenne for initial training. Start you right on the circuit full time during the season, then rotating between our corporate offices off-season. Lots of great travel. We could offer you a spot on the board as a junior member and keep you in the loop. Full bennies, too." Lenny paused. Then added, "Mr. Johnson?"

"Yeah, I'm here." Caleb thought furiously. If he took this job he'd have to be guaranteed Rosemary and Carson could travel with him when he hit the road. He'd request his local base to be Cheyenne, an easy drive from Dustin. "Listen, Lenny. Can I ask you something? I got a family here. They'd have to be included in my travel allowance, and—"

"You? A family? Since when?" Lenny's voice held amazement. "I remember you on the circuit, Johnson. You were a tomcat."

"Not any longer," Caleb replied firmly. "I got a little boy. Five years old. And my girl's going to marry me soon." *I hope and pray.* "I have to do right by them and that includes not leaving them behind."

"Well, I don't know, son." Papers rattled in Caleb's ear. Then Lenny sighed. "Let me see what I can do. But you gotta understand, it's a big deal being offered a job like this. The Commission folks do want you but they make all the final decisions."

"I understand. And if I were a single guy I'd jump on it. But I can't be the only one who's got a family."

"Well, now, son, you might just be. You know how rodeo is. Damned few get themselves tied down."

Right about then, just as Caleb opened his mouth to refute Lenny Folsom's opinion, his cell beeped in with call waiting. He pulled it from his ear and glanced at the display in time to see Rosemary's number flash.

Holy shit.

"Mr. Folsom, I've got an urgent call to take." Caleb disconnected before the man could utter a single squawk, and hit the button. "Rosie? Rosie!"

A rapid beep sounded in his ear. She'd already hung up. "Damn it!" His head ready to explode from the rush of emotion coursing through his body, he frantically pressed buttons. It went instantly to voicemail.

Frustrated beyond belief, Caleb let out an angry yell, then whirled around and pitched the phone across the room. Breathing heavily, and not feeling one damn bit better, he watched it bounce off the wall and skitter across the thin-carpeted floor.

Rosemary tucked her cell into her beach bag and stifled a sigh. Lifting her damp hair off her sweaty neck, she re-twisted the heavy curls and tightened the bright pink octopus clip that was supposed to secure the thick mass atop her head. When it flopped back over her shoulders, she yanked out what was left of the clip and stared at it. The spring mechanism was shot. "Ah, hell!" She tossed it aside.

"Now what?" Susan peered over the top of her sunglasses inquiringly. She sat up and reached for the bottle of suntan lotion they'd been sharing. "Here, make yourself useful and load me up."

"Well, turn around." As Susan presented her back, Rosemary slapped on lotion, rubbing it in with some of the aggression she was feeling, then rubbing harder when her best friend grumbled under her breath.

"Hold *still,*" Rosemary snapped.

"You're taking off a layer of my freshly-tanned epidermis. Boy, you're mean when you're sex-deprived." Susan grabbed the lotion out of Rosemary's hand. "I'll do it myself."

"I'm not sex-deprived," she denied.

Liar.

"Pissed-off, then." With a smug look, Susan finished coating one arm. "Or just generally pissy." She waved the bottle toward the lake, shimmering under endless blue skies. Children shrieked in the distance; birds cawed above, and a light breeze took the edge off the summer heat. "It's gorgeous here, Rosie. Carson's having fun, you're wearing my sexiest bikini, and at least twenty guys have eyeballed you, most with their tongues hanging out. *Carpe Diem* and all that." She plopped on her stomach and stretched out, a sleek cat soaking up the afternoon rays. "So stop wallowing and enjoy."

"I'm *not* wallowing." Abruptly Rosemary stood, brushing sand off her arms and legs. "You can carp their diem for both of us."

She didn't want to be here. Even though she knew it was unfair to make Carson leave so soon, her heart wasn't in it. Turning slightly, she assured herself that her son still sat at the edge of the blanket with his trucks and sand pail.

Slathered in the highest SPF sunscreen available, wearing his uncle's 'go to hell' camo bush hat and bright green board shorts, Carson looked adorable. As always. He toyed with a plastic shovel, occasionally digging up sand and pouring it in his pail. He seemed to be having fun, and earlier she'd seen him splashing around with a few kids his age, but for the most part her boy was quiet. Too quiet. From the serious expression on his little face, she knew sooner or later he'd come out with it. And she'd bet money he'd start asking questions about his daddy.

Trouble was, Rosemary had no answers for him . . . or for herself.

She'd escaped town in a big, angry huff, refusing Caleb's phone calls, ignoring the voicemail he'd left on her cell. In the more sensible part of her brain she knew her attitude smacked of unfairness, but she couldn't help it. The man just scrambled her emotions. And all her insecurities had surged front and center as soon as he'd said 'Rodeo

Commission.' Like waving a red flag before an enraged
bull.

I never gave him a chance to explain anything. Not her
most shining moment. Not very mature, either. So she'd
given him a call, only to discover he wasn't answering his
cell, and his voicemail wasn't engaging. She couldn't leave
him a message. A hard lump formed in her throat along
with a sense of *déjà vu* . . .

Because six years ago she didn't have a cell number
for him, either. No way to let him know he was going to be
a daddy. His folks had moved, their house sold to an
elderly couple with a bunch of cats. Rosemary had no idea
where the Johnsons had relocated.

How helpless she'd felt, sitting on the bed in her room
with her parents silent and furious downstairs. She'd
rocked back and forth on the edge of the mattress with her
cell phone in one hand, pressing against her still-flat
stomach with the other. Tears, so thick she could barely
breathe, had dripped everywhere as she tried to plan out the
most uncertain future she'd ever had to face. Seeing for
herself how miserable her mama was, married to a man
who didn't want to be tied down, Rosemary had made the
decision to just let Caleb go.

"Rosie?"

She jerked out of her stupor. "Huh?"

While she'd been standing there with bad memories
churning, staring depressingly out at the lake, Susan had
sidled up beside her, and held out a chilled bottle of water.
"Here. Drink some. Then I think we should head back to
the cottage."

They'd rented one of the lakeside cottages, snaring a
summer weekend special. The tiny three-room cabin was
rustic but at least had running water and some semblance of
power, although they'd popped a breaker twice when Susan
had forgotten to shut off the coffeemaker before blow-
drying her hair.

"I'm not thirsty." But Rosemary took the water anyway and drank a few gulps, wiping her mouth with the back of her hand. Then gained Carson's attention as he raised his head to look around. "Come get a drink, honey."

Obediently he rose to take the bottle. "Are we leaving yet, Mommy?"

She ruffled his damp hair. "Are you ready to leave yet? We can stay a little longer before we go back to the cottage."

"No. I mean, are we going home yet?" His face was bright, touches of pink on his rounded cheeks despite all the sunscreen they'd used and the too-big hat shielding his face. He guzzled the rest of her water and then dug a chubby toe in the sand, a sweet little guy with something big on his mind. "I had lotsa fun, but I miss Daddy. I think he's lonely. I think we should go home and be with him."

Sudden, harsh tears formed in Rosemary's eyes as she looked from her son to Susan. He wanted his daddy. *God, I want his daddy, too.*

"Susie-Q, I'm just so lost." She didn't know what else to say.

Her best friend since grade school slipped her arm around her shoulders and squeezed. "He's a pretty good man, Rosie. Most of the time," she amended, tempering her words with a smile. "As much as I'd still like to just haul off and punch him for the crap he put you through, he's a damned good father. Whatever the RC wants with him, I wouldn't be surprised if Caleb's plotting to figure out how to bring you and Carson along." Susan offered another, tighter hug. "He's gotten me really mad several times in the past, but I think now you owe it to Lil' Tuff here to see what's what." She pulled the bush hat down to Carson's nose and made him grin.

While her son leaned against Susan's legs and yawned, Rosemary took a few moments to deal with the jumble of uncertainty swirling in her head.

Her brother persisted in painting Caleb as a bastard who wanted nothing more than an easy lay between rodeo hookups. Mason refused to see beyond his own anger. Despite the hurt Caleb's desertion caused her from years ago, still difficult for her to release completely, Rosemary had to see this through. Trust never came easy for her but maybe it was high time she grew up a bit and tried harder. If he broke her heart a second time, so be it. She'd lived through it once, she could do it again.

At least she had Carson. She glanced down at him, her heart filled with so much love that she ached with it. As long as she had her son, she could handle anything.

With that decision made, she began collecting their beach gear, folding towels; sorting through toys and empty containers of soda pop and water. Offering Susan a grateful smile for her support, Rosemary quietly said, "Let's go home, and see what's what."

Chapter Thirteen

Where could he be? Rosemary rapped her knuckles on Caleb's motel door again, then checked the painted number above the deadbolt. Fourteen. She definitely had the right room. Caleb had mentioned he was staying in Nash's studio unit, and the man only had one.

She was determined to have it out with Caleb once and for all. Was he staying or was he going? She had a right to know, damn it.

When there was still no answer, she glanced around the area and worried her bottom lip. The sinking sensation in her stomach grew as a sense of fresh panic set in. *Had he left?* Already gone back to the rodeo? She shivered at the chill rolling over her, stark against the airless, muggy evening.

Noticing a slit in the curtains, she peered inside and saw a perfectly made up room, with nothing lying around to indicate it was still occupied.

Gone. Again.

Tears threatened and she blinked them away. She wouldn't cry again over a man who didn't even care enough to say goodbye. Something she should be used to by now. Yet a fist squeezed her bruised heart.

Turning from the window, she spotted DeeDee's down the street and decided she needed a drink. After a final afternoon at the lake, Carson was spending the night with his uncle. Mason had promised to take him to the kid's matinee in Hawthorn tomorrow, which was playing the new Disney movie, and he wouldn't be home until late afternoon.

Plenty of time to get shit-faced if I want to.

Rosemary refused to spend the night alone wallowing in self-pity after being dumped again by that aggravating cowboy. Marching toward the bar entrance, she breathed deeply through her nose and tried to calm herself.

She dug through her purse for her phone and punched in Susan's number. "Hey, wanna meet me at DeeDee's for a drink and a bite to eat?"

"Sure," her friend said. "When?"

"Now." Rosemary pushed through the doors, scoping out a seat at the bar. It was early yet, and the supper crowd was just straggling in. "I'll order a pitcher of margaritas to get us started." Her voice sounded strained, even to her own ears.

"What's happened, Rosie?"

Her throat constricted as utter despair flooded her, then, shaking it off, she climbed onto the tall barstool. "I'll tell you when you get here." Her voice broke at the end.

"I'm on my way. Feel free to start without me. Sounds like you need it."

She hadn't even finished her first drink when Susan came flying through the door. She'd switched her shorts for a pair of tight jeans, but still wore the slinky summer top from the beach. Her hair was pulled back into a ponytail and she had a pissed-off expression on her pretty face.

Spotting Rosemary, she hurried over and took a seat next to her. As she poured herself a drink from the pitcher, she asked, "So, what'd Caleb do now?"

"He left," Rosemary said simply, sucking her drink dry through the colorful straw. She held out her glass for Susan to refill.

Her friend froze for a moment. "You're shitting me. Are you sure?"

"Yeah. Pretty sure." Rosemary clenched her jaw. Her first drink had taken the sharp edge off her sorrow, but it was still hard to think about being deserted again. And this time around Caleb knew about his son, but he'd still left. That hurt the worst.

Susan's gaze narrowed as she proceeded to fill Rosemary's margarita glass. "That dirty bastard," she muttered.

"Yep. That about sums it up. Doesn't matter. I'm done."

Susan lifted her drink in a toast. "Good."

They clinked glasses. Rosemary loved margaritas, and DeeDee's made the best, just the right hint of tequila exploding on her tongue. She'd skipped breakfast due to her nerves, and only munched on a handful of snacks during the day. Already feeling the effects of the alcohol, this would be her last one, at least until she got something in her stomach.

Susan abruptly straightened and glanced around the bar. An amused grin spread across her face. "Hottie alert." She nodded toward the pool tables. "Up for a game?" She wiggled her brows suggestively.

Rosemary eyed the two men at the back of the bar, playing pool. Both attractive and about their age, neither one of them looked like a damn cowboy. For a moment she was tempted, and when the taller of the two met her gaze, she didn't immediately turn away.

He smiled at her, but all she could see in her mind was Caleb's smile; the way his eyes shone with happiness, crinkling at the corners and lighting up his entire face. She'd been sure he cared for her, and wouldn't leave this time.

Boy, was I wrong.

Only when the man handed his cue stick to his friend and began walking their way did she realize she'd been staring, lost in thoughts of Caleb.

Her stomach sank.

Glancing back to Susan, she mumbled, "Oh shit."

Her friend chuckled. "Cute. Maybe he'll invite his friend over."

Rosemary snorted, taking another long pull on her drink. "Not interested."

"C'mon, Rosemary. Have a little fun. It'll do you good."

She shook her head. "Not tonight, Susie-Q."

Susan blew a raspberry. "You're no fun."

The man reached them, and Rosemary, unwilling to appear rude, gave him a weak smile. Her pain in the ass friend wasn't so hesitant. "Hi," Susan said in a flirty voice, lifting her drink in a welcoming salute. "I'm Susan, and this is Rosemary."

"I'm Brad." The smile he gave them was nice, but she still wasn't interested. "Did you ladies want to join us for a drink?" He nodded his head toward his friend who hung out by the pool table, watching them with interest.

"We'd love to," Susan chimed, grinning broadly.

"No." Rosemary shook her head. "I'm waiting for my boyfriend." She tried not to cringe at the lame excuse, but jutted her chin in defiance when Susan cast her an amused glance.

Disappointment flashed over the man's face, before he returned his attention to her best friend. "How about you, Susan? Ready to play?"

The innuendo behind his words evident, her friend chuckled. "Sorry," she said. "Raincheck?"

Just then the front door opened and Dave walked in, glancing toward the dining room. "There he is now." Rosemary hopped off the stool with her drink in her hand. "Susan, why don't you go ahead and play a game of pool while I have a talk with Dave."

"You sure?" Susan studied her intently.

She nodded. "I'm certain. We'll be in the dining room. Should I order something for you?"

"Yeah, I'll take a burger with the works." She returned her attention to Brad. "One game."

Brad nodded, offering her his arm. "One game." They turned and walked off together.

Spotting her, Dave came over. "Hi, darlin'. Where've you been hiding?"

Her cheeks heated. Dave knew damned well she'd spent the last week shacking up with Caleb. She drained her drink, before asking, "Have you had dinner?"

"No." He gave her an intense once-over. "Everything okay?"

"No. Not really."

Dave took her elbow and led her to the dining room. After holding her chair out, he sat across from her. "So, tell me."

Rosemary stared into his compassionate eyes and once again called herself every kind of fool for falling in love with a wandering cowboy instead of Dave. "Caleb took off again."

His expression turned dark. "What happened? Last I heard you two seemed to be working things out."

After Adrianne walked over and took their orders, Rosemary played with the stem of her glass, then shoved it aside. "He was offered a job with the Rodeo Commission, and evidently took it, because when I stopped by the motel to talk with him about it he was gone."

There was no keeping the tears from her voice, though she refused to let a single one fall. Dave reached over and placed his hand on hers where they were busy shredding one of the napkins.

"Did he tell you he was leaving?"

"No. He just left."

"How do you know, Rosie? You should have a talk with him before jumping to conclusions. I ran into Caleb a few days back, and he seemed pretty damn happy to be in your life and spending time with his son. I don't think he'd just throw that away."

"I tried, Dave. I went to the Bronco Inn, but he was gone. Not even a goodbye." Emotion clogged her throat.

"Do you love him?"

Rosemary frowned. "It doesn't matter if I do or not, because he left again. He left his son. How am I going to tell Carson his daddy is gone?"

"Do you want my advice, darlin'?" Before she had a chance to answer Dave continued, "I think you need to find out why Caleb left. He might have a perfectly good explanation." He sat back in his chair and picked up the drink Adrianne set before him. "It's obvious to everyone you're crazy about each other, so don't let your anger and insecurities get in the way. That's all I'm saying."

A flutter of hope sparked to life in her chest. Maybe she had jumped to conclusions. But still, she was hesitant to trust.

"What am I supposed to do, Dave? Just wait around until Caleb decides to mosey back into town again? I don't think so. I deserve better and so does Carson."

He gave her a steady look. "Then don't."

Rosemary just stared at him for a long moment, as the words sank into her brain. *Then don't.*

Slowly, she pulled her cell phone from her pocket, swiped it open and punched in a number. "Mason, can you keep Carson an extra day or two?"

She paused for a moment listening to her brother's voice, then quietly stressed, "It's important."

Chapter Fourteen

Caleb stood and respectfully tipped his hat. "Thanks, Lenny. For everything."

After an enthusiastic handshake, his new boss slapped him on the back. "We're glad to have you with us, son. You're bringing a world of experience to the RC as well as a fresh approach." Lenny shrugged into his suit coat and smoothed the careful comb-over that hid most of his bald spot.

The man wasn't fooling anyone with that hairstyle, and he probably knew it. Still, Lenny Folsom was a nice guy who'd bent over backward to assure Caleb had a future for him and his family.

Even if that family seemed out of reach right now.

"So." Lenny kept pace as Caleb edged toward the wide doors leading outside of the State Rodeo Commission offices. "When do you want to start? Not tryin' to rush you," he hastily assured as Caleb raised an eyebrow. "Just need a general idea for my team. That's all." He jingled loose coins in his pocket, squinting up at Caleb in the afternoon sun. "That little ranch on the outskirts of Cheyenne is almost ready for you. Your gal and the boy— Carson, right?—well, they can move in anytime, and—"

"I don't know about that. I still need to talk to Rosemary." Caleb was beginning to feel that rush Lenny had promised wasn't coming from him.

Surprise wreathed the older man's face as he stared at Caleb. "You didn't tell her? You're kidding, right?"

"I wish I were." Caleb rubbed at his forehead, feeling the tension brewing under his fingers. "I'll need to get back to you on that." *Shit, on a lot of things.* He wasn't about to admit he'd lost track of his woman. It was just a matter of

location, because once he found her, he wouldn't be stupid
enough to let her run off again.

"Well, if I were you, I'd let your lady know she's got a
right nice place to call home once you start hittin' the
road," Lenny advised. "Hell, I'll let the boys on the
construction team know. They can slap on a fresh coat of
paint, too. Whatever she wants."

"Let me actually talk to Rosemary first, okay? Then
we can worry about paint." With another fast handshake
and a jaunty salute, Caleb bid Lenny goodbye and headed
toward the huge parking lot. He'd promised himself to
return Nash's truck before four-thirty.

An hour later Caleb swerved to avoid yet another pot-
hole. A repaving crew had been working on this section of
211, but it was a mess in spots. The back road was still the
fastest way to get to Dustin. He recalled how many times
he ridden the bus on this damned road, scraping up enough
money to ride to Cheyenne and catch the summer rodeo
circuit. He'd watch his heroes ride, and plot for the day he
could be shooting his own eight seconds on the backside of
the meanest bull in six counties.

*And I did it, didn't I? Rode those bulls, made that fast
money. Spent it, too.*

For him it was never the horses, though he certainly
enjoyed riding. It was always the bulls. And he couldn't
regret a single competition during those crazy years. He
didn't even regret the orneriest bull of all, breaking his leg
in two places; laying him off bull riding, most likely
permanently . . . because it also brought Rosemary back
into his life. Carson, too. He'd spend the rest of his days
thanking God for the second chance he'd been given.

When he bumped over that damned rut the county
never seemed to bother fixing, Caleb knew he was eight
miles from home. Reflexively he slowed to a crawl just as
he caught a flash of chrome and color up ahead, sitting at

an angle near the berm of the road. A familiar, dirt-streaked blue Civic.

He eased to a stop and killed the engine, squinting into the afternoon sun as he took in the sight before him.

Hot damn. God loves me after all.

Quietly, Caleb exited the truck, grabbing his hat from the seat and dropping it on his head. Leaving the door wide open, he stepped easy over road gravel so as not to startle the figure leaning into the open hood.

Shapely, long legs, covered in skintight, faded-out Levi's that were tucked into a pair of beat-up Dingos. One boot toe, squared off and scuffed, tapped impatiently in time with the sound of a hammer striking metal. Tendrils of smoke wafted from the vicinity of what was surely a dry and thirsty radiator.

He knew those red leather boots and those denim-clad legs; hell, he knew the heart-shaped ass attached to them. Rosemary Carmichael, love of his life, mother of his son.

Caleb felt himself slowing in anticipation, a dozen smooth opening lines bouncing in his head, a million things he wanted to say to Rosie starting with, 'I love you,' and ending with, 'Please never leave me.'

Instead, he walked up to the stranded car, grinning at the banging hammer mixed with a string of cuss words, and calmly—inanely—said, "Hi. Something wrong with your car?"

Cursing and pounding on the worthless piece-of-crap radiator, Rosemary never heard him approach until his low baritone voice flowed over her temper like a honey balm. Caleb Johnson, all six-feet-four of sex on a stick, sauntering over to her on those endless, muscled legs of his. He wore a pair of brown western-cut dress slacks, a white dress shirt with a "Hook 'Em" bolo tie, and polished Tony Lamas on his feet. He reached for his hat, a snappy, tan felt

Stetson, and took it off, holding it in both hands, turning the brim around and around as if nervous.

Caleb, nervous? She'd never known the man to be anything but smooth and supremely cool. Confident. Bigger than life. Certainly not the hesitant man who stood before her with his heart in his eyes.

His heart's in his eyes. For me.

The hammer slipped out of her fingers and hit the dusty ground. She couldn't look away. Seconds eased into a minute or more as they stood two feet from each other and stared. Finally, Caleb's lips parted on a tender, yearning, "Rosie . . ."

"I was—I was coming to you." Tears blurred her vision; she didn't bother to hold them back. "I figured you must be in Cheyenne so I took the last of my checking account money and spent it on a full tank of gas. I was going to walk right up to you and tell you to come home."

While her mouth quivered over the words, Caleb had stepped closer and set his hat on the fender of her doornail-dead Honda. Now he used his thumbs to wipe her damp cheeks, his palms curving along her jaw. He bent in, the merest inch, and rasped, "Then what were you going to tell me?"

"I—I—" Overcome, she turned her face into his hand and trembled.

"Would it help if you knew what I wanted to tell you?" he whispered.

She nodded.

A single tug brought her into his arms and up against his heart. With a sigh she settled there, one hand grasping his shirt and the other sliding over his shoulder to bury itself in his hair. Caleb pressed his mouth to her ear.

"I wanted to tell you I found us a future together, Rosie. A job with good benefits and a chance to be together most of the year, living in Dustin if you want. Traveling the circuit in the summer with Carson."

He brought his lips to hers and touched them, so very gently. His voice lowered to an aching breath that feathered over her tongue. "We'd find a house with a yard. Maybe a dog. Maybe a little sissy or bro, too. And it all comes with a promise and a ring."

Dropping to one knee, Caleb held both her hands; she could feel the tremor in his fingers. "I don't have the ring, just yet. But I got the promise and it's so big and so true. Marry me, Rosemary Carmichael." He swallowed visibly, hard enough to cause his Adam's apple to shudder. "For the love of God and my sanity, Rosie. Please marry me."

How she managed to force anything out when her throat was so clogged with emotion, Rosemary never knew. But she choked out, "Yes, Caleb. Yes."

Three seconds later she fell into his arms, her senses filled with warm cotton and hot man, kneeling on the side of the road eight miles outside of Dustin, while cars zipped by and horns honked.

Epilogue

Rosemary gazed up at her new husband as they stepped outside the church where they'd exchanged their vows to love, honor, and cherish each other for the rest of their lives.

Her heart overflowed with happiness. The road to this quaint little chapel may have been rocky, but their future soared bright.

He stared back at her with so much love shining from his sexy green eyes, their son settled on his left hip. Caleb's right arm wrapped securely around her waist as he held her close to his side.

"Whaddaya say, Mrs. Johnson?" He grinned from ear to ear like a little boy who'd just been given his favorite treat. "Ready for that honeymoon?"

Carson clapped his hands, wiggling with excitement. "Yeah! I'm ready, Daddy. I'm ready!"

She smiled at her son, reaching out to ruffle his carrot top. "Mommy and Daddy will pick you up from Uncle Mason's first thing in the morning, sweetheart, then it's off to Disney World."

"Whoopee!" Carson yelled as they passed through the small crowd of friends and family lined up outside the church to blow soap bubbles at them. Spying his uncle, he exclaimed excitedly, "I'm going to Disney World." Then, "Auntie Susie, I'm going to Disney World."

Grinning, Mason held out his hand for a high-five as Carson passed by. "Way to go, Lil' Tuff."

Susan laughed. "I know, buddy. You're going to have a great time." She gave Rosemary a big hug, whispering in her ear, "Be happy, BFF. I've decided he's good for you." Pulling back, and putting on a fake scowl, she wagged her finger under Caleb's nose. "I'm watching you, Caleb Johnson, and I know where you live."

Mason punched the arm Caleb had curved around her shoulder, and growled, "Ditto."

Rosemary wasn't too sure her brother was joking, but Caleb just laughed it off, leaning down to brush a kiss across her mouth. Glancing down at her feet, he teased, "Let me see those boots."

"These old things?" Lifting the hem of her handkerchief-edged gown, she showed off her beat-up Dingos, their silver-etched red leather vivid against the creamy lace.

His voice dropped lower, and he rumbled, "Damn, I love those things. You gonna wear them for me tonight?"

She shot him the sexy look she knew he loved best.

"Oh, yeah, cowboy," she purred. "Just the boots."

GUNSLINGERS AND HEARTSTRINGS
A Deadwood Tale

by
CiCi Cordelia

In the Black Hills of 1876, Dewey befriends the legendary Wild Bill Hickok and meets Melanie, a spirited young woman who awakens dreams he thought were long buried.

As gold fever sweeps through the frontier, a budding romance and the promise of a bright future begin to take shape.

But in the lawless West, tragedy can strike without warning.

Now Dewey must face the truth about the man he once was… and prove he has the courage to live as the man he's determined to become.

Chapter One

Northwest Nebraska - October, 1875

Dewey Bower's breaths came in short, ragged bursts as he rode hard alongside the members of the Red River Drifters, led by Clayton Harrow. The thunder of hooves echoing against the hard-packed earth mingled with the jingle of spurs and creak of saddle leather. Dark clouds cast shadows across the wide prairie, the breeze carrying the scent of damp earth and dying sagebrush.

A feeling of dread tightened his muscles as they approached the lower valley where a scattering of small homesteads had been erected over the past year. Buffalo grazed freely on the plains, huge beasts whose hides and meat were vital to these settlers struggling to improve and farm their land as they eked out a life here.

Unfortunately, Clay and his buffalo hunters had claimed the valley and its bounty for themselves. Four months of riding with the gang had soured Dewey's initial eagerness to join Clay's Drifters. Dewey had craved adventure, but with increasing dismay and disgust, he'd observed how the riders indiscriminately took down the massive creatures, only to leave the meat to rot. Most times they took the hides, but far too often it was just for the thrill of the hunt. It sickened him.

Now the Drifters headed for the front of a rough-hewn cabin where Clay had heard the family living there killed a buffalo or two that'd roamed onto their land. As they cantered around the side of the cabin, the evidence was plain to see: a hide, stretched on a rudimentary rack, almost fully cured.

Clay brought his horse to a hard half-turn. "Follow my lead, boys," he rasped. "I'm makin' an example of this sumbitch." He dismounted and stomped toward the door.

It burst open and a man wearing tattered dungarees ran out, barefoot, clutching a rifle in big, rawboned hands. "I done tol' you—Oh, damn." He came to an abrupt stop. "Mister—Mister Harrow, sir." His Adam's apple worked as he took in the mounted men surrounding the small cabin. Slowly, he lowered the rifle and laid it on the uneven ground.

Clay set his shooting hand on his holster. "Rawling. You been poachin', I hear." He tapped his pistol. "Know what happens to poachers?"

When Rawling tried to back up toward the half open door, it swung wider and a tow-haired boy slipped out, also barefoot, and wearing nothing but a pair of dingy smalls. "Paw?" He ventured closer to the edge of the narrow porch, shivering in the chilly air.

Even from yards away, Dewey could see how the youngster's ribs stuck out. By the size of the cured hide, the buffalo his father had killed wasn't very big. Dewey'd also wager the meat had been split between neighboring families. It was the way of these settlers, to share anything they had with those less fortunate.

"Go inside, son," Rawling urged, never taking his eyes from Clay.

A figure draped in faded blue suddenly appeared in the doorway, and Dewey shifted uneasily in the saddle as a young woman grabbed the boy, her other arm supporting a belly heavy with child. "Ben, come with me." The fright evident on her face was in stark contrast to her calm demeanor.

Clay's laughter mixed with a few other chuckles as some members of his gang eyed the woman and child. "You got yourself a nice family," he commented to Rawling who had edged to his wife's side and tucked her and the boy behind him. When he attempted to push them inside the cabin, Clay drew his pistol and aimed it. "Naw, let 'em see what happens when folks steal from me."

A cold shiver raced down Dewey's spine. When had these buffalo hunters changed their purpose to terrorizing innocent, God-fearing folk, threatening them?

It wasn't right, wasn't what he'd signed on for. It gnawed at his conscience.

Like a young fool, he'd believed Clay's vow that the gang hunted the herd for meat, with the hides a bonus livelihood. When they'd left a carcass behind, Dewey assumed local plains dwellers would benefit. He'd soon learned otherwise. The Drifters didn't share, nor did they help others who needed the meat for food and the hides for warmth. Led by Clay, they'd soon become more of an outlaw gang that reveled in buffalo slaughter.

The terrified faces before him served as a harsh mirror reflecting the desperados they'd become. His stomach churned with the realization.

I can't live this way a second longer.

Dewey spurred his horse forward, kicked-up dust stinging his eyes as he positioned himself between his boss's gun and the family trembling on the porch of their cabin.

Clay's eyes narrowed dangerously. "What the hell, Bower?" he ground out. "Move aside, this ain't your business."

Dewey pulled his own gun from its holster. "These folks are defenseless, Clay." He nodded toward the hide. "Look at it. A small adult male, I'd say. Not enough to feed hungry mouths for very long."

Clay sneered, "So what? They stole from me." His frown darkened. "You gone soft?"

The air grew thick with tension, a standoff that stretched on amid a child's whimpers and his mother's attempt to quiet him.

When other cabin doors started opening, Dewey figured things could get real dangerous, real fast. "Look, boss," he reasoned, "they ain't done you wrong. Shot a buffalo, is all. Just one, as far as I can see."

He gestured with his free hand, pointing out several other settlers who had begun sidling around the corners of lean-tos and poorly constructed sheds. Men who watched with caution, with fear–and holding weapons. Knives, rifles, even a pitchfork. "More'n blood makes a family out here. You want to go against that many kinfolk?"

His words echoed through the stillness, the truth of them resounding with a few of the gang members who shifted uneasily in their saddles.

One of them muttered, "We ain't murderers."

Another agreed with a terse, "Let it go, Clay."

The biggest member, a shaggy, unkempt hunter who called himself Mountain, took up the reins as the massive stallion beneath his bulk snorted and danced. "I ain't stickin' around when they's hides t' collect." He turned toward the trail leading into the hills, galloping hooves breaking into the standoff stretching on for what felt like an eternity.

Finally Clay, with a venomous snarl, begrudgingly lowered his gun. The air seemed to breathe again, though the settlers' rifles and makeshift weapons never faltered.

Yet, amidst the fragile peace, Clay's ugly glare was a silent vow of retribution. "Let's go," he growled, swinging into the saddle and kicking his horse to spur it forward.

Silence reigned as they rode toward the hills, Mountain and his stallion a dark blot in the distance. Every strike of hooves against rough ground and pebbles sounded like a death knell to the bond these men once shared. Dewey knew he'd just severed ties with the Red River Drifters.

If the rest breaks away, Clay'll blame me.

He'd just made a dangerous enemy, though it didn't matter; he was done. It was time to move on.

Chapter Two

*Late May, 1876, five miles outside Cheyenne,
Wyoming Territory*

Frederick Hayes gazed across the wide expanse of the
prairie. In his pocket was a pouch containing the balance
remaining from a cattle sale he'd finalized a mere week
ago. Half had gone toward a Schuttler covered wagon; the
rest he'd secure in a bank, once he and his daughter reached
their destination.

They'd packed carefully, following the Utter Brothers'
instructions on what provisions to bring for the one-and-a-
half-month wagon train journey from Cheyenne to
Deadwood.

"Where the gold is," Frederick whispered to himself.

He glanced at Melanie who sat by his side in the high
wagon, alight with anticipation. Pride burst in his chest. His
only child, motherless from the tender age of thirteen, had
grown into a spirited and intelligent young woman.

After his beloved wife, Beatrice, passed away, he'd
done his best by their daughter, building a comfortable life
on their modest ranch, raising beef cattle. He'd never
thought to leave Cheyenne for greener pastures, always
assuming Melanie would marry someday and begin a
family of her own. Wyoming would one day become a
state, and all they needed would be within their reach.

Then came the wagon train, bound for the gold mining
country. Organized by Charlie Utter, financed by both him
and his brother Steve, the train originated out of
Georgetown, in Colorado Territory, and would stop in
Cheyenne for a week, gaining more travelers and stocking
up on extra provisions. With good news of gold in the

Black Hills, the Utters assured all who listened that mining the bountiful vein would make folks rich.

Frederick was one who listened. With the sale of his cattle and land, his nest egg was quite bountiful. If gold mining didn't prove profitable, he would build a new ranch, bigger and better.

"Father." Melanie's soft voice broke into his whirling thoughts, and he turned to smile at his precious girl. In her green dress and dark cloak, a felted porkpie hat perched on her raven plaits, she made his heart swell with love.

He patted her hand as it rested on his arm. "Any regrets on leaving for the unknown?"

"Not a single regret." The wave of her hand encompassed the prairie and far away hills, her expression bright with excitement. "Just look at it. What an adventure we will have!"

Frederick smiled fondly. "I believe you have wanderlust in your veins, Melanie. Others your age might balk at attempting such a trek."

"Pssh," she retorted, her dimples appearing in a wide grin. "Never back down from a challenge. Isn't that what Mother always said?" Her mirth faded as sadness shadowed her blue eyes. "She would approve, Father. Onward, ho! 'Tis my new battle cry."

"That's my girl," he replied approvingly, her positive attitude helping to banish the last remnants of guilt he'd experienced in pulling her away from their settled lives.

The familiar landscapes of Wyoming soon gave way to the uncharted horizon. Their wagon followed fourteen others, with sixteen more behind them. Like sentinels of hope, the sturdy covered wagons rolled along over rough ground and brush, most pulled by teams of horses, several others with lumbering oxen.

Gamblers, prospectors, and other fortune-seekers manned the wagons. Spying a few 'ladies' of questionable repute sharing space with some of those gamblers,

Frederick found himself unsurprised. Whatever awaited them in Deadwood Gulch, he reckoned additional female company would come in handy.

Each person on this journey carried a story and a dream—

A dream of Gold Fever.

That evening, the wagons converged in clusters, four or more to a group. The Utters explained this to be a safety measure, as the surrounding wilderness held its share of dangers.

Frederick had halted beside a gaudy painted wagon owned by a rather flamboyant couple who had traveled from Georgetown and knew the Utter brothers well. On the grayer side of fifty, Lester and Lil Hamilton possessed as bad a case of gold fever as anyone Frederick had met so far.

"You'll take heed, Mister Hayes. I'd bet there'll be scoundrels afoot in those golden hills," Lester avowed, his silver hair blowing in the breeze.

Beside him, the plump Lil repeated, "Scoundrels, to be sure."

Frederick politely tipped his hat to her. "Yes, ma'am. I shall be as careful as possible."

Melanie smiled at the Hamiltons. "Father taught me how to shoot. He says I'm a dead-eye." She patted a pocket in her cape.

"Land sakes, missy! You've been carrying a loaded gun in that blanket you're wearing?" Lester exclaimed, while Lil looked suitably impressed.

"Well, it wouldn't do me much good if it were not loaded," Melanie reasoned. "But no, I left it in the wagon." She rose from the nest she'd made of her cape. "I should keep it with me. In case of scoundrels."

Before Frederick could stop her, she darted toward the rear of their wagon. Fondly, he commented, "Ever the vigilant one—"

Her sudden holler of, "Unhand my bag, you lout," had him up on his feet and running.

Rounding the corner of the wagon, Frederick gasped at the sight of his daughter trying to wrestle one of their carpet bags from a straggly-haired man. Even from a distance the thief's smell proved ghastly.

"Here, now," Frederick shouted, hurrying to her side. "Let go of that!" He got hold of the man's shoulder and tugged.

Suddenly there was a pistol in Frederick's face and a growling, "I reckon I'll take the gal and her bag," in his ear, as the thief attempted to back away with Melanie still clinging to the handle.

Unarmed and fearful of antagonizing the man holding a gun near his daughter's head, Frederick could do nothing but watch and shout for help as the thief dragged Melanie off into the deepening night gloom, her cries of anger growing louder.

Suddenly, a single shot rang out, and the miscreant dropped to the ground, releasing his grip on Melanie and writhing in pain as he clutched his leg.

Stunned, Frederick ran forward and caught her up in his arms. "Dear child, are you hurt?"

"Only my pride," she retorted, leaning against his chest. "I'll not leave my gun in the wagon again. Not in this rough company."

"A smart sentiment, young lady." The gravelly voice came from behind them.

Frederick and Melanie turned to see a tall, slender man in a set of worn buckskins. A dusty flat-brimmed hat covered his shoulder-length wavy hair, and his drooping mustache bracketed a wide, unsmiling mouth. In one hand he held a deadly-looking Smith & Wesson pistol.

Shrewd eyes narrowed on first Melanie, then Frederick. "You know," he stated as he holstered his gun, "that's the first time in a hell of a lot of Sundays I've had to shoot anyone." He tapped his temple with a long, callused finger. "Bad eyesight."

Gently setting Melanie aside, Frederick came forward, his hand outstretched. "Sir, you saved my daughter's life. I am in your debt. Frederick Hayes, from Cheyenne, at your service."

The stranger shook hands. "James Hickok. From just about all over the West." He nodded toward Melanie. "Glad to see you are unharmed."

She studied him closely. "Hickok? Your name rings a bell. In fact, I have read it in the paper."

"I suppose you have. And you can call me Bill," he replied. As her eyes widened and Frederick stared in recognition, Hickok gave a lopsided smile half hidden under his thick mustache. "Or Wild Bill, if you prefer."

"Mister—er, Wild Bill—would you join our campfire and share a meal with us? My daughter made trail beans and soda biscuits. There's plenty extra," Frederick offered.

"Two of my favorite things," the famed gunslinger and retired lawman answered, removing his hat and slapping the dust from the brim. "I'd be right proud to partake, soon as I dispose of this troublemaker." He prodded the wounded thief, who groaned and cursed weakly. "One of the prospectors, likely. Utters will send him packing. No room for this kind of lowlife in their wagon train."

Once the thief had been dealt with and the Hamiltons retired for the night, Frederick led their guest to the campfire he'd set earlier in the evening. While Melanie dished up their supper, he produced three tin cups. "Coffee, if that's all right with you. Melanie probably wouldn't object if I add a splash of whiskey to it," he said, winking at his daughter.

She laughed and held out the coffee pot, using her apron to protect her hand as she poured a measure of the steaming brew into the cups. "After my little, um, adventure," she stated, nodding toward the wagon, "I might just join you fellows."

They enjoyed the simple yet filling meal and warmed their bellies with the whiskey-laced coffee. Frederick found Hickok's tales of travel and tribulations vastly entertaining, though he could recognize the danger behind such a life. The man had been shot, thrown in jail, attacked and severely wounded by a bear, and came close to dying more times than even he could count. While Frederick had little doubt Wild Bill liked to exaggerate some–the way adventurous types were wont to do–he recognized the ring of truth, and knew he'd enjoy the man's company on the long haul to Deadwood.

Melanie excused herself for the night, brushing a kiss across Frederick's cheek. Others settled in their wagons, here and there raucous chatter and the occasional bark of laughter vying with the nickering horses and lowing oxen.

Frederick reached into his vest for a cigar, offering one to Wild Bill. They smoked at leisure, the conversation circling to Frederick's desire for land.

Hickok blew out a smoke ring. "You might want to speak to the Utters," he suggested. "They know where to stake out and purchase clear land."

"Clear land?"

"Yes, cleared of tribal possession," he clarified, nodding toward the dark horizon. "Closer to the Black Hills and Deadwood Gulch, I'd say. If you still plan on mining, the Gulch area might be your best prospect. Tomorrow you can ask 'em. I'm sharing their wagon. Be glad to drive the team while you boys have a chat."

Chapter Three

Mid-July, 1876, Deadwood, Dakota Territory

Melanie waited for her father to finish securing their
wagon, sighing when she spied the dust coating her boots.
Stomping her feet knocked off the worst of it.

Their arrival in Deadwood five days earlier had been a
blend of nervous anticipation and excitement for what new
adventures lay ahead. The town, buzzing with the clamor of
construction and the boisterous energy typical of a gold
rush, contrasted sharply with the serene atmosphere of their
previous home in Cheyenne.

They'd purchased several mining implements for
extracting minerals and would soon venture to the Gulch
camp right outside of town. For now, they settled some of
their wagon belongings in a room her father had rented in
the only operating hotel, a small, one-story establishment
nearby other hastily erected shanties and thick canvas tents.

She'd been grateful for the two narrow, yet
surprisingly comfortable pallets set against thin opposite
walls. A tin basin and water pitcher took up space on a
crude table. A single window, covered with oiled canvas,
lent scant light into the room. Mister Linden, the owner,
promised the future addition of real glass. In the meantime,
he had provided plenty of tallow candles.

Across from the hotel was a saloon owned by a gent
named Billy Nuttal. Realizing his patrons also needed food,
Nuttal offered items such as pickled eggs and dried buffalo
backstrap alongside his whiskey. After a few meals there,
Melanie had found the eggs more to her liking.

Her father soon joined her. "All buttoned down
tightly," he said, retrieving his pocketwatch from his vest to
note the time. "We're to meet a young fellow by the name
of Bower. Mister Utter, as well as Nuttal, assured me of his
qualifications as a carpenter."

"Are you thinking of hiring him to expand the cabin?" she queried. Two days ago, her father had signed for ten acres of land a few miles outside of Deadwood, mostly pasture with the added bonus of a small building. "Would he build our barn as well?"

"I believe it could be satisfactorily arranged," he replied, and crooked an arm. "Shall we, my girl?"

She clasped his elbow. "We shall, indeed."

Dewey leaned against the rickety wall of Nuttal's #10 Saloon as he waited for Frederick Hayes, one of the Utter Brothers' wagon train people. The man was in need of employing someone for an expansion of his newly acquired ranch. According to Nuttal, Hayes and his daughter had bought ten acres and a dilapidated cabin.

At least there'll be something to work with.

In the three months since he'd arrived in the Gulch area, he'd staked a claim, done a bit of gold panning, and found enough nuggets to rent a small room in the hotel across the street. At the time it'd been more of a shanty than a hotel, but an offer to help reinforce the lopsided building had provided Dewey with additional work as a carpenter. Word grew in Deadwood and soon he had people willing to hire him to fix what they'd started. Once the sawmill established itself, others joined the carpentry business, but there was plenty of work to go around.

Casting a glance in the direction of the open area where the wagon train had settled, Dewey spotted a stout fellow approaching, sporting a thick mustache and wool felted Homburg hat. This must be Hayes, for on his arm he guided a young woman, presumably his daughter, over the ruts in the road.

The young woman flung back her head and laughed at something her father said, causing her flat-brimmed hat to slip off and hang by its ribbons, revealing silky black hair bound in a single plait that fell over the bodice of her white shirtwaist.

Dewey straightened, a flutter of excitement—a feeling long forgotten—thrumming in his chest. The dirty, half-wild streets of Deadwood saw very few women, and those they did were of questionable nature. But even wearing the plainest of clothing, this sweet-faced miss was a breath of the freshest air.

"Mister Bower?" The gruff inquiry snared Dewey's attention. "I'm Frederick Hayes, and this is my daughter, Melanie."

Stepping away from the saloon wall, Dewey extended a firm handshake to Hayes. "Pleasure to meet you." His gaze shifted, settling on Melanie, intrigued by her unwavering stare, unusual for a gently reared female.

He tipped his hat with a murmured, "Miss Hayes," before refocusing on her father. "I understand you're looking to build on ranch acreage you recently purchased."

"That's correct," Hayes confirmed. "We bought ten acres with the promise of a fair price for whatever future land we might want. What we have thus far contains flat pasture. Eventually we will need a barn, but for now our horses require shade from the sun. There's a small cabin, only two rooms, and we'd like to add a few more, make it into something sturdy that can stand up to whatever this region might throw at us."

"Dakota Territory can be a demanding mistress," Dewey admitted. "But she's fair to those who understand her ways."

Miss Hayes stepped forward, her voice steady and sure. "We're prepared to meet her challenges."

Dewey had to admire her spirit. His lips curved into a warm smile. To her father he said, "Let me know when you've secured your supplies. Talk to Mister Linden about wood and nails. He might be able to get what we'll need, and at a fair price." He paused, curiosity getting the better of him. These folks had traveled with Utter's wagon train, after all. Upon seeing Deadwood and the stark realities of the mining camps, had they decided against digging for gold?

"Sir," he began frankly, "I know you came in with the Utter group. It may seem bold of me to ask, but are you still planning on mining in one of the camps?"

Hayes released a heavy sigh. "To be honest, I ponder the wisdom of subjecting my daughter to that rough life—"

"Father," Miss Hayes interjected, clearly irritated, "I am perfectly capable of dealing with 'that rough life,' as you put it. I consider myself quite plucky, in fact."

Dewey let his gaze wander over the lovely young woman, from the top of her raven hair to the tips of her dainty boots. Slender yet shapely, tall for a woman, she would still fit nicely under a man's chin. Innocence as well as intelligence shone from her wide blue eyes.

Indelicate as it might seem, he felt compelled to ask, "Can you shoot a gun, Miss?"

Her rosy lips curved in a smile. "I can, sir. With unerring accuracy." She patted her pocket. "Would you care for a demonstration?"

Now it was her father's turn to protest, "Melanie!"

A gentle laugh was her response as she took her father's arm and gave it a squeeze. "I can look after myself, you know."

"Heaven help me, I do know." Hayes turned to Dewey, who'd struggled to contain his amusement at their banter. "Bower, by any chance are you a miner?"

"I am, but it's been weeks since I visited the camps. Work in town has kept me very busy."

"Would you be willing to join us on our first panning attempt? Having someone of experience along would surely be appreciated."

"I'd be glad to serve as your guide," Dewey replied, managing—barely—to hold in his anticipation of spending more time in Melanie Hayes' company.

"Excellent!" Hayes took her elbow. "Is tomorrow too soon?"

"Not at all, sir." As Dewey watched Frederick Hayes and his daughter depart, excitement suffused him for the chance to return to mining combined with the challenge of showcasing his woodworking talents.

"I'll work hard," he promised himself. Standing taller, he vowed to make his mark in Deadwood and put his past transgressions behind him.

Chapter Four

The next morning, Melanie exited the hotel, stepping carefully over the uneven porch planks. Repositioning her hat to stave off the bright sunlight, she breathed in deeply, then coughed out air tainted with a mixture of horse manure and dust. Still, being outside was preferable to the closed-in feeling of the room she and her father shared.

She took in the bustle of her surroundings, how men shouted, horses neighed, and hammers pounded as more structures were erected, some little more than heavy canvas supported by split logs. The town would grow quickly from its rudimentary roots. In another year, barring the gold veins drying up, Deadwood might be quite the modern spectacle.

A clink of spurs caught her attention and she smiled to see Dewey Bower striding toward her. Over his shoulder he carried the sort of canvas bag that she had seen other miners toting on their backs, similar to what she and her father had also purchased.

The morning sun had already dampened his shirt with perspiration. Muscles rippled across his chest and down his sinewy arms. He cut such a manly figure, Melanie found herself unabashedly staring.

When she finally dragged her gaze away and met his twinkling brown eyes, her entire face burned in a flush. Still, she had never been the retiring sort and was far from a tittering maiden. Her chin lifted. "Good morning, Mister Bower." Her steady tone belied the mad flutter in her heart. "You are quite punctual."

He tipped his hat to her. "Morning, Miss Hayes. Please, call me Dewey." He patted the bag. "I took the liberty of purchasing some of Nuttal's eggs. In case you and your father get hungry."

"No backstrap?" At his sudden expression of distaste, she laughed. "Ah, not so fond of buffalo, are you? Well, I join you in that sentiment. I also thought to pack a few items. And you may call me Melanie." She was enjoying this chance to chat with the handsome carpenter.

"Thank you . . . Melanie. I must say you're smart to wear trousers instead of a skirt," he commented, glancing approvingly at her attire of pants and one of her father's old work shirts. "But you might want to tuck your hair up under your hat. Where we're going, it's best to look more like a lad than a lady."

"Ah, I see." Removing her hat, she coiled her plaits over the crown of her head and arranged the wide brim to shade her face. "Better?"

"Oh, yes." His low reply sent a pleasurable shiver up her back.

Just then her father stepped off the porch and joined them. "Bower, good morning. I admire a punctual man."

"As I do." Dewey shook the hand he extended. "It's about five miles to Gulch Camp. Some of the miners walk the trail, but we can go by wagon." He gestured toward a stable further down the rutted street. "There's one I'm allowed to borrow, plus a draft horse to pull it."

"Very much appreciated," Melanie said, impressed at how he'd thought ahead.

They neared the south edge of the mining camp, where the churned-up mud near Deadwood Creek had hardened in the heat. Dewey brought the horse and wagon to a halt a few yards away from one of the roped off areas where miners hitched their horses and stowed wagons. At one end an awning made of ropes and canvas sat nearly empty, indicating most of the miners working today had walked in or camped here all night.

He ground-tied the horse under the awning, then collected the bags, handing one to Frederick and slinging his and Melanie's over his shoulder.

"I can carry my own," she protested, trying to take it from him.

Dewey adroitly avoided her attempt. "You'll be too busy watching your step." At her questioning look, he pointed to the ground. "Holes everywhere. Some are big enough to swallow you whole," he teased.

"Oh, my." Careful to walk with care, she didn't protest further. He kept an eye on her feet, making sure she stepped carefully. When he glanced up, he caught Frederick's approving nod.

Hoping for the best, Dewey led Melanie and her father to his creek claim site, glad to see it undisturbed. Granted, it was a small claim, but anyone could have taken it over. He hadn't meant to abandon it.

"This is my original claim," he said, setting down his and Melanie's bags. "I thought it might be best if you get a feel for mining here. Then if you want to stake a claim for your own, the office at this camp can get you settled. The straw boss is fair and honest."

Surprisingly, only a handful of men worked their sites today, but for that Dewey was relieved especially when a few miners they encountered eyed Melanie as if they'd figured that she wasn't a lad after all. In all fairness he understood their attention, for the trousers and shirt she wore enhanced her delicate femininity instead of detracting from it.

Dewey's glower in their direction, coupled with his hand on his holster, was enough of a discouragement to make them mind their own business.

For several hours they remained at the creek, Dewey demonstrating how to sift through water and silt. Gold panning was a slow, methodical chore, yet there was no denying the satisfaction of unearthing nuggets, no matter how small.

"I found something," Melanie exclaimed, prodding a chunk of what appeared to be a slimy pebble. She swished it in some clean water, examining it closely. When she held it up and sunlight hit it, Dewey saw the yellowish sparkle.

He moved to her side and peered into her palm. It was indeed a gold nugget. "Looks like you struck a vein, Miss Melanie," he commented, finding her excitement contagious.

Frederick had also crouched next to her. "Let's see that treasure of yours."

She handed it to him, watching as he turned it between his fingers. "Could it be fool's gold?" she asked. "I have read about miners finding such a thing."

Dewey shook his head decisively. "No, not here. The gold found thus far in the Black Hills has been verified and registered. It's one of the straw boss's duties."

Her success had fueled his own fever, and he eagerly resumed his position at the creek. "Ready to find more?" he asked, dipping his pan into the water.

Having retrieved her nugget from her father, Melanie tucked it into her pocket. Her smile threatened to outshine the sun. "Most assuredly!"

"Another hot day," Melanie commented to her father as she used her hat to fan her face. "I am glad we didn't choose to pan gold again." She fumbled for the handkerchief she kept tucked in the watch pocket of her skirt and blotted the back of her neck.

Yesterday's mining attempts had yielded two more nuggets, both found by her father. His whoop of delight had echoed over Deadwood Creek. A quick meal of pickled eggs, paired with the soda biscuits and huckleberry jam left over from their wagon train days, had been an enjoyable affair, fueling them for another hour of panning before they'd given up and traveled back to town.

They had plans to meet with Dewey at Nuttal's and discuss the additions to the cabin as well as the new barn and stable. Knowing she would soon see him again sent so many nerves tumbling inside her, Melanie had to force herself not to clutch her stomach like a girlish ninny.

Feigning a calm front, she took her father's arm as they crossed the street and entered the saloon.

Nuttal's was—as usual—noisy and filled with the sounds of clinking tin dishes and hearty laughter. Dewey was already there, seated at Wild Bill's table and engaged in a quiet conversation with the legendary gunslinger. At her entrance, he jumped up with a wide smile and pulled out a chair, seating her carefully before greeting her father.

Wild Bill inclined his head politely. "Good to see you, Frederick, Miss Hayes. I hear you dipped your toe in Deadwood Creek and panned a few nuggets."

"We have, sir," her father affirmed. "And I see you have met young Bower. He's a solid, hardworking sort."

While Dewey flushed at such praise, Hickok regarded him thoughtfully. "I have heard good things about you, Bower. Been watching you around town. You've got a keen eye and a steady hand. Ever thought about law enforcement?"

Visibly surprised, Dewey pondered the question before meeting the older man's eyes squarely. "I can't say it hasn't crossed my mind. With all that's going on in Deadwood, a man could make a difference."

Wild Bill nodded. "How about I show you some of the ropes? Someone of your capabilities could be invaluable in keeping the peace around here."

Melanie's father turned to Dewey with obvious approval. "That's a fine offer. You'd do well to learn from one of the best."

"I agree." Dewey accepted the hand Wild Bill held out and gave it a firm shake. "Thank you, sir. I wouldn't think of refusing such a generous offer."

The retired lawman's grin softened his usually fierce demeanor. "My friends call me Bill."

Chapter Six

Dewey wiped the sweat from his brow as he hammered the last nail into the new addition. He stepped back to admire his handiwork, a sense of pride swelling in his chest. In barely a week—and with Frederick Hayes' help in raising the walls—he'd significantly enlarged the cramped, modest cabin.

With a bedroll and lantern waiting for him each night in the temporary, three-sided lean-to he'd erected in the clearing where the new barn would sit, Dewey hadn't needed to travel back and forth to town each night. Mister Linden had been kind enough to allow whatever time was needed in which to complete the work on the Hayes property.

Now the cabin boasted a new wing, making it into a more comfortable dwelling. Though crude on the inside, Frederick's assurance that he could finish the inner walls himself afforded Dewey the freedom to return to Deadwood and continue working for Mister Linden as well as starting an apprenticeship with Wild Bill.

As Dewey wiped the sweat from his brow, a familiar feminine voice called out, "Supper, if you're ready."

Turning, he saw Melanie emerging from the cabin. She carried a roughly woven basket, her steps light and graceful on the uneven ground. Her father followed behind her, holding a few horse blankets to use as a place to sit.

"Evening," he greeted them, his voice echoing slightly in the open space.

Frederick clapped Dewey on the shoulder. "It's such a beautiful sunset, we thought we'd enjoy our meal outside."

Melanie set the basket down on an old stump doubling as a makeshift table. The mouthwatering fragrance of meat wafted out. "One of the miners gave us three hares in exchange for some of the quince preserves I brought from

Georgetown." Her dimples flashed in the lowering light. "There's also corn cake and apple butter. I hope you're hungry."

Dewey couldn't hide his grin as his stomach rumbled. "I could eat."

Frederick spread out the blankets, one of which held tin plates and some forks. They served themselves, finding comfortable positions on the cushioned ground. The rustling of the wind through the trees provided a soothing backdrop, occasionally punctuated by the distant yip and lonely howl of a coyote.

Dewey paused mid-bite, tilting his head slightly at the coyote's call. "The wildlife seems to be speaking to each other tonight."

Melanie smiled, her pretty eyes reflecting the last rays of the setting sun. "I love to listen to them. It reminds me that we're just a small part of this world, sharing it with everything from the tiniest critters to the mightiest beasts."

Frederick gave an approving nod. "You've got the right of it, daughter."

The next few minutes passed in companionable silence as they enjoyed their meals against the backdrop of nature's best music.

With a final scrape of his fork, Frederick laid down his plate on the edge of the blanket. "Delicious as always, my girl." While Melanie blushed at the compliment, he turned his attention to Dewey. "Young man, how is the extension coming along?"

"Just finished up. Tomorrow, I'll start working on framing the barn." Dewey gestured with his fork. "Might need to rustle up a few men from town to help raise the trusses once they're built."

"You've accomplished so much in a short amount of time," Melanie commented as she collected their empty plates. She cast him a smile that lit up the world. "It's hard to believe it's the same place."

He met her gaze, warmth expanding in his chest. "Thank you, Melanie. It's been a good challenge."

As the sky further darkened, Frederick stood. "Well, I suppose we should call it a night. It's getting late."

Melanie nodded, helping to fold the blankets. "Yes, Father."

"I can't thank you enough for including me in your evening meals. It's a true kindness." Dewey addressed them both, though his eyes lingered on Melanie as he hefted the basket. "I can carry this for you," he added, gaining him another sweet smile.

And he realized the sense of camaraderie and belonging both Melanie and her father had afforded him made the harshness of life in Deadwood far less daunting.

Together they walked the short distance to the cabin, a lantern's glow spilling softly from the uncovered windows. "I heard it'll be a month or longer before any buildings around here will have actual glass," Frederick said, laying the horse blankets over the new hitching post. "Is there any oiled canvas left in town?"

"There is, sir," Dewey answered. "I'll fetch some tomorrow before I get started on the barn frame. Might not be enough for the add-on but I know how to make shutters. It'll help fill in those openings."

As they reached the cabin door, Melanie stopped and faced him. "Goodnight, Dewey," she murmured.

"Goodnight, Melanie." Dewey held out the basket. Their fingers brushed momentarily, a spark of connection in that brief touch. As she stepped across the threshold, the light from the cabin's interior outlined her silhouette.

Just before the door closed, Dewey caught Frederick's eye. The older man offered a knowing chuckle, a gleam of approval in his eyes, before he followed his daughter inside.

Chapter Seven

August 1, 1876
Deadwood, Main Street

Gripping the newly installed newel post, Dewey gave it a firm shake, nodding in satisfaction at its sturdiness. Deadwood might be coming together in a hurry—out of necessity—but anything he built in this town would hold up. He'd make sure of it.

Stepping back, he surveyed the reinforced porch of the hotel. It'd taken two extra hands, local boys whose folks had been part of the Utter wagon train, but they'd been eager to learn and glad to help out for the coins Linden paid them. Dewey was grateful for the labor; it meant he could return to the Hayes ranch site a few days sooner and resume work on the barn.

And I'll get to see my darling Melanie.

He missed her something awful. Had it truly been less than a week since he'd walked in the summer moonlight with her? In one single unforgettable moment, their lips had met in a first tender kiss.

Days later he could still feel her mouth against his, sweet as ripe peaches and softer than a rose petal. She'd kissed him back, her arms linking around his neck when he'd pressed her close.

"Dewey," she'd sighed when they broke apart.

Just his name, that was all, yet the look in her eyes had told him everything he needed to know.

After several more impassioned kisses, he'd walked her back to the cabin, tucking her hand in his, guiding her carefully over the rough ground. At the half open door, he'd wished her goodnight with a tremble to his low voice, thrilled to hear the quiver of longing in her response. Retreating to the lean-to, he'd curled into his bedroll and dreamed of the day he'd ask Frederick for his daughter's hand.

Smiling at the memory, Dewey set aside his hammer. Another two days in town, and he would head back to the ranch site. With the extra wages he'd earned from the hotel reinforcement and other odd tasks, he could begin planning the sort of future Melanie deserved.

His contentment had grown with the three meetings he'd enjoyed with Wild Bill, soaking in the man's vast experience and ideals. Despite his dangerous past, Hickok had a reputation of being tough but fair when it came to upholding the law. Dewey found his mentorship fascinating and invaluable.

Craving a drink to ease his thirst, he headed across the rutted dirt street toward Nuttal's saloon.

Inside, the air was already stiflingly hot. A few men stood at the makeshift bar, sipping their whiskey from tin cups. Three of Nuttal's four rickety tables sat empty, the other occupied by a brisk game of poker. Dewey spotted Wild Bill, facing the door as was his habit, studying his cards, a thin cigar clamped between his teeth. Two of the men at his table were unknown to him, but the third was an unpleasant surprise.

"Jack McCall," Dewey muttered under his breath as he crossed the room to lean against the wall. Unobserved by the saloon's occupants, he studied the man who swayed in his seat even as he brought a half-empty bottle of whiskey to his thick lips and guzzled.

The last time Dewey'd seen McCall was in late May at the mining camp deep in Deadwood Gulch. Drunk, staggering around, picking fights, McCall had a reputation for stealing anything he could squirrel away without getting caught. He'd finally been chased off and told never to come back.

Dewey doubted anyone at the table, including Hickok, knew what level of rotten they were currently playing with.

McCall would cheat for sure. The drunker he got, the meaner, not to mention dishonest as hell. Determined to inform Wild Bill, Dewey stepped forward just as McCall threw his cards to the floor and half-rose in his seat.

Even in the dim room Dewey could see the glaze of alcohol in the man's eyes.

"Bastards, all a' you," McCall snarled, leaning so heavily on the table, poker chips and empty cups slid across its scarred surface. "Cheatin' sumbitches—"

"Son, you're drunk," Wild Bill replied calmly. "Not the best time to be playin' poker, you understand." Reaching into his pocket, he withdrew a handful of coins and held them out. "Why don't you take this and get a bite to eat, soak up that whiskey? Maybe come back when you're sober, win back some of your losses."

Glaring at Wild Bill, McCall managed to fully gain his feet, ignoring the outstretched palm and its assortment of coins. "Go t' hell," he slurred, pushing back from the table and stumbling out the door.

Dewey strode over to the table. "I know that man, and he's a drunkard, a thief. As dangerous as they come."

Hickock frowned. "I figured as much. He drained two bottles of Nuttal's best, right here at the table. If he can ride without falling over, I expect he'll leave town and not come back. Troublemakers like him aren't welcome in Deadwood." Nodding toward the bar, he offered a faint smile. "How's about you and I get a few of Nuttal's pickled eggs and some of that tree bark he calls backstrap? I'm buyin'."

"Well, as long as you're buying, sir," Dewey replied with a chuckle, taking a seat at the table.

Chapter Eight

Aug. 2, 1876
Hayes Ranch Site, Outside Deadwood

Melanie folded laundry she'd pulled off the makeshift clothesline her father had erected from a length of rope attached to one outer wall of the cabin and an abandoned fence post.

"Father, we should go to town today," she commented, smoothing the wrinkles from his favorite shirt.

"And why is that, darling?" His question was innocent enough, but she caught the mischievous twinkle in his eye. "Perhaps you might want to meet with a particular young man?"

She slapped both palms to her flushed cheeks, emitting a groan tinged with laughter. "You know me too well."

"That I do." He paused, meeting her gaze with silent understanding. "Dewey is a fine man. A hard worker and dedicated. I couldn't ask for a better fellow to be courting my only daughter."

"Father, we haven't—that is, we only—oh, let's just ride into town and see what's what!" Flustered and reluctant to reveal more of her feelings, she hurriedly stacked their clean clothes on the slab of wood currently being utilized as a table, before adding, "Aren't you curious about what's been built this past week?"

"Of course I am, since Deadwood is growing like weeds in a garden. I believe I'd like to have a visit with Wild Bill, too." Her father reached for his hat, hanging on a nail near the door. He placed it on his head and gave her unruly braids a brief glance. "Better wear a bonnet, child. The sun is fierce today."

Behind the cabin, her father and Dewey had put up a temporary shade awning for the horses, enclosing it with enough wire and odd pieces of wooden planks to create a corral. A makeshift gate worked as an entrance and exit. Until the barn was built, it would have to do. So far, their well-mannered beasts had not tested the boundary by trying to push against it or jump over it. Two troughs filled with water and grain crowded one side of the awning.

The horses nickered softly as Melanie approached, nuzzling her for the sugar cubes she had in her apron pocket. "Greedy, aren't you," she cooed, sharing the cubes between the handsome pair. Taking their leads, she guided them beyond the fencing to the wagon and helped her father hook them to the neck yoke.

He boosted her onto the seat and took his place next to her, snapping the reins lightly as she removed her apron and smoothed her skirt. Then gave her a wink. "Let's go see your young man."

"Thanks, Mister Linden," Dewey said, accepting the wage pouch from his employer. "You're a fair man to work for."

Linden slapped him on the back. "And you're a hardworking son of a gun, for sure. I ain't never seen anyone who could get things built so fast and so well." He led the way out to the porch of the hotel, squinting into the afternoon sun. "You headed back to the Hayes place?'

"Yessir." Dewey dropped his hat on his head. "But if you need me for anything else, I'm happy to take it on."

"Good to know." With a final handshake, Linden retreated, leaving Dewey on the hotel porch with a heavy coin pouch and anticipation lighting him up from inside.

After subtracting basic necessities from his total wages, he had a substantial nest egg started, courtesy of not only Linden but Nuttal, the Utter brothers, and now Frederick Hayes as well. Half the town had already benefited from his carpentry know-how. He'd heard talk of other businesses coming to Deadwood, in addition to the sawmill. The steady work plus the additional law apprenticeship he'd received from Hickok would lay the foundation of a solid profession.

Anxious to see Melanie and speak to her father, Dewey turned toward the smithy. He'd reinforced and expanded the shanty himself, until it provided enough shade and water troughs for six or so horses. Now the business was run by a former miner who'd arrived in town with a bag of gold nuggets and big plans. Dewey had been happy to forego payment for his labor in order to secure a permanent trough spot for his horse, especially as summer's heat could be unbearable.

As he re-tucked his shirt into his trousers, he glanced toward Nuttal's, and thought he'd stop by for a visit with Wild Bill, who usually played poker in the afternoons. Dewey paused to let a horse and rider pass before stepping into the rutted street—

And two things happened, almost at once.

He spotted Jack McCall advancing toward the saloon, his hat tilted precariously on his head and fingers hovering over his gun. A potent mix of determination and menace emanated from him, each stride charged with the unmistakable threat of an upcoming showdown.

At the same time, Melanie and her father strolled along from the other direction, mere yards from the saloon entrance, oblivious to any possible trouble.

The entire town buzzed with stories of Wild Bill's afternoon poker games at Nuttal's saloon, his table always surrounded by eager spectators. As the door swung open, McCall's hand moved away from his holster and gripped his gun.

"Oh, no," Dewey rasped. "No, no, no."

Time seemed to grind down to tiny seconds as he sprinted forward just as Frederick stretched out a palm to push at the door. Melanie laughed in that bright way she had about her, the sound soft and sweet.

Frederick's booted foot stepped over the threshold, followed by Melanie's dainty laced up shoe—

Dewey's legs couldn't move fast enough as he flew across the street. *Please, please, God.* "Melanie!"

She paused, turning her head to glance his way. Her face lit up with a dimpled smile, her lips parted in a greeting, then her eyes grew wide, noting his frantic pace.

Just as he reached them, a shot rang out, loud and sharp and deadly.

Dewey flung himself at them, shoving both Melanie and Frederick to the hard-packed floor at the entrance of the saloon, covering them with his body.

The sound of men yelling turned the air blue with curses. Melanie's ears rang from the piercing punch of a gunshot in the crowded room. She groaned, bruised from the hard fall to the dirt floor.

Her father stirred, muttering, "What—what's going on?"

"Keep down," Dewey ground out.

She blinked, focusing on his perspiring face a mere inch from hers. "Who?" She licked her dry lips and tried again. "Who was shot?"

"I don't know." He rose, pushing away from her, then tugging her up. Her father quickly scrambled to his feet and drew her into his embrace.

"Both of you stay here," Dewey ordered, as he strode further into the dimly lit saloon.

Melanie swayed on her feet from the rush of nerves coursing through her. "I want to see what happened," she protested.

"No you don't, child." Her father tightened his arms. "Whoever shot his gun probably killed somebody. He might still be nearby."

"Ah, damn it, he's dead," a gruff voice shouted. "Git that sumbitch!"

"He ran out the back," someone else hollered, punctuated by thumping boots and jingling spurs.

Dewey appeared suddenly, urging her toward the door. "Been a killing," he announced tersely. "No place for you, Melanie—"

"Who?" She craned her neck to see around his shoulder and caught a glimpse of a man slumped over a table, a pool of blood mingling with cards and chips, darkening a curly, light brown mane of hair. His hat had tipped over on the floor.

A familiar-looking hat.

"No. Not Wild Bill," she whispered hoarsely, feeling her throat close up with grief as Dewey guided her outside into the afternoon sun. Her shoes dug into the dirt, forcing him to halt. "Why would anyone do this?"

"I don't know, sweetheart, but he won't get away with it." Dewey sighed roughly. "It was Jack McCall who shot Hickok. He escaped out the back. Men went after him and they'll catch him."

Heartbroken, Melanie stiffened her spine against the need to curl up and sob aloud at the loss of such a good man. Tears rolled down her cheeks. "He needs to pay for what he's done."

One Week Later, Hayes Ranch Site, Deadwood
Dewey threw down the copy of the *Black Hills Pioneer*, its cheap ink already smudged. "Acquitted, by God. I can't understand the stupidity of men, that they'd believe a criminal over actual facts."

Frederick picked up the single sheet newspaper and scanned its contents. "Says here McCall killed Mister Hickok in retribution for the murder of his brother." He adjusted his spectacles and quoted, "'*Should it ever be our misfortune to kill a man . . . we would simply ask that our trial may take place in some of the mining camps of these hills.*'"

"I doubt McCall ever had a brother. And we can only hope the truth comes out. He killed Wild Bill for no other reason than in some sort of mad rage." Dewey shook his head sadly. He'd heard through the town grapevine that McCall had bolted from Deadwood immediately after the sham of a trial held at McDaniel's Theater. With such a murderer on the run, one could only reckon he'd commit another crime, something that would ultimately bring him down.

Melanie carried the coffeepot from the stove, refilling their cups, then took the only remaining chair at the table. Weariness darkened her pretty blue eyes, attesting to more than one sleepless night. In the week since Wild Bill's murder, they had all grieved. Dewey moved to her side and placed a bolstering hand on her shoulder, relieved when she graced him with a small smile.

Over her head he met her father's gaze. In a short span of time, Frederick Hayes had become a father figure, and Dewey held the man in high respect. His original plan, of asking for Melanie's hand in marriage, had been derailed by Hickok's death. It hadn't seemed right to pursue happiness in the face of such tragedy.

But if he had learned nothing else, he'd discovered the fragility of life. Of how a person might think they'd have many years to marry, produce children, build a future.

He parted his lips to speak, but the older man only smiled and nodded. Somehow without words he conveyed his approval of Dewey's suit. It meant a great deal.

"I'll just take a bit of a stroll over to the stable, check on the horses," Frederick said. As he passed Melanie, he dropped a kiss on her head.

He offered a wink to Dewey before heading to the door.

Heart near to bursting, Dewey bent to take his beloved's hand, kneeling there on the rough floor next to her chair. Bringing her slender fingers to his mouth, he kissed them, one by one.

As her beautiful eyes widened in surprise, he murmured, "My love, marry me . . ."

Mount Moriah Cemetery, Deadwood, Dakota Territory
Aug. 3, 1879

A breeze flowed through the air, offering respite from the otherwise stifling summer morning. Frederick Hayes removed his hat and held it to his chest as he gazed at the wooden grave marker.

> **Wild Bill, J.B. Hickok.**
> **Killed by the assassin**
> **Jack McCall in Deadwood,**
> **Black Hills, August 2, 1876.**
> **Pard, we will meet again in**
> **the happy hunting ground to**
> **part no more. Goodbye.**

Beside him, Melanie pulled a handkerchief from her pocket and blotted her forehead. "Such a hot day, isn't it? But I would not miss paying our respects." She pressed her cheek against his arm. "He was a good man. May he find eternal rest here."

"Amen," Frederick murmured, clasping his daughter close.

Thinking back to that awful day, three years ago, could still send a shiver through his frame. If not for Dewey's swift actions, he and Melanie might have walked right into the path of McCall's bullet. The bastard had shot only once, but no one present at Nuttal's that day could have known his full intent. Perhaps he'd plotted to shoot everyone, not just Hickok.

In the end the man had been tried a second time, then hung for his crime. Justice had been served. But it did not keep Wild Bill's friends from mourning him.

The clomping sound of tiny boots roused him from his musings, and Frederick smiled down on the raven-haired tot who threw himself against his legs with an excited, "Grampa!"

"There's my boy." Frederick swept an arm under his grandson's rump and hefted him up. Eyes the color of the sky held the sort of mischief only a rowdy young'un could get himself up to. But for now, he laid his curly head on Frederick's shoulder and yawned.

Dewey joined them at the gravesite, doffing his hat for a moment, eyes closed as he offered a silent prayer of his own. With a brief touch of two fingers to the rough-carved wood, he paid his final respects before turning to Melanie and kissing her lips gently.

"I spoke with Calamity." He gestured in the direction of the famous sharpshooter, standing with her head bent, callused hands clasped behind her back. "She's claiming the right to be buried next to Hickok, if possible."

"If that's what she wants, then her wishes should be honored," Melanie replied. "She cared very much for him."

For a few additional minutes they stood together in the quiet cemetery, while William James Bower—named in honor of their departed friend—dozed on Frederick's shoulder and Dewey held his wife gently, one hand on her burgeoning belly.

There'd be another grandchild to dote on, come the fall, one more blessing. Frederick reckoned they'd had their share of those, starting on the fateful day he and Melanie chose to join Utter's wagon train. And look where it took them. A new life in a rough-and-tumble place. He couldn't imagine living anywhere else, especially now that Dewey and Melanie's ranch adjoined his.

They departed the cemetery, Dewey carrying their slumbering son. Frederick clasped his daughter's arm, guiding her carefully over the uneven ground. At her sigh, he murmured, "Are you weary, my girl?"

"A little. I shall be quite relieved the day I hold this babe in my arms," she replied with a soft laugh, "instead of my poor old tummy."

As they reached their wagon, she turned to give him a hug. Into his ear she whispered, "If it's a girl, Dewey wants to name her Beatrice, after Mother." She drew back to peer into his face. "Is that all right with you?"

"Oh, child." Overcome, Frederick embraced his precious daughter. "Most assuredly."

SAVED BY THE DEPUTY
A tale of western romance and rescue

ROBERT
Deputy Robert Blackwood has held a tender spot in his heart for Magnolia "Maggie" Sanders since the moment they met at her Uncle Knight and Aunt Hannah's wedding in Little Creede. Knowing Maggie will soon return to her home in Atlanta, he longs for the chance to court her properly.

MAGGIE
Choosing to remain in Little Creede through the winter of 1881 gives Maggie Sanders the opportunity to enjoy a lighthearted romance with the handsome deputy. But just days before Christmas, a fierce winter storm strands them miles from town in a tiny, dilapidated cabin.

SURVIVAL
With danger closing in and temperatures dropping, Robert and Maggie must rely on each other for warmth and safety. As the storm rages outside, the closeness they share may turn a budding romance into something far deeper—if they survive long enough to claim it.

Chapter One

Little Creede, Colorado
December, 1881

"Mind the corners, boys." Knight Gleason's voice boomed out of the partially open front doors of his Galleria, just as Robert Blackwood gained the planked porch and knocked the mud and slush from his boots. Between the heavier snowfall throughout the past few days and the thinner, crisp mountain air Little Creede was known for, he found himself fighting back the urge to cough.

Removing his hat, he pushed the door wider, his gaze following four burly fellows maneuvering a massive mahogany table into a side salon whose archway didn't look as if it'd handle the table's girth. Judging by the straining grunts and muttered curses, the thing was heavy as hell.

Fascinated, Robert followed the sweating quartet's progress as Gleason approached and slapped him on the shoulder. "Mister Gleason, what is that thing?"

Gleason looked as proud as a brand-new papa. "That, suh, is mah newest gamblin' acquisition. Roulette, all the way from New Ah'leans. Ah look fer opportunity an' growth, yessir. Lawd knows ah love our bustlin' lil' town."

"How in blazes—when did you get it here?" Robert studied what he could see of the gleaming table, noting a large hole in the center of the tautly stretched felted wool covering the top. Two more men staggered in, carrying an ornately carved wheel between them.

"Well, now, that was an undertakin'. A couple of mah associates bought it fer me, right off'n a Mississippi riverboat. Loaded it on a West-bound train, even arranged fer a special coach bringin' it the rest of the way. One of mah men traveled with it. Ah spared no expense, nosir." Gleason fingered the lapels of his dark green superfine coat, looking mighty pleased with himself. "Name of Singleton. He's gonna stay heah an' head up mah security, run the games fer me, too. If'n roulette catches on, ah've got plans for a few dice tables."

Robert frowned at the mention of more serious gambling. Poker was one thing, but dice games tended to get rowdy. And rowdy could escalate fast to dangerous. As the town deputy, the possibility of trouble concerned him. "Mister Gleason, I'd be cautious about the dice—"

"Ah know what yer thinkin', son. And ah promise yew ah've got mah customers under control."

No sooner had that assurance left the big man's lips than a loud slap, followed by a muffled curse, came out of the dining salon where the Galleria served drinks and a complimentary breakfast for its patrons. Robert strode toward the open doorway, prepared to break up a fight.

Instead, he found himself confronted by Gleason's niece, the very same lovely woman he'd met and been instantly smitten with at her uncle's wedding. Since then, they'd crossed paths a couple of times, once at a church social and again at a barn dance. On both occasions, he had found himself drawn to her lively personality and the way her laughter filled the air. Now, as they stood face-to-face once again, he couldn't help but feel his heart skip a beat.

Magnolia Sanders' cheeks sported high color as she shook out her hand. She halted in the open doorframe, perfectly turned out in a dove-gray gown that lovingly followed the curves of her body. The polished image was offset somewhat by the tumble of heavy red curls down her back and the fire in her blue eyes. That fire met his gaze briefly before she made to step around him, still favoring her hand. A glance at her slender palm, reddened against the pretty alabaster of her skin, and Robert knew she'd just whacked somebody, hard.

Instinct had him reaching for her hand. He cradled it in both of his. "What happened, Miss Magnolia?"

Her fingers tensed, then relaxed in his hold. "I set someone straight, that's all." She shot a fast glare over her shoulder toward the shadowy interior, where a man stood as if hesitant to step into the light. "Now he's probably afraid I'll tell on him."

"Who is it?" Robert growled, surging forward, ready to lay the fool out for whatever he'd done to upset her. "Did he touch you?"

"No." She pulled her hand away and quickly stepped in his path. "He didn't get a chance. I slapped the stupid grin clean off his face as soon as he opened his mouth. I expect Uncle Knight will send him on his way darned fast."

"Yeah, he will. I'll make sure of it." Spotting the cur trying to slip out the back exit, Robert dodged around her to get at him.

Magnolia caught his arm in a surprisingly firm grip. "Mister Blackwood, you've no call to defend me." She held his frown with one of her own. "Although I appreciate your chivalry, I am perfectly fine and safe."

"You're a young, sheltered miss," he began, only to pause when she uttered a laugh that sounded like musical chimes.

"I attended a strict finishing school back East. You might not know this about young ladies of quality, but they can be as vicious as any common dockside fishwife." She tucked a loose curl behind her perfect ear. "What fortitude I gathered in that place will surely assist me when I begin the next stage of my education in the spring."

"I don't understand." Robert stared at the elegant Southern belle, wondering how this woman could be anything but treasured, sheltered, and cherished. "You are beautiful and refined. You'll no doubt attend a genteel university—"

"Oh, but didn't Uncle Knight tell you?" She tilted her head to one side; a coy maneuver Robert had seen other young ladies employ. "I'm apprenticing in Law. Probably back in Louisiana, once a seasoned attorney is secured for me. My uncle has connections there."

Apprentice? Attorney?

"There are no women lawyers."

Her face lit with a teasing smile. "Oh, you won't be saying that for much longer."

With a sweep of skirts, Magnolia sauntered from the side salon.

"Darlin'." Uncle Knight laid a hand over Maggie's as she reached for the sugar bowl. "Yew know yew kin stay heah foreveh, don'tcha?"

She squeezed his thick, callused fingers. "I surely do, Uncle. In fact, I'd like nothing better than to visit far longer in this quaint little town, with you and Aunt Hannah. But you know as well as I how difficult it is for women to be taken seriously when it comes to higher learning. I'm grateful for your assistance in finding someone to apprentice me. Or should I say, your persuasion?" At his raspy chuckle, she grinned. "Once I've received my certificate, I'd also like to see where I'm most needed."

The swiftly indrawn breath across the breakfast table gave Maggie pause, and she regarded her uncle's new bride with affection. "Aunt Hannah, I'll be fine."

"Oh, I am certain you will, dear child." Aunt Hannah's gaze held steady as she passed the basket of sweet rolls. "You're such a bright young woman. It's just—well, I've heard things about Louisiana. Baton Rouge can be a wild place, and it's growing so fast. Knight and I just want you to be safe."

"Father will come with me." Maggie's assurance was more to herself than to her anxious relatives, sitting there with concerned expressions.

Her uncle's bushy red brows drew together as he stirred his coffee. "Yew asked him already? Ah was under the impression yer daddy was fixated on Atlanta an' his practice theah."

"He'd move his office for me." Even as she said it, Maggie forced back a cringe of denial. Her father loved Atlanta and his law practice was booming. He'd been stepping out with a widow as well, a very nice lady close to his age who'd lost her husband during the war. Everyone in town knew 'Bubba' Sanders was a fair attorney who worked hard for his clients. His honesty and work ethic had been the driving force behind her desire to follow in his footsteps.

"Ah wouldn't be too sure of that, darlin', but yew know yer daddy better n' me. Whatever yew do, ah'm in yer corner. Yer auntie Hannah, too."

As her aunt nodded vigorously, Maggie sprang from her chair and hurried around the table to give her uncle a hug. In his ear she whispered, "I love you, Uncle Knight."

He didn't reply, but the hard swallow she felt against her cheek, and the way he squeezed her breathless, was answer enough. With a smacking kiss on his bearded jaw, she pulled away, turning to press her lips to her aunt's soft cheek. Heart full of emotion, she exited the room before she dissolved in tears.

Most undignified for a future attorney.

As she emerged from the dining salon into the lobby, she spotted Robert Blackwood at the front desk, squatting in front of Dolores Lund's daughter, Luellen. The little girl's sweet giggle, coupled with Robert's deep tones, made for a charming contrast as he listened intently to her chatter. It warmed Maggie's insides to see how the tough deputy took time from a busy day to make a child happy.

Robert straightened as she approached, an easy smile on his face as he held Luellen's hand and swung it back and forth. "Afternoon, Miss Magnolia." He winked at her before glancing down at Lulu's pigtailed head. "Looks like I've found me a new sweetheart."

"So I see." Maggie maintained a serious demeanor. "I hope you'll do right by Miss Lulu."

"Oh, he will," Luellen assured earnestly. "My new beaux brought me cookies and said we'd have a tea party." She danced in place for a moment, then leaned in to confide, "'Cept not right now, 'cause I need to use the privy." Tugging her hand free, she darted across the gleaming pine-slatted floor, calling out, "Bye, Missy Maggie. Bye, Mister beaux!"

Maggie's laughter burst forth, and she clapped a hand over her mouth to hold it in as Robert issued an exaggerated sigh. "Seems I've been ousted by a potty."

"Well, it couldn't happen to a more deserving swain." Maggie wiped tears of mirth from her eyes. "Did you really bring her cookies?"

"Yep. I brought her a dozen. Had to promise to drink pretend tea out of a pretend teacup, too, in order to get a few back." He regarded her with sudden interest. "You want to join us? I'll give you imaginary tea, and a real cookie."

"Um . . ." She felt her face heating up at the low words that should have rung innocently but for some reason sounded anything but. Meeting his intense gaze, Maggie couldn't look away. "Only a cookie?"

At the way his eyes darkened, she could have kicked herself.

What on earth am I thinking? She wanted to sink into the floor.

She'd actually started to retreat when Robert said, "I stopped by for something other than chatting up my new best girl." His lips broke into a wide smile. "Although she's mighty charming, if a mite too young for me. I wanted to ask you . . ." He paused, catching her gaze again, pinning her where she stood. "I'd like to take you out for a meal. At the Stage House. Tonight, if you're willing. It's their annual Yule dinner. The proceeds go toward the families at the Carter Mine, and over at Rocky Gulch."

The way he said *willing* shot a bolt of heat up her spine and a touch of panic to her nerves. She'd never stepped out with someone like Robert Blackwood. The fellows back in Atlanta, with their dandified ways and overblown sense of importance, had been acceptable to dance with at this or that evening gathering, but their attitude toward the 'place' women were expected to hold in society only frustrated her. If she'd voiced her intentions aloud—that she planned to follow in her father's path and practice law—she would've been laughed off the dance floor. Or, more predictably, banished from society altogether . . . and by the same people who sought out Bubba Sanders for their legal needs.

But here in Little Creede, a woman's life seemed less constricting. More free. If she brought her certificate back to Colorado and hung a shingle here, what would her life be like?

"Miss Magnolia?" Robert's low rumble dragged her out of her scattered thoughts, and Maggie mustered a smile. Pointless to ponder anything so life-altering right now. Not when a handsome man who already made her heart flutter asked her to step out with him, and for such a worthy cause.

"I would enjoy your company at Yule dinner, Mister Blackwood." At his quirked brow, she hastily added, "For the benefit of those women and children, of course."

Chapter Two

The wooden boardwalk beneath Maggie's high-topped boots had become so slick that she was forced to take tiny, shuffling steps. As the air grew colder, the wind intensified, causing the shingles of the overhanging building awnings to rattle. Snowflakes drifted from the sky, gently caressing her cheeks, serving as a fleeting introduction to the formidable storm looming on the horizon.

With a sigh, she buried her chin into her muffler and trudged along. Winter had grown ugly so quickly here in the lower mountain range, she wondered what, if any, sort of holiday festivities the town could supply.

Just a few days ago, lively chatter bounced off the walls of the Stage House during Yule dinner, when ideas for an impromptu Christmas Day dance was the talk of the evening. She had happily joined in the discussion, while logs snapped merrily in the enormous salon fireplace, and fragrant pine boughs and berries lent their beauty as center-pieces for each table. When Robert walked her home, the evening sky had been clear, the air crisp as a newly plucked apple.

Then, almost overnight, snow had released its frigid wrath over the town. Now, on Christmas Eve morning, the streets were bare of man, woman, or child—or horse. It would likely be a quiet day and evening, with everyone huddled before their hearths and stoves.

The scrolled awning and wide front walkway of the Galleria came into view, and Maggie sped up as much as she dared, anxious to reach the swept-off porch before she grew any more chilled and wetter. A tickle formed in her nose and she let loose with the most unladylike sneeze, then glanced around guiltily. Other than an occasional whinny from Mister Jaworski's smithy and stable, not a living soul existed out in this white, icy world but her. She wiped her nose on her mitten and forged ahead.

I have probably caught that blasted cold going around, she thought, brushing ineffectually at the thick snowflakes collecting on the shoulders of her winter cloak. The heavy felted wool, lined with padded satin, kept the worst of the chilblains away. Under her walking skirt she had donned the sturdiest petticoat she could find, a thin lambswool that protected her legs from the bitter wind.

Maybe the weather was beyond awful, but she had the appropriate clothing to wear, and her comfortable suite at the Galleria contained everything she needed. She had no earthly right to complain.

Bracing herself against the brisk wind, she shoved her mittened hands in her pockets and felt the crinkle of the receipt for the list of supplies the Galleria kitchen staff had requested from the mercantile. She'd have toted it all back in one of the hand wagons they provided for the customers, but the owner had shooed her off with the promise of delivering everything himself.

She huffed out a resigned sigh, thinking of how her uncle was determined to put on a fancy Christmas Day feast for folks who might not have anywhere to go for their holiday meal. With the Stage House closed for the holiday tomorrow, Catherine Carter and her mother-by-marriage, Lucinda Blackwood, had volunteered to help Dolores, the Galleria's excellent cook, and several Stage House servers would assist. Maggie had volunteered for shopping chores, fearing that Dolores might insist on coming out in this nasty weather herself. Based on the poor woman's cough over the past few days, Maggie didn't want her becoming any sicker.

Outside, the breath-stealing wind and stinging cold had increased. Maggie tucked her chin into the muffler around her neck as she trudged through the snow. Glancing around at the silent town, she could just make out the smithy, then Henry Tipple's barber shop, and the town jail—

Which sent her thoughts directly to Robert Blackwood. A flock of butterflies took flight in her belly.

Stop it, she silently scolded.

Though she enjoyed the handsome deputy's company and stepping out with him for Yule dinner had provided a lovely evening, it wouldn't be fair of her to encourage his affection. She'd meant to tell him exactly that—

Then he'd kissed her, right beneath an icicle-encrusted eave on one side of the Galleria doors. His warm lips had moved against hers as his gloved hands framed her face, his wide shoulders blocking the kerosene lamps glowing along the entryway. She'd tasted passion for the first time, unable to protest or make a sound other than a soft moan at the way that single kiss made her feel. After a low, "Good-night, Miss Magnolia," followed by a final kiss to her cheek, Robert had escorted her inside before taking his leave. Maggie had stood inside the open doorway, letting in cold air, and trembled as she watched him stride away.

Head down, her thoughts still on Robert, she was un-prepared when someone ran into her and nearly knocked her off her feet. Gaining her balance, Maggie looked into Dolores Lund's tearstained face. The woman wore only her cook's uniform, drenched from the snow. "Dolores, my goodness, what are you—"

Dolores' raspy wail cut her off, as she collapsed into Maggie's arms. "Luellen. I can't find my sweet baby."

The coughing behind her panic worried Maggie almost as much as the words themselves. "What? What do you mean?"

She placed a protective arm around the woman's shak-ing shoulders, guiding her back toward the Galleria. As they hurried up the slippery path leading to the kitchen, Dolores gasped out, "She ran outside after her dog, and by the time I followed, I'd already lost her in the whiteout. I looked and looked, but I couldn't find her." The last words were barely recognizable behind her sobs, as she completely fell apart.

"Shh, we'll find her." Maggie strove to offer comfort even as she tensed with worry for Luellen's safety. Shoving open the Galleria's kitchen door, she urged Dolores inside, calling out to anyone within earshot, "Quick, someone help."

From the main hallway, Uncle Knight's head housekeeper, Etta, hurried toward them. "Oh, my goodness. What happened?"

Samuel Singleton, the gunslinger her uncle hired to handle troublemakers in the Galleria, appeared at the top of the stairs, his cool gaze assessing the situation.

Maggie settled Dolores into the nearest chair, unable to stem her panic despite trying to remain calm for the distressed cook. "Luellen is missing in the storm. We need Doc Sheaton. And men to go out looking for the child."

While Etta did her best to soothe Dolores, Singleton descended the stairs two at a time. Although he'd never been anything but polite, the man always made Maggie nervous. It was something in his dark eyes, a hardness that verified he was more dangerous than his quiet demeanor indicated.

Giving her a curt nod, he drawled, "I'll fetch him, and the sheriff too."

As he strode to the front and shoved through the Galleria doors, Dolores grabbed Maggie's hand. "Please—"she sucked in a shallow breath"—find her. You have to—"

"I will," Maggie assured her. "She can't have gone far." She turned and headed for the kitchen exit.

"Maybe you should wait for the sheriff." Etta followed, worry creasing her round face.

"There's no time. Stay with Dolores until Doc arrives." Maggie had to get to Luellen before it was too late. Already the storm was growing in intensity, and Dolores' quiet sobs ripped at her heart.

"I promise, Dolores," Maggie called over her shoulder as she flung open the door, stepping into the storm, "I'll bring your little girl back to you."

The freezing wind took her breath away, but she braced against the cold and hurried to her uncle's stables, stumbling in the deep snow. In the first stall, piebald Fury stomped his hooves impatiently as if feeling the urgency. Maggie threw a saddle over the stallion's wide back and tightened the straps.

There wasn't time to wait for the sheriff to gather a search party. Luellen wouldn't survive much longer, and the air grew colder by the minute.

Mounting quickly, she rode into the storm.

"Luellen," she shouted. "Lulu, answer me." What power her voice contained ripped away by the wind, it took every ounce of courage Maggie had to continue, as the snow fell faster, nearly blinding her. Wiping at her frost-encrusted eyelashes, she searched for the girl, losing track of the time, as each second seemed like an eternity.

Shivering against the bitter cold, soon all she could see was whiteness, the town disappearing from her vision. The desire to turn around, and hopefully find her way back to her uncle, paled as thoughts of sweet Lulu kept her going.

She'd find the child. There was no other recourse.

As Robert brushed the heavy snow from his shoulders, a nagging uneasiness settled within him. The biting cold only served to heighten his concern for anyone who might be caught out in the storm.

He'd finished dealing with a loner who'd shown up at Rocky Gulch with guns drawn, thinking he'd steal what ore had been retrieved and set aside for rendering. How in hell he thought he'd cart it all away, Robert hadn't a clue. Obviously, the dolt hadn't plotted that far ahead.

Davey Bentley, the Gulch's foreman, had caught the thief red-handed and had locked him up in one of the inner mine boxes where the carts were stored. By the time Robert had arrived, the man was rattling the bars and begging for his life, thinking he'd be left for dead in the storm. Not about to drag him around in the snow, Robert had tossed him a chamber pot, a bag of dried venison, and a canteen. A few extra horse blankets thrown in would keep the man's worthless hide thawed out. With enough food to last him several days—unless he gobbled it all at once—he'd make it through until the storm eased and Robert could bring him to the jail in Little Creede, notifying Territorial as well.

It'd started snowing in earnest halfway between Rocky Gulch and Little Creede. The last thing Robert wanted was to stay out any longer in the worsening winter storm. He patted Gypsy, his prized paint mare, in an attempt to soothe the high-strung animal. The snow, easily over a foot deep, worried him. "Shouldn't be much longer, girl."

At the slow pace they were going, it'd be another hour before they made it back to town. He blinked against the flakes blowing in his eyes, not sure Gypsy could handle much more in this weather. Her back was so blanketed in snow, he could no longer see the pretty pattern of black against the pale cream of her coat.

"Hell, not sure I can take another hour," he muttered, as more ice and snow slid down the back of his neck despite his efforts to keep his collar up as protection. If it didn't let up soon, he'd have to find shelter until the storm passed. He knew of an abandoned cabin not far from the south end of the Carter mine. He'd hole up there for the night if the weather didn't start improving.

By the time he reached the trail leading to the cabin, the snow had slowed somewhat. *Might as well continue on to town.* More minutes crawled by—he'd lost track of how many—when he spotted something dark in the distance.

"What the hell?" Robert squinted, frowning as the object grew closer and he could make out a horse.

Nudging Gypsy forward, he swore when he recognized Magnolia Sanders swaying in knee-deep snow, clinging to the reins of a shivering stallion.

Dismounting in one quick leap, he raced to her side. "Magnolia!"

Her glazed eyes met his for one instant, with a spark of recognition. "R-Robert?" she stuttered, her slender frame shuddering hard. With a pained moan, she collapsed.

His arms clamped around her before she could hit the ground. His grip tightening, he swung her into his arms. "Shit."

He glanced up at the sky, trying to gauge how much longer the storm would last.

Not good.

Finding shelter was urgent. In this frozen mess he couldn't take the time to search for the right trails back to Little Creede. They—as well as the horses—needed immediate warmth if they were to survive. Striding over to Gypsy, he managed to get himself and his precious cargo back on his mount and clicked his tongue to the stallion. The beast had enough sense to edge closer, enough for him to snatch the loose reins.

Robert urged both horses toward where he estimated the cabin was located. The one-room structure contained a hearth. It wouldn't be much but it was better than nothing.

Fear for Magnolia lodged a hard knot in his gut. She remained limp and unresponsive in his arms, tremors wracking her body. As Gypsy plodded through the snow, Robert struggled to hold on to her, the stallion's slippery reins clenched in his other hand. Finally, the cabin came into view.

"Thank God," he muttered.

The mare held still as he swung a leg over the saddle, clutching Magnolia tightly, worried he'd drop her if he wasn't careful. Easing to the ground, he strode toward the cabin. Noting the crooked lean-to, attached to one side and shrouded by an old conifer evergreen, Robert sent up fervent thanks. The ground appeared mostly dry, with very little snow blowing in. A rickety trough held a broken bale of hay, and he could melt snow for water. More importantly, the horses would be out of the storm.

"We'll be all right," he whispered to the unconscious woman in his arms, as he carried her inside and pushed the door shut with his boot. "We're safe here."

Lord, I hope I'm making a promise I can keep.

Chapter Three

Oh, my head. Maggie struggled to break free from the suffocating and stale air inside the scratchy weight that covered her. She pressed a hand against her throbbing temple, her thoughts sluggish, as if moving through molasses.

Struggling to open her eyes, she squinted as she glanced around an unfamiliar room, dimly lit by a half-gutted candle and low firelight. The air on her head felt cold, but beneath the heavy thing covering her—a horse blanket, judging by the smell—the rest of her was warm.

She rose stiffly on sore elbows, wincing. *What on earth did I do to myself?*

Catching hold of the blanket, she tugged it aside and gasped when she looked down at herself. Her skin prickled with goosebumps, and she wrapped the horse blanket tightly around her body. The realization that she was only wearing a petticoat and camisole filled her with a sense of unease.

Maggie shivered, both from the cold air and from a creeping sense of fear and confusion. *Who undressed me?* She glanced around the shabby cabin, her brows furrowing. *For that matter, where am I?*

As her eyes focused in the dimly lit room, sleet pinged against the roof like a chorus of angry fists, echoing through the small, smoke-filled space. The meager lighting cast a flickering glow on the rough-hewn walls, making the shadows dance like ghosts. Against one log wall, a small table and two chairs leaned at an awkward angle. A makeshift counter, roughly nailed to the opposite wall, held a dirty bucket and several burlap sacks that looked like they had been there for ages.

Maggie shifted her weight, feeling the lumpy straw mattress beneath her. It was thin and offered little cushioning for her aching body. As she peered closer, she spotted rips and chew-marks in the outer ticking. Her stomach churned at the unnerving thought of rodents or other varmints making a home in the bedding.

Her clothing, though, remained missing. Frantically she twisted round, then found her dress and lambswool petticoat hanging on a couple of nails near the fire hearth, her cloak draped over the edge of the mantel.

Gritting her teeth in frustration, Maggie pressed the heel of her hand against the persistent, pulsating throb in her temple. Her mind raced, anxiously grasping at any fragment of memory, as she desperately tried to recall what had happened—

"Luellen. Oh, my Lord." *Where is the child?* When she forced her memory, another wave of pain hit her between the eyes. As she untangled her legs from the smothering blanket, the door burst open, and a snow-coated figure entered.

Panicked, Maggie shrieked and fell back. A sudden jolt of pain shot up her spine as she landed hard on her tailbone, scrabbling for the blanket to shield herself.

"S-Stay away," she gasped.

As the figure strode into the firelight, she recognized Robert Blackwood and slumped with relief. The tension in her body eased as he knelt at her feet and removed his heavy coat.

"It's all right, Miss Magnolia," he said gently.

The coat fell to the ground with a soft thud, revealing clothes drenched in various spots, the wet fabric clinging to his body, outlining his muscular form. The soggy muffler around his neck dripped with the icy remnants of the harsh weather outside.

Maggie's gaze lingered on his face, taking in the concern etched into his features. His eyes met hers. "I didn't mean to frighten you."

She put out a hand to grab his wrist. "Where's Luellen?"

He blinked at her, wiping melted snow from his hair and face. "Lu—you mean, the little girl from the Galleria? Back in the kitchen with her mama, I assume."

Maggie frantically shook her head. Fear for the child's safety churned in her stomach. Her gaze darted toward the window, picturing the little girl alone amidst the howling winds and driving rain.

"She was out in the storm. I went after her." She looked back at Robert and pushed unsteadily to her knees. "We have to find her, we have to go, *now*."

"Whoa, there." Robert gripped her arm, forcing her back down on the blanket. "We can't go anywhere. The storm is ten times worse than it was."

"I don't care. We have to go look for her." Tears blurred her eyes as she tugged to dislodge his hand. "I was riding Fury." Her voice cracked with worry. "Where's my horse?"

Robert caught her shoulders as his concerned eyes met hers. "We're stuck here. The horses took off. Something spooked them, maybe a coyote or wolf. Hard to be sure what scared them. I've been out looking, but in this weather it's near impossible to track them down."

"G-Gone?"

"Yes. Now, tell me about Luellen."

Haltingly, Maggie whispered, "She ran out in the storm after her pup. Dolores couldn't find her and begged me to go after her. Mister Singleton went for the sheriff and a few others, but I couldn't wait around. It's so cold, and she's just a little girl all alone in the storm . . ."

Her throat tightened as she fought back tears. "We have to try, Robert."

"Shh." Curling a finger under her chin, he peered into her eyes. "If Singleton went for Sheriff Lang, then they'd most likely have already found her. I bet she's tucked in bed right now with a cup of cocoa and one of those cookies she hoarded from our pretend tea party."

His firm voice offered her a glimmer of hope. "You think so?"

"I know so." He tugged the blanket around her shoulders and maneuvered her to face the fire. "I want you to sit here and stay covered up. There's a decent supply of wood we can burn, and I melted snow to drink. I even found some root vegetables that aren't too badly shriveled. It's not a feast, but we won't starve, and tomorrow—or the next, depending on this rotten storm—we'll head back to town."

"What about the horses?"

Well, Gypsy's pretty smart, and I'd bet Fury will follow along. Wouldn't be surprised if they make it to town on their own." Robert got to his feet and pointed a finger at her. "Do not move from here. I'm going to build up the fire and then figure out what to do with the carrots and taters I found. The mattress will keep you off the floor. It's mighty drafty."

As her emotions calmed, she eyed the lumpy thing with distaste. "Do you think it's got bugs?"

"Not this time of year." As her worries eased, he added, "At least not any live ones."

"Oh, ugh." But she pushed her revulsion aside. It *was* better than the hard floor.

While he worked to sort through the wood bin, Maggie caught a glimpse of her dress and cloak. Heat crawled up the back of her neck. "Robert, did you— I mean, did you remove my, um, apparel?"

As Robert turned to face her, a smile formed on his lips, revealing a slight dimple in his cheek. Maggie's heart raced at his mischievous expression, and when one dark brow arched teasingly, her pulse quickened even more.

"I did. You were soaked and shivering, Miss Magnolia. But I covered you up before I started unhooking things. Mostly," he added with a wink.

Maggie's eyes widened even as amusement curved her lips, betraying her own attraction to him. Though she wondered what he meant by "unhooking things."

"Mostly, what? Mostly you covered me, or mostly you didn't look?" she asked, trying to keep her tone playful.

"Yes," he replied, chuckling softly as he crossed the room to retrieve the kindling he had stacked near the door.

Her cheeks flushed as she watched Robert depart. Clearly her feelings for him were growing, intensifying with each passing moment they spent together.

Placing the rinsed carrots in the battered cast-iron pot he'd found outside of the lean-to, Robert added water and then dried his wet hands on the seat of his trousers. He hung the pot over the fire. Soon, steam rose from the pot, carrying the aroma of carrots throughout the room as the sound of boiling water filled the small cabin.

He gave the room a onceover, checking for drafts and spots where gaps could let in the snow. Oiled canvas had been nailed over the two windows and appeared sturdy enough to keep out the worst of the wind. The floor offered no comfort other than the narrow straw mattress, and he couldn't find a broom to sweep away the varmint droppings and tiny bones of whatever once hibernated in here. Discovering a few other moth-eaten horse blankets in one corner, he'd spread them out close to the fire to warm them. The place looked like some sort of hunting cabin and held that peculiar gamey smell he associated with venison and elk meat.

There wasn't much they could use, if by chance the storm forced them to linger more than a few days. Judging by its overall condition, the cabin had most likely been ransacked several times over the years. A handful of extra candle stubs poked out of a crooked cabinet hanging off one wall by a single nail. Another cabinet had crashed to the floor and lay barren of anything resembling foodstuffs. By pure luck he'd found the crude, shallow cellar, half-hidden under a piece of ratty carpet, and unearthed the burlap bags containing the taters and carrots. How they'd remained unmolested by foraging critters, he'd never know.

While Magnolia dozed by the fire, Robert had braved the howling wind and snow outside for another load of wood, currently stacked near the hearth and drying out. With most of the bigger logs already split, they'd burn through the supply fast, and he hadn't spied an axe anywhere with which to chop more.

He crossed to the crumbling mattress and knelt, laying the back of his hand against her forehead. She'd thrashed some in her sleep and he'd worried she might be feverish but so far, her skin remained cool to the touch. If either of them got sick during this little venture . . .

Not gonna think about borrowing any trouble.

She stirred against his hand. Eyes heavy with sleep blinked open, and he roused a smile for her benefit, still worried about how flushed she appeared. 'Hey there, Miss Magnolia."

Her lips curved in a faint smile. "You can call me Maggie, you know." She struggled to rise, and he hastily assisted, coaxing her to lean back against his arm. "Do I smell carrots?"

"Yep. I'm boiling them." He nodded toward the old pot. "I found a rabbit warren when I was outside looking around. Got two before the rest scattered. Already stripped and dressed them. I figure we can eat them tomorrow."

At her frown, Robert sighed. Some city-dwelling families kept rabbits as pets. Maybe Magnolia—*Maggie*, he corrected—had, too. But they desperately needed food, and wild hare was good eating. Reluctantly he moved away. "I think your clothes are dry. Want them?"

Please say no.

"Yes, please." She held out both arms.

He mumbled, "Damn," but rose to collect her dress and petticoat, handing them to her. As he turned to retrieve her boots, he couldn't resist asking, "You need any help, er, fastening anything?"

Her sweet laugh settled some of his worry over her health. "I think I can manage."

A few minutes passed, while she muttered under her breath and the sound of rustling fabric had his imagination spinning. Finally, she huffed, "I can't quite reach—can you help me?"

"Of course." Berating himself for his lascivious thoughts when she was at her most vulnerable, he swiftly fastened the hooks running from waist to neck. He did his damnedest not to stare at the silky bit of exposed flesh as she held her hair out of the way but failed miserably.

Swallowing hard, he edged back. "There, all neat and tidy."

Nudging her boots within reach, he took her elbow to steady her while she pushed her feet into each one, not bothering to unlace them first. "They seem to have shrunk a little."

"At least they're dry." Needing to distance himself from the temptation of the lovely Maggie Sanders—before he did something stupid, like kiss her soft, rosy lips—he made for the door. "I have to secure those rabbits so nothing gets at them before we can eat them."

"Poor little critters." Her mournful tone stopped him in his tracks.

He sighed. "I understand, Maggie, but we need to eat to stay alive, and these rabbits will give us the sustenance we need."

He squashed a pang of empathy as her bottom lip quivered. Determined to keep them both strong and resilient, still he longed to gather her into his arms, to hold her close and soothe her worries. Seeing her unhappy hurt him in a way he couldn't quite understand. He knew they were in a bad situation, but he couldn't bear to see her suffering. Even from across the room, he could sense the bone-deep exhaustion that weighed heavily upon her, increasing her emotional state.

And I'd lay money, she'd once had a rabbit as a pet.

He gentled his voice. "I know it's not much, and it's not something a lady would want for a meal, but will you try to eat?"

"I—" She sighed. "Yes, of course I'll eat."

The wind howled incessantly, whipping against the fragile walls of the cabin. Inside, Robert eyed Maggie carefully, noting her flushed cheeks, worried she might have a fever after all. She had been coughing, too. Though their situation was dire, she hadn't complained once. He was impressed by her strength and determination.

He stoked the fire with a thick piece of kindling, the crackling wood adding to the shriek of the blizzard outside. "I can't believe you went out in this storm to find that little girl,"

Maggie gestured toward the door. "Listen to that. I couldn't just stand by and do nothing. She's just a child." Her brows scrunched with worry. "I pray Sheriff Lang and Mister Singleton found her."

Robert admired her selflessness. "You're a remarkable woman, Magnolia Sanders."

"You're not so bad yourself, Deputy Blackwood."

For a moment they gazed at each other. Robert's attraction to her had already grown by leaps and bounds. In the firelight's glow, she looked so beautiful, his heart pounded like mad. He tried to focus on something else and shifted on the mattress. The aroma of burning wood intermingled with the alluring scent of Maggie's natural perfume.

Eventually they fell into a comfortable silence by the fire. Despite their dangerous circumstances, there was a

sense of peace between them. Robert knew that when they
made it out of this storm, he would find a way to tell her
how he felt about her. But for now, they had to focus on
surviving.

Maggie's fever had sapped her strength, and she found
herself grateful for Robert's protective presence. He took
such excellent care of her, always seeing to her comfort,
making sure she ate something even if it wasn't more than
a couple of boiled carrots or potato chunks. The man had
saved her life.

When the snow began to threaten the roof, Robert
stepped outside to clear it away.

"Be careful," she called after him.

"Always," he replied, the reassurance snatched away
on the wind.

Maggie twisted her fingers in her skirts, feeling an
overwhelming fear for his safety. She wished they had
more resources to help them survive this storm. The limited
supplies and her own illness had rendered her weak, and
she hated it.

As Robert returned to the cabin, Maggie spotted concern in his eyes. She silently patted the mattress, and he understood, taking off his coat and shucking his boots before
joining her, slipping an arm around her shoulders.

Grateful for Robert's presence, Maggie huddled closer.
In the silence, she found herself lost in thought. She wanted
to be brave and strong like him, but she couldn't shake the
sense of vulnerability that came with her illness. Unwilling
to ruin their camaraderie with her own uncertainty and
fears, she sat quietly as their intimate moment together
spun out.

Yet she wondered if he felt the same way about her.
She had noticed the way his eyes lingered on her. Uncertainty warred with excitement that swirled throughout her
body.

Robert cleared his throat, breaking the silence. "You know, Maggie, when we finally make it out of here, I'd like to take you out for another proper dinner." His eyes held a glimmer of hope.

Maggie's heart skipped a beat at the suggestion. A smile crept across her face. "Yes, that sounds lovely," she said, her voice hoarse from coughing.

Robert's grin widened, and he leaned in a little closer. "It's an outing I will very much look forward to."

A flutter tickled her chest. "Thank you for coming to my rescue, Robert."

His gaze softened, and he cupped her cheek. "Of course, Maggie. I couldn't just leave you out there in the cold."

The tenderness in his touch sent shivers down her spine.

Could there be more between them?

Oh, I hope so.

Chapter Four

Maggie peered up at the creaking roof as the wind pounded the thin walls of the cabin, cold air seeping through the cracks in the walls. "Are you sure it'll hold?"

The storm had only grown in intensity. Though Robert constantly tended the fireplace, the cold breeze sneaking through the cracked wood walls threatened to smother the meager flames, leaving them both freezing.

He tossed another log into the fire, then turned back to her with a look of reassurance. "It should be fine for the night. Hopefully the storm will die down by morning, and we'll head home."

Rubbing her arms in an attempt to stay warm, her gaze skittered around the cramped interior. "Do we have enough firewood?"

"I brought in all I could find. If we're careful with it, we should have enough until morning."

"What if the storm doesn't let up by tomorrow?" The knot of pessimism lodged in her chest tightened, stealing her breath.

Robert crossed the room and took a seat next to her on their makeshift bed. A shiver shook her, and not from his nearness this time. It seemed no matter how hard he tried to keep the room comfortable for her, Maggie couldn't seem to shake her chills.

His features tensed and he placed a cool palm against her heated forehead. She knew her fever hadn't abated much though she strove to ignore it in hopes it'd go away.

"Why didn't you tell me you were still sick?" The note of disapproval in his voice was offset by the concerned way he snatched the horse blanket up and wrapped it around her shoulders, before tucking her against his chest. His hands rubbed up and down her back, creating heat.

"I'm f-fine," she stuttered, as goosebumps overtook her. Maggie snuggled in tighter, tucking her arms between them.

With a low curse, Robert scooped her up and placed her sideways onto his lap. He grabbed the remaining blanket and covered them both, then leaned against the wall. "We need to warm you up, Maggie."

She wanted to argue, but he was right. The way he held her would be deemed inappropriate by most, yet the heat from his body offered her what she so desperately needed. In a search for more, she drew her legs up under the blanket and nuzzled her head beneath his chin. "T-Thank you," she said on a sigh of relief.

He pressed a kiss to the top of her head. "You're welcome, honey. Now why don't you try and get some sleep."

With his endearment still ringing in her ears, Maggie closed her eyes. The crackling fire offered a bit of relief from the frigid air, and Robert's body heat kept the worst of the shivers away.

It feels so good to be in his arms.

She was acutely aware of Robert's broad chest sheltering her from the cold. Just like Uncle Knight, he was a gentleman to his core. A deep affection for the man settled into her heart, and she had to fight the urge to lift her head for a kiss.

His rumbly voice interrupted her thoughts. "Stop squirming."

"I'm not," she denied, trying to hold still. Thinking about kissing him had caused a peculiar throb inside her body, causing her to move restlessly on his lap. The feel of his manhood growing hard against her leg sent a tremor of a different kind through her.

"Oh my," she murmured, biting her lower lip as her gaze flew to his face.

Tight-jawed, his eyes pinned her. A visible swallow rippled his throat. "I apologize for that."

Maggie opened her mouth to say something, but no words came out. Did he truly want her in an intimate way? She was no prude and knew what went on between a man and a woman. What she hadn't expected was how he made her feel, all achy and needy. As if she would die unless he kissed her, touched her in ways she knew were forbidden.

Her gaze fell to his mouth, and she unconsciously licked her lips.

"Maggie," he growled out.

"What?"

"Don't look at me like that."

"Like what?" she asked weakly.

"Like you want me to kiss you."

"And if I do?"

His gaze narrowed, those full lips of his pursing as he rasped, "What are you saying?"

"What if I do want you to kiss me, Robert?" She ignored the little voice in her head that protested Uncle Knight—heck, her father, too—would be horrified at her boldness.

He gave a short shake of his head. "Not a good idea."

"Why? You've kissed me before. When you took me to the Yule dinner." She couldn't quite keep the pout out of her voice. Maybe it was the situation they found themselves in, or possibly her resurgent fever was worse than she thought. But she'd never wanted a man to kiss her as badly as she wanted Robert to kiss her right now.

His gaze softened. "Because, sweet Maggie, for one, your uncle would shoot me dead if I touched you. Two, you're still running a fever and not thinking straight." His brown eyes darkened. "And three, the first time I kissed you was gentle. Tender. The way I'm feeling right now, if I kiss you, I may not be able to stop."

While the storm raged outside, Robert gritted his teeth and forced his lips to remain off Maggie's pretty mouth. No matter how much he wanted her, he'd never take advantage of her. Yet, how he was supposed to hold her all night and not accept what her eyes so freely offered?

It'd be a challenge, but one he was determined to win. Lifting his hand, he pressed her head back to his chest. "Get some sleep. You'll need your energy because we're going to have to walk out of here once the snow stops."

She burrowed into him, and he bit back a groan at the feel of her pressed intimately against him. This innocent beauty had no idea what her actions did to him.

He wanted more from Magnolia Sanders than just her body; he wanted her as his wife. Robert had known from the moment he'd set eyes on her at her uncle's wedding. Beautiful and sweet, with a streak of independence he found admirable, she deserved to be wooed the proper way, with flowers and dinners. *With respect.*

Breaking through his thoughts, Maggie mumbled sleepily, "I can do it, Robert." Determination rang clearly in her voice. "And I'm sure Uncle Knight is out there looking for us."

Listening to how the walls creaked under the onslaught of the wind, Robert seriously doubted it. No one would be foolish enough to be out in this weather. Not wanting to crush her hopes, he only nodded, though she couldn't see him. "You could be right. But either way, you're going to need your rest."

"I suppose." Her fingers played with the buttons on his shirt. "Tell me, Robert, how long have you been the deputy for Little Creede?"

They had a long night ahead of them, and if she wanted to get her mind off their predicament by chatting for a bit, that was fine by him. "'Bout a year now. Right before you got here, as a matter of fact."

He smiled when he felt, more than heard, her big yawn.

"What'd you do before that?" she mumbled.

"I worked the mines, like most men in the area do. Richard and I helped stake out Rocky Gulch after Harrison and Frank Carter bought the plot."

"Mmm," was her drowsy response. She nestled closer. "Is it morning yet? It's so dark in here."

"I don't know, sweetness. I left my pocket watch in my other trousers." Explaining how dark the storm rendered any sky, daytime or not, made no difference now. "But in case it's morning, Merry Christmas."

Her breath stirred against his chest. "Merry Christmas, Deputy Blackwood." The soft salutation was accompanied by another yawn and harder shiver that shook her slender frame.

Robert frowned as he bent to peer into her face. Her cheeks were red. He felt her forehead and found it hotter than before. "Damn it." There wasn't anything he could do for her tonight except keep her comfortable. As she relaxed into sleep, he carefully repositioned her onto the uncomfortable sleeping area he'd created on the floor and stood.

She looked small and fragile against the backdrop of this shitty cabin. The need to get her safely home roiled fiercely inside him, the force of it even surpassing the storm outside. Each time the roof shuddered, he worried it might not survive the snow accumulation until he could clear it in the morning. More wintery blasts of air blew in through the gaps in the old log walls, causing Maggie to shiver again, though she didn't awaken.

Moving over to stoke the fire, Robert decided he'd better take care of the roof now before it fell in on them. Though he didn't look forward to going back outside, he snatched up the hay shovel he'd found earlier and brought inside. As carefully as possible, so as not to wake her or let too much air inside, he tugged on his coat and laced up his boots, preparing to brave the blistering snowstorm.

Maggie came awake slowly. Every muscle in her body ached, and when she brought up a hand to rub her nose, it felt frozen enough to break off in her palm. "Robert?"

The room was empty. Had the slam of the door woken her? Did the fire go out? She squinted to focus on the hearth, relieved to see flames, though they danced alarmingly. If she didn't add wood, surely the remaining coals wouldn't be enough to keep—

A sudden crash, and a muffled curse, made her struggle to her feet. "What on earth . . ." Stumbling her way to the door, the rough, cold floorboards snagging her stockings, she reached for the latch just as the door blew inward with a rush of whirling snow. "Robert!"

"I'm here, Maggie. Get back to bed." Robert loomed in the open doorway, stomping his boots before hurrying through and forcing the uneven boards shut. The door wouldn't close straight, and he groaned, "I was afraid of that."

Maggie pressed both hands to the door, pushing hard. ""What can I do?"

Robert chuckled. "I'm afraid it's not gonna budge, but thanks for the offer."

Before she could utter a protest, he shed his heavy coat and urged her back across the room and onto the mattress, swaddling her in a blanket. Gathering an armful of split logs, he tossed them in the sputtering flames and banked coals.

Maggie frowned. "I'm not helpless, Robert. I can help." She shoved the blanket off and began to rise.

Robert hurried back and sank to the mattress next to her, halting her progress. "Get under the blankets, Maggie. We can't waste any more of our energy." He glanced over at the fireplace which had caught, slowly gaining flames. "We'll have to be careful of how many logs we use, so they last until the storm breaks."

"What was that noise I heard? What's wrong with the door?" Maggie offered a corner of the blanket. "Here, you look as cold as I feel."

"Thank you." He covered his feet and legs, then held his hands out to the heat. "I tried to clear the snow from the roof. It was a miracle it hadn't collapsed yet. Got the worst of it, then when I went to jump off, I slid halfway and landed on my a—uh, backside."

He raked a hand through his wet hair. "It could still fall. There's nothing I can use to reinforce it. As for the door, the roof has sunk in over the frame, and the door no longer fits right. All we can do is keep our fingers crossed."

"Our toes, too?" As humor it fell short, but she'd do anything to banish impending disaster from his mind, and hers.

"Yep, toes, too." He finished drying off his fingers. "Let's check your temperature again." He laid the back of his hand across her forehead. "You feel a lot cooler. You been coughing? Sneezing?"

"Not much. Though I'm still cold." When he held out one arm, Maggie crept nearer and snuggled beneath it, savoring the heat his body generated. "Do you think the roof will really hold?"

"I hope so. I'd hate to think of the alternatives."

Arms entwined, they stared into the flickering fire. Robert pressed his lips to her tangled hair. "If I had to get stuck out here with someone, I thank my lucky stars it was you."

Startled at the confession, Maggie sought his gaze, melting at the tenderness she found there. Resting her cheek against his shoulder, strangely content, she whispered, "I'm glad it's you too, Robert. I don't think I could handle this alone."

Chapter Five

Frigid air and stabbing ice swirled around Robert's head, jerking him out of the half-doze he'd fallen into. He sat up, dislodging the blanket covering Maggie's slumbering form, awareness knocking the remaining dregs of sleep from his brain when what meager fire remaining in the hearth sputtered and winked out.

"Damn it to hell!" Whirling, he took in the flapping oilskin over the nearest window. One of the corners had torn and snow now poured in, chased by the wind still howling outside.

Hastily Robert scrambled to his feet, wincing at the chill coming up from the worn floorboards, and crossed the room, pushing on the shredded canvas where it had ripped clean off the nail.

"Let me help." Two slender, pale hands joined his, holding the oilskin in the middle where an additional tear had formed. "Are there any more nails?"

"Maggie, get back under the covers." If her condition worsened before they could trek out of here, Lord only knew whether they'd make it to town in one piece.

"I feel much better," she shouted over the whistling canvas, offering him a confident smile even as her hands shook.

Robert sighed in exasperation. *Stubborn woman.* But right now he needed her help, much as he hated exposing her to the dangerously inclement blizzard.

"Hold the center tightly with one hand if you can. Press the other, here," he instructed, indicating the torn corner. "I'm going to see what I can find."

"All right." She positioned herself, hands grasping the slippery material, and stood firm. "Hurry."

The first day there, he'd hunted for nails and came up empty. But he'd seen a hank of thin rope hanging off one end of the mantel when he'd placed Maggie's sopping cloak near the hearth to dry. He could knot the rope onto the ripped corner of the oilskin and tie it down, try to bring it as close to the wall as possible.

With no additional canvas anywhere to be found, repairing the center gash would be difficult. Fisting the rope, he hurried to the window and stood next to Maggie, shielding her from the icy wind.

"Hold that corner steady." Swiftly he tied one end of the rope above the worst of the ragged edge and lashed it around the nail which blessedly held firm.

"What about the center?" Struggling to bring the pieces together using both hands, Maggie's voice echoed the strain her muscles must be feeling. "It's getting worse."

Casting about for a solution, Robert spied the raggedy carpet that'd covered the root cellar. "I've got an idea."

He felt in his pocket for the lockblade knife he was never without, thankful it hadn't gotten lost in the snow when he'd slipped off the cabin roof. Catching one edge of the carpet, he dragged the ancient remnant to the window and hoisted it up.

"Let go of the oilskin, Maggie, and grab the side of this."

While she dug her fingers into the rough weave, shivering violently in the blast of wintry air, Robert poked a hole in the top edge and stabbed the knife through the opening, straight into the wall.

Quickly, he pulled up on the trailing piece of rope tied to the nail, whooping in relief when it stretched far enough to wrap twice around the knife's handle. "You can let go, honey. Ain't much, but it'll hold."

Stepping back, he eyed his handiwork, slipping an arm around Maggie to stave off here shivers. The rope, diagonally taut against the carpet remnant, helped to press it over the tear in the center of the oilskin. Already, the air in the cabin felt better.

He led her back to the mattress, covering her with her cloak and both blankets as soon as she sank to the bedding and curled on her side. "I'll try to get the fire going again."

"A-All r-right," she replied through chattering teeth.

With barely enough kindling to use for a starter and only two matchsticks left, Robert set wood and splints carefully. The first matchstick sputtered but held a spark, and he touched it to the thinnest splint, muttering thanks when the tiny flame caught and grew. He fed in broken splint pieces, then a few bigger, until the fire would hold an actual log.

"I can feel that," Maggie said sleepily, staring at the hearth and then at him. She rose on an elbow and held out her hand. "Come under the blankets, Robert."

The need for additional warmth drove her entreaty, but Maggie acknowledged it was more than a physical ache. It had become emotional as well.

This man had saved her life. Had kept her from freezing, fed her, eased her distress when fever and aches overcame her in the midst of the most difficult and dangerous time she had ever faced. He'd reassured her when she fretted about the safety of Luellen Lund, had calmed her when she panicked, and never made her think, for one moment, they wouldn't make it out of the icy hell in which she'd inadvertently thrown them both.

She wanted his heat, desired it above all.

Robert stood as if turned to stone, staring at her hand. The longing in his expression, the need glittering in his eyes, revealed to her how he wanted the same things, too. But if she'd learned nothing of this man, his moral standard and his gentlemanly ways were ingrained and always at the forefront.

I know what I want.

"Robert, please." Her plea vibrated softly in the tension-filled room. "Please come under the blanket and warm yourself. Warm me."

His mouth opened and closed. A visible swallow rippled his throat even as he edged closer. "You still have a fever. And we need to eat something."

"My fever broke earlier. I truly do feel better," she assured him, wondering if he heard her over the tangible worry that hung in the air. The last thing she wanted was for him to run out in the storm, scrabbling for rabbits. They'd eaten the last of the carrots and what taters they could salvage from the root cellar. Tomorrow they might very well walk out of here. Or the storm would worsen further, and they'd have to rethink their survival.

Either way, she didn't need food right now. "I'm not hungry."

In the firelight his eyes reflected such tenderness, it stole her breath. Another step brought his feet up against the tattered mattress which had become their bed. Patiently, she kept her hand extended to him. Waiting.

Wanting.

Lord, give me strength.

Nothing in his experience had ever tempted Robert as deeply as the sight of Maggie, rosy from the fire, holding out a hand to him. He'd already compromised her reputation by being alone with her in this intimate manner, never mind cuddling next to her and embracing her while they both slept off their exhaustion, innocent as it had been.

Her uncle and her father would never understand. They'd come after him with a shotgun aimed right between his eyes. And he'd deserve their fury, because what could a simple deputy in a tiny boom town have to offer an educated young lady whose ultimate goal included becoming the first woman lawyer of the West?

She thought he could hold her and not act on other, baser desires. Safe in his arms, they might ride out the rest of the storm and then walk out of the wilderness together, neither the worse for it. He'd bring her back to her uncle, perhaps be allowed to call on her the proper way a suitor wooed the object of his affection. It could happen exactly that way—

If I can keep my damned paws off her, first.

"I should hunt for more hares," Robert murmured desperately. "You need your strength, Maggie."

As a defense against the irresistible lure of holding her lush body, Robert knew his reasoning was pathetic. If he took her into his arms, most of his noble intent would fly out the window and he'd have her beneath him, kissing her. Touching her. And more, much more. "You must be thirsty, too—"

"I'm cold, mostly. And so are you, Deputy Robert." She sat up, and though modestly covered, he easily recalled what she looked like with only her delicate undergarments accentuating her beauty.

I'm sunk.

Robert knelt and took her hand, let her guide him, until they both reclined on their sides, face to face, only a hair's breadth separating them. She pulled the blankets up over their shoulders. Cocooned together from head to tingling toes, he lightly touched his mouth to her forehead. She wasn't feverish, though her condition could return if they weren't careful.

Her lips trembled into a smile. "Stop worrying so much."

"That's rather hard to do." He rubbed a thumb along her elegant jaw and knew if he died this very instant, no heavenly angel on high could compare to Magnolia Sanders.

They lay there together, the heat from the fire and their closeness in the cramped cabin increasing their intimacy.

Robert curved his arm around her and she snuggled into his embrace as if it was the most natural thing in the world.

When she raised a hand and stroked the back of his neck, Robert could only think of how desperately he wanted to kiss her. Unable to deny her, or himself, any longer, he took her lips, gently at first, then more urgently as her eager response both shocked and delighted him. Her fingers tightened on his neck as her body arched, bringing her full length against him, soft breasts and slender waist, shapely hips, long legs.

Breaking their kiss, Robert gazed down at the woman in his arms, her remarkable eyes heavy-lidded, her lips reddened and glistening. Thick tendrils of silky hair framed her face, shimmering a deeper red in the glow from the fire. His hands held a tremor as he caressed her, the loosened fastenings of her dress slipping off one creamy shoulder. Her cheeks blushed sweetly but she didn't retreat from his touch. Instead, her arms twined around his neck and clasped him closer. Her face lifted to his, her lips an offering he couldn't possibly resist.

The kiss they shared contained so much passion, his head spun.

Shifting her onto her back, he leaned over her and stroked her tongue with his. She whimpered and boldly returned the gesture. What breath he retained in his lungs depleted, until with a gasp he released her lips and buried his face in her hair, panting into her ear as he strove for some sense of balance.

Now was the time to declare himself. Before anything else happened and he compromised her further. This very instant, when she could accept his promise to her had nothing concerning duty and everything to do with love.

They would marry and live in a fine house he'd build for her on the outskirts of town. There'd be children, boys who took after him and girls as lovely as she; rambunctious and smart, happy and carefree.

In a fulsome daze Robert could see it all in his mind. Years of loving, decades of happiness, supporting each other's dreams and aspirations.

Right now, he'd ask her—

Cupping her face with one hand, he parted his lips to speak.

The door suddenly crashed open on lopsided hinges, and a huge mountain of snow-coated fury erupted into the small, dimly lit cabin.

"What in seventeen worlds of *hell* is a'goin' on in heah?"

Robert grimaced at the sight of Maggie's uncle. It was impossible to miss the overprotective anger in Knight Gleason's voice, and he had every reason to beat Robert bloody. Though fully clothed, he and Maggie were far from the image of respectability.

His fault. *I should have never touched her, kissed her.*

The desire he'd read in her eyes, only moments earlier, had been replaced with distress, a deep blush coloring her cheeks. The knowledge that he'd compromised the woman he held in such high esteem settled into his gut like a heavy rock.

"Oh, shit. This isn't good." Richard's amused voice collided with Gleason's threats of unmanning Robert with the hay shovel leaning against the wall.

"It'll be all right, Maggie," Robert promised, releasing her. Yet as he stood and confronted her uncle, he wasn't sure that was a promise he'd be able to keep. "Mister Gleason, don't go jumping to conclusions now. Nothing happened here."

Maggie scrambled to her feet, her lips still damp and red from his kisses, and Robert groaned under his breath. She flew across the small space and flung herself into her uncle's arms. "You found us, oh thank God."

Though Gleason gathered her close, his heavy scowl remained locked on Robert. The threat of death—or a well-deserved beating at the very least—shone from the man's narrowed eyes.

Robert opened his mouth to try and dig out of the hole he found himself in with the big, burly gambler, but Maggie's voice broke in before he could form any words. "Lulu. Uncle, did they find Lulu?"

Gleason's stormy glare finally eased, his expression softening as he gazed down at his niece with obvious love and affection. "We sho' did, darlin'. That lil' pup of hers barked like the dickens 'til we found 'em, shortly after yew ran off, matter o' fact." The last words were said in a scolding tone.

With a beautiful smile, Maggie turned back to Robert. "Did you hear that?" She sprinted across the room and laughingly launched herself against him. "They found Lulu!"

Robert caught her, one arm encircling her waist as she hugged him, her soft body pressed tightly against his. Her uncle's muttered curses, and his brother's bark of laughter, sounded over her voluble delight over the young girl's rescue.

Meeting Gleason's blistering scowl over the top of Maggie's head, Robert tried an unassuming smile, which only made the man's thick brows dip even more threateningly. Her spontaneous action certainly wasn't going to help calm matters any.

Robert discreetly disentangled himself from Maggie and stepped back, ignoring for the moment that her uncle deserved an explanation of the compromising position he'd found them in. "Maggie's running a slight fever and we need to get her to Doc Sheaton's right away."

"I'm fine," she insisted. "I just need to get out of this drafty cabin."

Richard poked his head out the door briefly, before ducking back in. "Still coming down some, but we shouldn't wait around." He strode over to extinguish what remained of the fire. "Wind's brisk. Take those blankets and bundle her up good."

Gleason was already advancing toward the bed they'd created on the uneven cabin floor, snatching up both blankets with visible force while Robert buttoned Maggie into her cloak and bonnet. "Mah niece'll ride with me."

Wisely, Robert didn't argue, though it pained him to let her go. He'd grown accustomed to caring for her over the last two days and he wanted to continue as her protector. Judging by the way her uncle squeezed the rough horse blankets in two ham-like fists, pushing the issue wasn't smart.

Securing the wide bonnet ribbons under her chin, Robert longed to feel her happy smile beneath his lips as he kissed her. When her eyes darkened and began to glow, he found himself bending to her—

Then Gleason roughly shoved him aside, wrapping one of the horse blankets around her shoulders. "Keep lookin' at mah sweet niece like that, Blackwood, an' ah really *will* hafta kill yew."

"Uncle," Maggie scolded, as he flung open what was left of the cabin door.

Robert shrugged into his own coat as his brother came up behind him and slapped him on the back. "Looks like you'll be riding with me."

"Looks like," Robert agreed. A blast of cold air hit him, making him shiver. The ground was covered in a thick blanket of white snow that crunched under his boots. In the dim light, he saw two horses standing in the lean-to, their snorting breaths forming visible clouds in the frigid air.

He recognized Jester, their uncle Dub's beloved stallion, and eyed him appreciatively. The horse was a magnificent creature, with a glossy black coat and strong muscles rippling under his skin. Robert scanned the area but didn't see Buster, the horse he usually rode. He turned to Richard. "Where's Buster?"

"Threw a rock and twisted his left fetlock. Aunt Lucinda's been babying him." Richard mounted Jester, holding him steady while Robert swung up behind him.

The snow had slowed to light flakes, and fortunately the worst of the wind had died down, though he still worried about Maggie's exposure to the cold. Her uncle had covered her with the second horse blanket until only her eyes and nose could be seen. She rode in front of him, leaning against his barrel chest.

Richard shot a smirk over his shoulder as they rode away from the ramshackle cabin. "So, you and Magnolia Sanders, huh?"

Robert's jaw flexed as he nodded. "I intend to marry that woman."

"Does her uncle know that?"

"No. But if you'll ride a little closer, I'll inform him right now."

"You sure you want to do that? The man looks like he'd rather take your head off than welcome you into the family."

"I'm certain."

"Your funeral, little brother."

Robert's fist clenched at the soft chuckle, but when Richard added, "She's a mighty fine woman, and you'd be fortunate to have her as your wife," some of his frustration eased.

Richard flicked his reins, gently nudging Jester forward, until they rode alongside Knight Gleason, whose enormous draft breed stallion, Rounder, easily handled his additional rider.

For a brief moment, Robert's eyes met Maggie's sparkling blue gaze, which peeked out from the cozy cocoon of blankets covering her face. The crisp air lent a rosy tint to her cheeks.

He gave her a reassuring nod, reveling in her warm regard even as he turned his attention back to her uncle. "Mister Gleason. We need to talk."

"Ah'm listenin'." The man sounded less angry than he had at the cabin.

Robert cleared his throat. "I want you to know that I care about your niece."

"That's a damn good thing, Blackwood, since yew best be fixin' to marry her."

"Uncle!" Maggie snapped, her back straightening with indignation, the horse blanket slipping off her shoulders. She half-twisted and glared. "Why would you say such a thing?"

"Because, darlin', yew spent the last two days alone with this fella, doin' God only knows fer certain. They's no other choice to save yer reputation."

"Poppycock," Maggie exclaimed, with such displeasure that it brought a smile to Robert's lips. One of the things he loved most about the woman was her confidence and fortitude. "It's almost the twentieth century. You need to be more enlightened."

Before Gleason could respond, Robert broke in. "Sir, I understand your concern, but I refuse to marry Maggie out of a sense of obligation."

At her sharp inhale and her uncle's low snarl, Robert's gaze locked on hers, easily reading the hurt there.

Richard mumbled, "You must surely be the stupider brother."

Robert blew out a disgruntled breath. Somehow, he had to get the rest of this out before he created a mess he wouldn't be able to clean up.

He held up a hand when Gleason's snarl grew into a growl. "No, let me finish. I meant that I want to court Maggie the proper way. And if one day I'm lucky enough to

have her accept me as her husband, I'll be a fortunate
man."

Secure in her uncle's grasp and comfortable despite the frigid air, Maggie had dozed a bit on the ride back to Little Creede. Expecting to be peppered with questions, instead he let her be, affording her time to think about Robert's words.

If one day I'm lucky enough to have her accept me as her husband, I'll be a fortunate man.

Heart pounding, she pondered the significance of a life with him. He'd never leave this town; it was his home and contained all his family, his friends. Entrenched here, Robert had everything he needed to be happy . . . the way she'd thought herself to be back in Atlanta.

But he doesn't have me.

"Yet," she murmured, absurdly giddy at the thought.

"Yew say somethin', darlin'?" Uncle Knight's gruff query rumbled against her ear.

Maggie leaned back until she could focus on his face. The poor man looked exhausted, deep rings around his eyes as if he'd not had a lick of sleep. "I'm so sorry. I shouldn't have gone running off that way—"

Now, don't yew start frettin'." He cuddled her gently. "Ah know how tenderhearted yew are when it comes to children. Yew did the right thing." He paused, staring ahead at the trail, while Rounder picked his way through the deep snow. Expelling a sigh, her uncle asked quietly, "Yew love this man?"

"I—"

"Enough to git yerself hitched to a lawman an' live a diff'rent life than the one yew been claimin' to want?" he pressed on.

Maggie huddled beneath the damp blanket, suddenly chilled, when before, she'd been feeling cozy and safe. Marriage to Robert would change everything; she mustn't allow herself to think otherwise. The law apprenticeship she sought was her goal, her life's passion. Making her father proud, following in his esteemed footsteps, meant the world to her. How could a husband fit into that world? Women went where their men dictated, not the other way around.

Having no simple answer to her uncle's complicated question, she remained silent, and he didn't ask again.

Ahead of them on the winding trail, Robert's muted voice meshed with his brother's as they traded bits of conversation. A shiver rushed up her spine, recalling their time at the cabin. Under the blankets, entwined together, his embrace and reassurances had kept her fright and worry at bay. He'd be a wonderful husband and father, a strong provider.

An amazing lover . . .

Stop that right now, she chastised herself. *Think of something else.*

Raising her head to see their whereabouts, Maggie realized they'd reached the edge of the knoll where the trail descended into town. Those now-familiar streets, lined with weathered wooden buildings, their facades painted in muted shades of brown, gave Little Creede a homey, unpretentious feel.

The Galleria, with its large windows and elegant sign, stood out as one of the more prominent structures. She could just make out its side roof. "Uncle Knight, we're almost there," she exclaimed, sitting up straighter in the saddle.

"We sho' are, darlin'. Safe an' sound." He gave her a squeeze as Rounder picked up speed, cantering easily over the tamped ground.

Closer now, she spotted the outline of shops and buildings, the mercantile and Millie's Milliners. The Miner Stage House, too. Further along on the other side, through spitting snow she spied the bank, the jail, the barest silhouette of the schoolhouse.

Smoke billowed from chimneys, the scent of burning wood filling the air. Despite the cold and snow, the town bustled with life, and Maggie felt a deep sense of belonging as they rode down the sloping trail.

All familiar to her now, they'd become somehow dear to her, which was silly. Only buildings, after all—

Then she gasped as the doors of the Galleria were flung open and people poured out, some bundled up against the weather and others wearing hastily donned hats and shawls. Tears filled Maggie's eyes at the cheers that rang in the wintry air, which all of a sudden didn't feel cold, but warm and welcoming.

Her uncle pulled up on Rounder's reins, the stallion churning up snow as he pawed the ground and snorted. Hands reached for her, and Maggie blinked to clear her blurred vision when Robert carefully swung her down. He kept a steadying hand on her shoulder as friends greeted her with hugs and kisses to her cheeks.

Unable to sort out the happy salutations and excited chatter, she let it swirl over her like a healing balm, the cacophony narrowing down to a single, comforting yet sobering thought . . .

I'm home.

Over the scent of mulled cider and fresh-baked bread, Robert kept an eye on Maggie. She looked happy, though a bit peaked, her face unusually pale, her hands trembling now and then as she lifted her cup and sipped the tea Catherine Carter insisted she drink.

"Take that away, husband," Catherine had instructed, when Frank approached with a mug of mulled cider. "No liquor. I know darned well there's bourbon in there."

Grumbling about interfering women, Frank had backed away, while Maggie accepted the tea and murmured her thanks in the soft, cultured drawl Robert swore he'd never get out of his head.

Now and then throughout the day, he'd caught Knight Gleason's appraising frown, as if expecting him to make some sort of declaration. Unwilling to speak of such private things when a room filled with nosy neighbors could overhear and over-embellish, Robert kept his lips pinned. Sooner or later he'd find a moment alone with Maggie, and they'd discuss their future.

"You holding up, Blackwood?" Harrison Carter dropped onto the settee next to him and held out a tumbler, whisky by the smell of it.

Robert took it but set it on a low side table. "I'm all right. Just thinking."

"Yes, I can imagine." Harrison stretched out his long legs and balanced his own drink on his thigh. "This town has a history of happily married couples who started out in compromising positions."

Harrison snorted softly, nodding toward Frank and Catherine, canoodling in a far corner while their daughter, Charity, babbled at their feet and twisted her rag doll into knots. "My lovestruck brother, for one. Joshua and Vivian, too. Even Maude Adams, by God. She once confided to Retta that Buck married her with her daddy's shotgun pointed dead center of his forehead."

Robert chuckled, picturing such an event. "Nothing untoward happened with Maggie, I promise you."

"Hey, don't bother promising *me*," Harrison retorted. "Figure out what you want to do, then do it. Maggie has feelings for you, that's no secret. I reckon you've got the same for her. Just don't let time get away from you."

He straightened, draining the last of his drink, and set the empty tumbler aside. "Magnolia Sanders is going places. She's got a goal in sight, and if you want her, you also accept those goals. It's a different world, my friend, and a new century looms on the horizon. Best keep that in mind."

With a bolstering slap on Robert's shoulder, Harrison rose and crossed the room to join his wife and children.

Sighing, Robert dropped his head back against the settee, his gaze finding Maggie—

And a smile curved his lips when she gazed back at him. Rising gracefully to her feet, she carried her teacup with her as she left the room, heading for the kitchen.

Determined to benefit from Harrison's advice, Robert stood and followed.

Maggie's hands shook as she set the cup and saucer in the speckled dish tin. Dolores or one of the kitchen helpers would have collected the pretty china, allowing her to remain behind and continue to enjoy the belated Christmas celebration the thoughtful townsfolk had planned, just for her.

The ever-thoughtful Catherine had left out the fragrant pine garlands from yesterday's holiday meal and set her tables with her best linens and dishes. The aroma of roast fowl and spiced apples filled the air. In one corner, Dub Blackwood plied his fiddle in a soft Irish reel she recognized from her childhood.

It was lovely, and she should be in there enjoying it right now. Except Maggie wanted to see if a certain deputy would follow her—

Boot heels clicked, then paused on the polished wooden floor near the kitchen entrance, and she knew Robert stood a few feet away.

Taking a deep breath, Maggie gathered her courage and turned.

He was closer than she'd thought, one hand stretched out yet not touching, palm up. Like a question she might not be ready to answer.

Slowly, her gaze holding his, she placed her hand in his and allowed him to pull her against his chest. Oh, that male scent, bay rum and cotton, teasing her nose as she leaned into his shoulder. His arms came around her, a haven and a thrill.

"We shouldn't be alone like this," she whispered, even as she clung.

"No, we shouldn't." He trailed his lips along her temple and over her ear, giving her shivers.

"I have to leave in the spring, Robert." She edged away, until she could look up into his eyes. Deep brown and tender, they held hers steadily as she strove to explain. "I want to apprentice, become a lawyer. I want to make my father proud—"

"Your father is already proud of you, honey." Robert slipped one hand up her back and into her hair, soothing under the heavy curls. "Are you worried I wouldn't understand your wants and needs? Because I do."

"Then where does that leave us? My uncle expects a wedding in order to save my reputation. Which will come into question anyway as soon as word gets out that I have chosen the law as a profession. Women don't become lawyers."

"This one will." He cupped her cheek gently. "This one will, and when she does I'll be there, cheering her on."

Her shock must have shown on her face, because he chuckled. "Did you think I'd stop you?" Bending, he pressed his lips to hers, and Maggie helplessly returned his kiss, drowning in the sensation of being treasured and cherished.

For long moments they kissed, until she reluctantly broke away, breathless and aroused. She stared up into his handsome face, wondering how on earth she had gotten so lucky. "You mean it?"

"I mean it, Miss Magnolia Sanders. I can be a lawman anywhere. But I understand your prospects of finding an attorney willing to apprentice you might be somewhat limited. We'll figure it out." He gathered her close, whispering in her ear, "Just know I love you. That's enough, for now."

Heart near to bursting, she nodded, feeling his mouth smiling against her temple. "I love you, too. And you're so very right, Deputy Blackwood. It's enough for now."

The Miner Stage House, Little Creede
December, 1885

The sound of cheering and applause filled the Stage House's dining salon as Maggie stepped through the double doors with Robert by her side. Still chilled and damp from the snowy carriage ride to Little Creede from Silver Cache, right then it didn't seem to matter one whit how disheveled she was.

The clapping and whistling echoed off the ceilings, punctuated by excited whoops and hollers from her family and friends. It was a joyful and boisterous noise, like a chorus of happy pride.

"Well, let's see it!" Catherine Carter called out. Turned out in an impeccable deep green day gown that enhanced her lovely eyes, she stood next to Frank, who let out a wolf-whistle while young Charity, their daughter, clapped both hands over her ears.

"You heard the boss, Missus Blackwood. Show 'em," Robert murmured in her ear.

"I couldn't have done it without your loving support, Mister Blackwood."

He gently tilted her face up, his expression tender as he spoke softly, "I must respectfully disagree. You have a spine of steel, Maggie, and it's an honor to be on this journey with you."

She stared into her husband's loving eyes, still awed by her good fortune to have wed such a fine man. With a smile that threatened to split her face in two, she pulled the scroll from beneath her winter cloak and held it high in the air amid fresh applause and whistles.

"Madame Attorney." Uncle Knight strode up to her and scooped her into his brawny arms, swinging her around in a dizzy circle. "Ah'm so proud of yew, darlin.' The first lady of law in Colorado."

He kissed her cheek and squeezed her until she laughingly let out a squeak. Snatching the scroll from her hand, he unrolled it, beaming, while the adults gathered around to see for themselves.

Maggie had barely removed her outer garments when her nieces and nephews—and a few second cousins—ran to her and clung, babbling noisily. The younger ones had no idea what she'd accomplished, but the older children sure did—

Because whenever she and Robert brought little Duncan to the Galleria for a visit, she carried the law and theoretical tomes she'd borrowed from Maxwell Berger, her mentor and teacher, using Uncle Knight's office as a quiet place to study. Their older cousins often stopped by, peppering her with questions, constantly curious about her progress. They'd probably never know how much those questions actually helped her, for she used them as a kind of test, determined to always answer correctly.

Each time Maggie returned to Silver Cache, she would eagerly draw on Mister Berger's intellect and wisdom. After three years in his office and a year of internship in Silver Cache Court, Maxwell proudly presented her with her certification two days ago.

As they made their way toward their seats, the aroma of roast beef and meat pies wafted through the air, making Maggie's stomach growl with hunger. The inviting scent mingled with the sweet fragrance of fresh-baked bread.

Addie Carter ran up and flung her arms around Maggie's waist. The adorable girl was almost as tall as her mother, Retta. "You're gonna make history, Cousin Mags."

Maggie snuggled her gently. "You think so?" She cupped Addie's freckled cheek. "Maybe you'll discover a passion for something only a man has ever done. What do you think about that?"

Addie's eyes grew big. "I could, couldn't I?" She pulled away and danced in a circle. "Look out, menfolk!"

Nate was next to hug her. At thirteen, the handsome boy was almost a head taller. "I'm proud of you, Cousin Maggie." He glanced to the side where Addie still danced and whooped. "What did you say to the heathen?"

Maggie bit back a laugh at the nickname he'd given Addie years ago. "You know, sooner or later you'll have to stop calling her a heathen."

"Well, sure. As soon as she stops acting like one."

News of Maggie's remarkable achievement had spread like wildfire. Always happy to have something to celebrate, Little Creede converged upon the Stage House, donating everything from homemade wine to fresh eggs and poultry for Mary Rush, Catherine and Frank's cook, to prepare. Half a dozen women, led by Betsy Loman and Dolores Lund, came to help out, taking over the kitchen and churning out all sorts of deliciousness.

When she ran out of tables and chairs, Catherine simply spread tablecloths on the polished lobby floors and served folks picnic-style. Nobody complained, too busy enjoying the mounds of food erupting from the kitchen, a feast for the eyes as well as the stomach. Rich colors and textures abounded, with platters of roasted meats glistening with savory juices, bowls of vibrant vegetables steaming in the cool air, and decadent desserts piled high with fresh fruits and clotted cream.

Guests eagerly filled their plates, savoring every delectable bite and marveling at the culinary prowess of Mary Rush and her team of helpers.

The Stage House rang with laughter and joy, the sounds of clinking glasses and heartfelt toasts filling the air, echoing the sense of camaraderie that had always been at the center of their tight-knit community.

Sitting with Uncle Knight and Aunt Hannah, holding her nephew Alexander—who for once seemed content to snuggle rather than tear up and down the hallways—Maggie's eyes glistened with unshed tears of happiness. "This is wonderful, Uncle. I'm so glad I stayed here and apprenticed rather than traveling East to some stuffy law school."

"Yer aunt an' Ah would've missed yew somethin' fierce, darlin'," Knight replied gruffly, patting her shoulder.

Aunt Hannah leaned in and kissed her cheek. "You couldn't have done better than Mister Berger. Why, he studied in England, I'm sure you knew that. Such a brilliant man."

Robert dragged a tassled footstool over and sat next to her, slipping an arm around her waist. "Your son is playing poker with his namesake."

"What?" Maggie tried to see over her husband's shoulder. "Duncan's only a year old!"

"You can never start too young, Wife," he intoned somberly.

She shook off his arm and jumped to her feet. "I am going to kill Uncle Dub."

At Robert's burst of laughter, she realized his jest and settled back into her seat with a shove to his chest. "Maybe I should just damage you."

He eyed her teasingly. "Anytime, sweetness. Go ahead and damage me. You just say the word and name the place."

The adults mingled and shared stories while the children played in a cleared area, their easy laughter a testament to the enduring bonds between their families. Amid games of tag and cup and ball, age differences didn't seem to matter, for they all knew each other and cared for one another.

Watching them at play, Maggie and Robert exchanged a knowing glance. This new generation of Little Creede would carry on the legacy of their parents, forging their own paths and overcoming whatever challenges life might throw their way.

As snow fell gently past the windows and coated walkways and rooftops, Robert stood, raising his glass. "To new beginnings and a bright future."

He cast his contented gaze over the room as one by one, glasses clinked together. "And to our children, too," he declared, his voice filled with emotion. "To the paths they take. May they continue to build on the foundation we've laid and make their own mark on this world."

The gathered crowd echoed his sentiment, their glasses raised high as voices murmured, "Hear, hear."

The winter sun dipped below the horizon, setting on one chapter of their lives as the next began to unfold.

We'd like to share an excerpt from our award-winning Brides of Little Creede Series

The Substitute Wife by Cici Cordelia

Chapter 1

Chicago, Illinois

March, 1878

The earsplitting whistle made Retta Pierce choke up as she hugged her sister goodbye on the train platform. Jenny's slight frame trembled in her grip, and Retta fought back her worry.

Too thin. Too frail. Shoulders drooping, as though too heavy to hold up.

"There must be a better way, Jenny," Retta murmured, stricken. "It's just not right—"

Her sister's features took on that stubborn look Retta knew so well, indicating there'd be no changing her mind. "And what would be right, Retta? For Papa to really hurt you the next time he feels the urge to beat the devil from your soul? For him to finally slip and hit Addie?"

Tipping up Retta's chin with two shaking fingers, she smiled gently. "That sweet child is the best thing that ever happened to this family, no matter how her father ran off and left you."

Jenny's gaze slid to Aunt Millie, standing under the train station's metal portico, holding two-year-old Adeline in her arms. The desolate flapping of a loosened, rusty panel, noisily vibrating in the chilly breeze, only added to the solemnness of the day. Moisture gave a sad sheen to her aunt's eyes as she cuddled the toddler closer.

Retta's sigh was as broken as her heart. "No, of course not. But to leave you when you need me the most . . ."

The dark circles around Jenny's blue eyes gave her complexion a grayish cast. She shouldn't be standing out in the wind like this, as sick as she was. She could barely stay upright. But Retta knew all too well her sister's inner core of strength, because Jenny was cut from the same cloth as their beloved mother, gone three years now.

"Mama wouldn't want me to desert you," Retta began, only to be silenced by her sister's dismissive wave of one skeletal hand.

"Mama would do exactly what I'm doing." She shoved a wrinkled pouch into Retta's shabby reticule, ignoring her protests. "Take it. You think I would leave Mama's rubies to rot in Papa's strongbox?" She snorted weakly, but her disdain was evident. "It's your future, darling." Her voice dropped to a wisp. "It's my legacy to you."

Fighting back tears, Retta held on to her sister's fingers when she would have pulled away. "You can't go back. Papa will know you took Mama's necklace and will beat you for it." She gripped her bag between whitened knuckles, then gasped at the clinking sound coming from within. "Are those coins? Jenny, where did you get them?"

Jenny drew herself up, straightening her shoulders, and for a shining moment Retta saw her sister as she'd been, before consumption ravaged her body. "My dowry. Yours, now."

She patted the reticule in Retta's fist. "There's a letter folded inside with the coins. You take that letter to Harrison. It explains everything. Tell him, I wish for him a happy life. Tell him I'm sorry."

Jenny dashed thin locks of dull-brown hair off her perspiring forehead. "I'm going to stay with Aunty until, well, until . . ." Her chin firmed. "I will be safe and well-cared for. By the time Papa sobers up enough to realize we both left him, it'll be too late to do anything about it."

"Oh, Jenny," Retta murmured sadly, blinking away fresh tears as Jenny gave her hand a final squeeze, before she eased away.

Aunt Millie edged closer and transferred Retta's sleepy daughter into her arms, then whispered in her ear, "I know, child. She wouldn't admit anything but I know how sick our Jenny is. I'm taking her back to Dewfield with me. I promise you I will never say a thing to your father, and I'll care for her faithfully."

"You'll keep in touch? You'll write?" Retta clung to her aunt's vow, even as everything inside her demanded she remain to care for Jenny herself.

"Yes, indeed. Have no worries." Millie curled a supporting arm around Jenny's narrow shoulders. "I'd best be getting you back to the house, darling girl. A nice cup of cocoa and a nap will do you wonders. Just you wait and see."

An errant tear tracked down Jenny's pale cheek that she quickly batted away before offering an encouraging smile. "Harrison is a good man, Retta. Be happy. All I want for you and Addie is to have a good life. Promise me you'll give him a chance."

Retta's stomach clenched with fear and uncertainty, even as she hesitantly agreed. For the love of her sister, she'd acquiesce to her final wish. Though it'd been four years since Jenny had last seen her fiancé. Who knew what kind of man he was now?

Jenny traced a slender finger down Retta's cheek. "I love you, little sister."

Blinking through a flood of tears that fell silently against the top of her sleeping daughter's head, Retta whispered, "I love you, Jenny. I'll hold you in my heart forever."

There were no final goodbyes, just an assortment of promises and encouraging murmurs, before Aunt Millie guided Jenny from the platform, toward a waiting hackney.

Struggling for composure, Retta held Addie close. As the March wind whipped around her ears, she watched them go until their figures merged into a single, blurred image, and the train whistle blew its final, 'All Aboard' warning. Only then did she allow the conductor to help her with her baggage.

Harrison had reserved a sleeper for Jenny, an extravagance to be sure, but safer for a woman traveling alone. *What will he do when I arrive instead?*

Blinking furiously, Retta guided Addie through the doorway. Inside the cramped compartment, she laid the sleepy child on the narrow bed and covered her with the only blanket she could find. Addie cuddled into a ball, snoring lightly. Retta brushed the tangled golden curls from her fair brow, trying to envision what sort of future awaited them out West.

Love for her child stiffened her spine. Her baby—her world.

I'll make a better life for you, I promise.

Even if she had to travel halfway across the country and marry a stranger to do it.

Outside Little Creede, Colorado

April, 1878

"Well, Copper," Harrison Carter said soothingly, stepping onto the wagon plank and settling himself on the wide wooden seat, "time to pick up our girl."

One of the first things he'd done when coming out West was to capture and tame his wild mustang. But even after years of building trust with his old friend, the burnished stallion still had a bit of a rebellious streak. Tossing his silken mane with an indignant whinny, Copper turned his head and gave Harrison an annoyed stare, while adjusting to the pull of the wagon straps. The horse was more than capable of handling the heftier burden, though Harrison knew Copper hated it. Three other horses—two mares and another stallion—were stabled at the ranch, but Copper remained Harrison's favorite.

With a cluck of his tongue, he steered the horse and wagon toward town.

Jenny was due in before dusk, and Harrison would be there, waiting. It was the least he could do after the brave girl traveled all this way to marry him.

She's not a girl any longer.

No, Jenny would be all grown up. But he'd bet she was still that sweet, innocent young lady he'd met at Missy Brower's wedding in Bolster. Harrison had known right off she was the one for him. After a short courtship, he'd proposed, and she'd shyly accepted, allowing him to steal a kiss from rosy lips he swore he could still taste.

A scant few months of betrothal adjustment had gone by too fast, before he and his brother Frank left Illinois. For a chance at a better life, they'd set off for Colorado Territory to make their fortune in silver, from the mines their uncle left them in his will.

Faithfully, Jenny had waited for him. Very soon, she'd be in his arms.

As the wind died down and the air stilled, Harrison whipped off his Stetson and blotted the sweat from his brow with his forearm. He hadn't expected it to take so long to get the silver mines up and running. Talking Frank into joining him had been tricky enough, without years of struggles and hardship adding to the mix. At times, they'd come close to chucking it all and returning to Bolster with their tails between their legs. Only the dread of having to listen to a multitude of 'I told you so' from family and friends, kept them out West.

Harrison studied the barbed wire enclosing the south border of his land and caught the last glint of the low-hanging, late-afternoon sun. The fencing, brand-new, surrounded most of the three hundred acres Uncle Norton had left him. With the mines producing strongly, Frank's house almost finished, and Harrison's lacking only a few pieces of furniture, the Carter Brothers' future shone brightly. A plan to buy up more of the surrounding land was in the works as well.

And not a moment too soon, for a man needs room to grow a family. Harrison broke out in a wide grin as he raised his eyes to Bountiful Mountain and its lower summit that served as a backdrop to their ranchland. Judging by the sun's angle against the closest ridge, he should reach Little Creede in plenty of time to meet the stagecoach . . . and finally put his arms around Jenny.

Closer to town, the rough-scrabbled trail smoothed out and widened. Low brush and dried-out clumps of prairie grass gave way to greener patches speckled with late-spring wildflowers. Bonney Creek bubbled noisily, its runoff from the higher range dumping the last of the melted snow from the previous winter into its generous rock bed. Once he and Frank secured those extra acres, North Bonney would cross neatly over their extended property line. Someday his and Jenny's children would play in that creek.

Maybe even Frank's children too, if the cranky bugger ever cheered up enough to attract a woman who'd be willing to marry him. Harrison chuckled at the thought, and Copper snorted loudly as if in response.

Higher grasses opened to a trail fork leading to several other smaller silver mines located in the hills. Carter Brothers Mining sat higher than most, where the ore formed deeper but proved more plentiful. Yes, their workers had to toil a bit harder, but the rewards had been great. Satisfaction settled in Harrison's gut like smooth whiskey as he clicked his tongue and urged Copper into an easy canter, the wagon rolling along on well-oiled axles.

Up ahead, Little Creede's assortment of outbuildings and newer structures came into view. The town was growing a mite too speedily in his opinion. Harrison guided Copper along the rutted street, nodding to several miners he recognized as they ambled the wooden sidewalks. A pair of older women paused in front of Lomans' Mercantile and tittered behind work-roughened hands as he tipped his hat to them. He tried not to frown at the sight of their worn, faded day-dresses and shawls. No doubt these were miners' wives, come to town for supplies.

The life of a miner wasn't easy. He knew that firsthand. But his Jenny wouldn't suffer callused fingers and mud-stained half-boots. He'd make sure of it.

Harrison's mood lightened as the carriage station came into view. Excitement grew in his chest and he urged Copper at a faster clip down Main Street, noting the dust churning in the distance. The stagecoach, six horses pulling its load of travelers and baggage, would arrive very soon. The north end of Creede Station came into view and he couldn't wait a second more. He eased Copper into the wagon lot, barely pausing for a complete stop before he jumped down and flung the straps around the nearest post.

"Ho, Carter, you collectin' that lil' gal of yours?" Moe Parker called to Harrison as he strode toward the station.

Harrison didn't even slow down, passing the grizzled miner who owned one of the larger spreads between Little Creede and Silver Cache. "That I am, Parker." Harrison managed a perfunctory nod as his legs ate up the distance and the dirt path gave way to wooden planks, ignoring Moe's raspy cackle behind him. He probably looked like an overeager young fool, but it'd been nearly four years, and he could almost taste his Jenny's welcoming kisses . . .

The coach doors flew open and a few men jumped out, striding off toward the Lucky Lady Saloon down the street. Anxious for his first glimpse of Jenny, Harrison watched as two more travelers disembarked. The stage held roughly six to eight people and so few women traveled West by themselves. Surely Jenny would be easy to spot, with her silky brown curls and those huge blue eyes—

He hurried along the platform, squinting, worry forming along with the anticipation of seeing her again. What if something happened along the way? Ten days on a train was difficult enough, but over two weeks stuck on three different stages held its own kind of danger. Anything could have gone wrong.

A slight young woman with a crown of golden hair stepped from the coach. Something about her rang a distant bell in his memory. She held out her arms, a soft smile forming on her face. Harrison found his lips curving at the sight of a little girl with thick, bouncy curls as bright as the sun. The child jumped into her arms with a squeal of laughter and she swung the tot around amongst happy screeches.

Then she turned toward Harrison and her big blue eyes locked onto him. Her smile faded as she perched the tiny lass on her hip and slowly walked toward him.

Glancing over her head at the gaping door of the stage, Harrison frowned when no one else stepped out and the drivers began unloading baggage from the roof of the coach.

What the hell—?

He started for the nearest driver, when a gloved hand touched his arm.

"Are you Harrison Carter?"

The slender, golden-haired woman had stopped before him. Looking down, Harrison stared into eyes the exact same color and shape as Jenny's. But there the similarity ended. This woman was very young, barely big enough to carry the little girl who gazed at him with deep-brown eyes, her thumb in her mouth.

"Is your name Harrison?" the lady repeated, drawing his attention back to her delicately lovely face.

Harrison nodded briefly. "It is."

She expelled a breath and fished in her bag with her free hand, drawing out a slip of badly-wrinkled paper. "This is—I mean, I'm—" She stuttered to a stop, held out the paper with fingers that visibly trembled, and whispered, "I'm Retta. You might not remember—well, I'm Jenny's sister." She waved the note.

With a sudden sense of foreboding, Harrison took it from her.

Slowly he opened it, while she fidgeted beside him and the toddler she carried yawned and snuggled against her shoulder. Harrison started reading:

Dearest Harrison, please forgive me—

His head came up as a horrible, breaking sensation tore through his chest. He didn't want to read any further.

He had to.

Meeting the eyes of Jenny's sister—who would have been just a tad short of sixteen, last time he saw her—Harrison spotted the glitter of tears on her cheeks before he managed to return his attention to the letter.

A few minutes later, he crumpled the note in one shaking fist. Unable to spare another glance toward the bearer of the most agonizing news he had ever received, Harrison strode toward a trio of shabby bags piled on the platform, hefting two of them under one arm and grasping the third in his free hand. "These all you've got?" he ground out.

"I don't think I should—"

"*Are these all you've got?*" He tried and failed to keep the fury from his voice.

"Y-Yes," she stammered, as the child in her arms fussed.

Above the roaring in his ears he managed a rasping, "Fine. Follow me." He stomped off toward his wagon.

After several moments, he heard the hesitant click of her boots on the wooden platform behind him, the sound of the child's soft whimpers echoing in the gentle, early evening breeze.

Chapter 2

Dying. Grief held Harrison in an iron grip, and his heart ached at the thought of the beautiful girl he'd fallen in love with, wasting away over fifteen hundred miles from here. This was not how he'd envisioned the day ending. He flicked the reins to encourage Copper to get moving. Clamping his jaw, Harrison ground his back teeth together, struggling to keep from snarling at the girl, his supposed 'substitute bride,' sitting meekly on his right.

The sound of her timid voice reached his ears, along with the jingling of coins. "Jenny sent along her dowry." There was a short pause, before she hesitantly continued. "She wanted you to have it, Harrison."

He didn't dare look at her. Not yet. If he did, he might lash out in anger, and she was already frightened enough. She'd put as much distance between them as the wagon's bench seat allowed, holding her child protectively in her arms. Sucking a thumb, the little girl clutched the front of her mother's dress. Her big eyes filled with wariness as she stared at Harrison, before she finally gave in to sleep.

"Keep it," he gritted out, snapping the reins to get Copper moving faster.

He'd never harmed a woman or child in his entire life, and he wasn't about to start now. But how in the hell was he supposed to take this stranger as his wife, when his heart belonged to Jenny?

Jenny. Images of her lovely face flashed before his eyes, and he inhaled deeply, trying to control his pain and anger at the loss of his dream. Jenny had spoken fondly of her sister in their letters, and he knew all about the drifter who'd passed through their little hometown, seducing Retta and leaving her with child, before riding off again. Considered a loose young woman, she'd become a disgrace in Bolster.

Now she was his burden. What was Jenny thinking?

Am I really going to marry her?

Did he even have a choice? In her letter, Jenny had pleaded with him to wed Retta. She'd called him a good and honorable man. A man she could trust to provide for her sister and niece so she could die at peace, knowing they'd be well cared for. What kind of a man would he be if he threw them onto the streets?

A real bastard, that's what. Rounding the bend, Reverend Matias's church came into view, ending Harrison's internal conversation. "Let's just get it done," he muttered under his breath, tugging on Copper's reins.

Hopping to the ground, he finally met Retta's blue-eyed gaze, reminding him so much of Jenny's. Which angered him all over again, and for a moment he couldn't speak as he fought to reel his temper back in. But he was angry with everyone right now.

Jenny.

This girl and her child.

God.

Even the damned Reverend for what he was about to do, tying him to a woman not of his choosing.

Squaring his shoulders, Harrison walked to her side of the wagon and lifted his arms. "Give me the girl." The words came out gruffer than he'd intended.

Retta lifted her chin in a defiant manner. Her clear blue eyes clouded with suspicion. "Why?"

He blinked. Her sharp response wasn't what he'd expected. Retta's timidity so far hadn't been very inspiring, but now it was as if he saw her for the first time. The woman staring down at him appeared ready to do battle. Pink stained her pretty cheeks and her lush full lips pursed in annoyance. Long, pale curls escaped from her bonnet, framing a very appealing, sweet face.

His blood heated.

And that, too, angered him.

"We're getting married." Harrison didn't even try to hide his annoyance when he spoke to her. "Now, give me the girl."

For a moment, he thought she might refuse, and almost hoped she would, even if that meant letting Jenny down. But then Retta's shoulders drooped, transforming her into the meek woman he'd met at the coach station. She nodded and handed down her daughter.

A sliver of guilt tamped his anger to a slow boil as he took the sleeping child and tucked her in the crook of one arm, holding his free hand up to help Retta from the wagon.

Twenty minutes later, he exited the church a married man. The Reverend hadn't blinked an eye when Harrison showed up with a stranger to marry, though he must have wondered. But he didn't so much as ask whose child

Harrison held throughout the ceremony, while a tearful bride spoke her vows.

What have I done? Retta couldn't quite believe she'd wed the grim man at her side. He'd barely spoken a word to her since she'd arrived on the stagecoach. And when he did, he seemed furious. During the short ceremony, hard steel threaded his vows. It'd taken every ounce of strength in her not to snatch Adeline from his arms and run out of the church.

"Mama," Addie said sleepily, snuggling into her arms, "thiwsty."

Retta pressed a kiss to her little girl's forehead, then gathered much-needed courage, addressing the man she'd married only hours earlier. "May I have some water?"

Her breath froze in her lungs when she met his icy gray eyes. A scowl darkened his face. "There's a canteen tucked under your seat," he growled.

"Thank you," she whispered, hating the insipid sound of her own voice. She'd spent years being ridiculed by the 'good' townsfolk of Bolster. Abused by her father, too. Yet she'd managed to hang on to her pride, keeping her head high and her eyes level with every scornful stare she'd met.

What was it about *this* man that intimidated her so?

Breaking contact with his piercing stare, she placed Addie onto the wide spot between them, then reached under the wooden bench to locate the canteen. After quenching her thirst, her daughter snuggled back down in her arms and fell asleep.

Retta tenderly brushed the curls from Addie's face. *Poor darling.* She hadn't yet napped this afternoon. Overwhelmed with love for her babe, she pressed a kiss to her chubby little cheek.

When Harrison spoke again, the deep resonance of his voice sent a tiny shiver through her. Wondering what her wedding night would bring, her thoughts flashed back to her experience with Addie's father, Cal. Unpleasant memories, not something she was eager to repeat.

Will I have a choice?

"Retta, are you listening?" Harrison's exasperated tone snapped her mind from thoughts of the past.

She met his eyes over the top of her daughter's sleeping head, hugging her tighter as though that'd save her from her husband's temper. It hadn't worked against Papa and she doubted it'd work against this man either, who appeared upset with her. The question was, how bad would it be?

As long as he doesn't touch my baby, I can survive anything.

He scraped back thick, brown hair with a broad, long-fingered hand. "Tell me about Jenny."

Retta found it impossible to look away from his commanding stare. She wet her dry lips before saying, "Everything should have been in the letter."

Harrison's eyes lowered to her mouth. His jaw flexed before he slapped the reins to get the horse moving faster. "Humor me."

With a deep breath to settle her nerves, Retta spent the next hour, the length of time it took to reach his ranch, to talk about her sister. The happiness they'd shared growing up, the sorrow of their mother's death, and their father's downward spiral into a bottle. Jenny's sickness that'd come upon her so viciously. Everything, all the way up to Retta's departure at the train station. The only thing she didn't discuss was her father's escalating need to 'beat the sin' out of her, and her disastrous liaison with Cal.

Retta's voice cut off when she caught sight of Harrison's home, tucked at the foothills of a low mountain range. A medium-sized ranch nestled in a cluster of trees, with a wide, shaded porch facing the magnificent view. Jenny had said Harrison was successful in the silver mines, but this was more than she'd envisioned.

The buckboard rolled to a stop before a long iron gate, and without saying a word, Harrison hopped down to open it, then pulled the wagon through, closing the gate behind them. It was getting late and the setting sun graced the area in soft shadows of reds and golds, giving the home a calming, picturesque quality. In contrast, a cloud of tension hung in the air between them, growing thicker and darker with each passing minute.

Retta nervously licked her lips again, uneasiness churning harder in her stomach. Shivers snaked up her spine. What would this man expect of her tonight? Their wedding night. *You can do this, Retta,* she assured herself, *just close your eyes and think of something else.*

Harrison took Addie from her before helping her down. The jostling movement woke her daughter, and a few drowsy moments passed before she realized she wasn't being held by her mama any longer. With a wail, her lower lip trembling, she held out her hands as fat tears fell from her big brown eyes, so identical to Cal's.

Frowning fiercely, Harrison eased Addie back into Retta's arms. Collecting her bags from the bed of the wagon, he strode up the steps and deposited them on the wide-planked porch before unlatching the sturdy split-door and flinging both open.

Rooted to the spot, Retta told her feet to get moving, but they weren't listening. As hard as she tried, she couldn't force herself to enter his home, and into a life she didn't choose, a life with this implacable stranger. All the things Jenny told her about him had been wrong. He was neither kind nor gentle. Whoever he'd been years ago, he wasn't that same man today.

Too late. There'd be no going back for her now. That'd ended when she'd allowed Cal to doggedly coax her into submission under the stars on a hot summer night.

Harrison pinned her with stony eyes, brows drawn down. "Coming?"

Retta gulped, but slowly stepped onto the porch like a prisoner on her way to the gallows, which was exactly how she felt. By the time she approached the threshold of the narrow but functional foyer, anger seemed to ooze from him.

Silently he scooped up her bags. "This way."

Trying to ignore her rising anxiety as he led her into the house, Retta took in the spacious parlor. Harrison lit one of the wall lamps, filling the dim interior with the faint smell of kerosene and a soft golden glow. Although lacking any sort of feminine touches, the room appeared comfortable. A stone fireplace covered part of one wall. A tufted sofa and matching chair took up space across from a lovely formal dining set, framed by a huge picture window, perfectly smooth without a single ripple. She couldn't conceive the cost of glass for such a window. Many of the fancier houses in Bolster couldn't boast an extravagance like this.

Harrison strode from the room and she followed, more intimidated than ever. He brought her to a long, wide kitchen, taking a moment to light another sconce. Floor-to-ceiling shelves on one side of the sink area held an assortment of pottery and dishes. A simple block table and four chairs filled the middle of the room. On the other side, a thick wooden slab with a satiny finish provided a functional place to knead bread. Shiny copper pots and pans hung from a rack near the cast-iron cooking stove, which looked new and unused.

Her gaze lingered on its fancy scrollwork. Cooking on such a luxury would be a true joy, and for the first time since she'd boarded the train in Chicago, Retta felt a rush of anticipation. She loved to bake.

One corner held wooden barrels, and a narrow door against the far wall had been left ajar, cracked open a good six inches. She stared curiously, and ventured, "Root cellar?"

"Yes. Could be bigger, deeper. More shelves, too. But it's enough for now." He eyed Addie, snoring softly on her shoulder. "I suppose the girl still nurses?"

Retta felt her cheeks heat at the very private question. "N-No, Adeline can drink milk from a cup."

Her new husband grunted. "Might consider an ice box, then. I'll order one from Silver Cache."

"Where would you get ice?"

"Got access to plenty of ice up there." Harrison jerked his chin toward the window and the mountain range beyond. Along the higher elevation, she spotted snow. Mesmerized by the sight, she perused the craggy dips and soaring summits.

Then she started when Harrison advanced toward her, his eyes on Addie.

Retta stiffened. As exhausted as she was, if he tried to harm her girl in any way, she'd fight him.

A gruff chuckle near her ear indicated he'd reached her. "Relax, Retta. I don't bite."

He smelled of leather and dark spice. Such a combination under different circumstances would have appealed to her. Right now, she just wanted it, *and him*, to go away.

His broad chest brushed her shoulder when he continued past her, carrying her bags down a short hallway and disappearing through a door. Her heart raced as apprehension filled her, wondering if the room was for her and Adeline, or her and Harrison.

Of course it's for me to share with Harrison. I'm his wife now.

A heartbeat later, he returned, a determined expression on his face. Stopping in front of her, far too close, he peered down at her with unreadable eyes. "It's getting late. Put the child down for the night. Use the room across from ours, on the left. Then go to bed, you've had a long trip."

Across from ours . . .

That answered her question about the sleeping arrangements. She ran her tongue across her teeth, searching for some moisture so she could speak. "Maybe I should stay with Adeline tonight. She might wake up frightened, being in a strange place."

Harrison's face hardened. "No. You're my wife, your place is with me." He indicated a back door at the end of the hallway. "I'm going to tend to my horse. When I return, I'll expect to find you in my bed."

With that, he strode away without a backward glance and slammed out the door.

Retta sucked in a deep breath, her legs shaking beneath her as the finality of her situation crashed down on her.

Oh, Lord. What have I gotten myself into?

Pausing outside the back porch, Harrison stomped the excess dirt from his boots. He'd remained in the barn far longer than intended, brushing Copper until he gleamed, then lingering while the feisty mustang chomped oats and hay. Scraping out hard-packed muck from Copper's hooves, digging stones from the wagon wheels . . . it all took time.

Stop stalling. He had a wife waiting for him inside. Not the one he'd expected, but she was his nevertheless. He had to deal with her sooner or later. *Later, preferably.*

With a self-deprecating snort, he entered the hallway leading to the kitchen. Prying off his boots, he dropped them next to the stove; first one, then the other, each dull *thud* on the floor echoing his bleak mood.

What now? The woman was afraid of him, not that he blamed her. He hadn't exactly been welcoming toward her or the girl.

The girl. The child had a name. *Adeline.*

He scrubbed a hand through his hair and blew out an impatient breath.

Not only was he wed to a woman he didn't love, he was an instant father. To a dainty little female, no less. Hell, if he were a bettin' man, the money would have been on his brother ending up in a shotgun marriage. Frank was as wild as Harrison was steady.

And there'd be no living with the ornery cuss when he found out.

Enough moonlight filtered through the window that Harrison didn't bother with a lamp as he headed for the sink. A few hard jerks on the pump filled the tin washbowl halfway to the rim, enough to scrub his hands and soak his head. Straightening, he tossed back his damp strands, sending drops flying. Harrison sluiced the excess off the back of his neck, the cool water soothing some of his tension.

The lone wall sconce in the parlor still glowed, and he strode over to lower the wick until it blinked out. Women didn't much like the smell of smoldering kerosene, so he flipped the snuffer in place to keep the smoke from stinking up the air, then headed down the back hallway toward his room.

Our room.

Harrison found himself dragging his heels as he thought of the woman who waited for him in the big feather bed he'd ordered from Silver Cache a few months ago. When he'd built the frame and set the bed-slats, he'd anticipated the happy reaction of his bride-to-be. Maneuvering the thick mattress in place and smoothing on the soft linens he'd dried in the sun, he'd pictured the delight on her beautiful face. A handmade quilt he'd also found, bright with embroidered flowers and tiny birds, completed the marriage bed he'd share with—

Not Jenny. Pausing at the half-open door, Harrison inhaled deeply. Squeezing his eyes shut, he pinched the bridge of his nose between his finger and thumb. His bride's pale, frightened face etched onto the backs of his lids. *I can't do this.*

Turning, he trudged back to the kitchen and the bottle of Old James he kept under the sink. Pulling a tumbler from the side cabinet, he splashed in two fingers of bourbon and downed it in a single gulp. Harrison eyed the remaining fifth, which looked to be a goodly amount. He had bought the bottle right before Christmas, and he'd never been much of a drinker.

That might just be changing tonight.

Wiping his damp mouth on the back of his sleeve, Harrison poured another.

Chapter 3

Retta came awake abruptly, jerking upright in the bed. She must have dozed off despite the attack of nerves that had kept her hunched in the pillows, clutching the bedsheets until her knuckles throbbed. Exhaustion had gotten the better of her.

Shoving tangled hair out of her eyes, she peered across the room toward the door she'd propped open so she could hear Addie if she awoke anytime throughout the night. Earlier, half-spooked, she'd set a lamp burning on the low dresser against the opposite wall before climbing into bed.

She strained to hear any noise, any tiny sound of distress. When Addie's sweet little snores reached her ears, a sign she slept deeply, a hiss of relief escaped Retta's lips.

The darling hadn't raised a bit of fuss when Retta had laid her down, asleep almost before she could fasten a fresh diaper and pull a nightgown over her girl's curly little head. She'd trimmed the wick in the wall sconce until it burned low, then tucked Addie in securely.

Fully awake now, Retta did her best to relax into the pillows. A futile attempt. She wouldn't easily fall asleep again. A faint clinking in the kitchen told her Harrison had finally finished his nighttime chores. She couldn't imagine what he might be doing. She only knew he'd soon enter the bedroom. Once here, would he shed his clothes and pounce on her?

Fresh panic had her breaking out in icy chills. *Maybe if I pretend to be asleep, he'll leave me be.*

His image flashed in her mind. The man was so big and brawny. Much larger than she remembered from the one time she'd caught a glimpse of him back in Bolster when he'd shown up to collect Jenny for a barn dance. Hard-muscled from laboring in his mines, no doubt. His wide hands, long-fingered and work-hardened . . . how would they feel against her tender skin? Would he be gentle or cruel? What if those hands slapped and his fingers pinched and probed, instead of caressed?

Like Cal.

God, stop thinking about it. She was married now, legal and binding. Her husband could do as he liked and nobody would stop him. A wedding ring gave him power over her.

Nausea gripped Retta's stomach, pushing bile up into her throat. It was all so unfair. First Cal. Then her sweet sister falling ill. Now this. Trapped forever in a loveless marriage to a hard man.

Her eyes burned with unshed tears as she tortured herself with a litany of the ways Harrison Carter could cause her pain, and it didn't matter what Jenny had said about his warm, caring nature. Nor did it matter how gently he'd held her little girl while they'd stood before the preacher and repeated vows neither one of them might ever be able to keep.

Scuttling across the bed, her cotton nightgown snagging around her knees, Retta's singular thought was to scoop up her child, the only bright spot in her otherwise drab life, and escape out the door. To run as fast and as far as her legs could take them.

She managed to untangle herself from the voluminous material and gain her feet, only to shrink back in apprehension when the hallway floorboards creaked, closer and closer.

Then, a heavy exhale right outside the slightly ajar door. *Harrison.*

Teeth chattering, Retta dove for the bed and burrowed under the covers. Eyes squeezed closed, the phrase *pretend you're asleep, pretend you're asleep, pretend you're asleep* became a mantra in her mind.

The sound of the door clicking shut sent her into fresh panic. A few seconds later, the mattress dipped on the far side of the bed. In the anxiety-laden quiet, she heard the rustling of clothes, the chink of a belt buckle, the whisper of a shirt. She breathed in and out as quietly as possible. Biting her bottom lip to stop it from trembling, Retta curled into the tiniest ball of shivering flesh possible, trying to will herself into unconsciousness.

Sudden heat engulfed her shoulders, her spine, the backs of her legs, as she felt him nestle close. One large, muscled arm curved around her waist and tugged her against his *completely* naked body.

She swallowed a whimper, her limbs locked so tightly she ached. He adjusted slightly, as if searching for the most comfortable dip in the feathers, his wriggling movements fusing him against her quaking frame.

"I know you're awake, Retta." His deep rasp vibrated in her ear.

Startled, she jerked, which brought her even closer to his hot, firm flesh. Refusing to contemplate the meaning of that heavy firmness, now pressing into the small of her back, Retta froze. Still, a tiny sob burst from her throat.

He stroked her arm with fingers every bit as rough-hewn as she'd imagined. "Shh. You don't know me." His mouth stirred the hair at her nape. "I don't know you." He brought her around to face him, and the shock of this new position made her gasp and slam her eyes shut.

Sighing, he cupped the side of her head with one wide palm and pushed her cheek into his shoulder, his thumb rubbing along her jaw. His other hand slipped over her nightgown and rested lightly on her hip.

The heat of his fingers burned through the thin cotton material. His nakedness, pressed against her, was terrifying, yet at the same time the gentle way he held her was a comfort.

"Look at me." The command in his tone left her no choice but to obey.

With a nervous gulp, she opened her eyes and met his level gaze. In the dimness from the lamplight, his eyes glittered, their expression shrouded. The smoky hint of bourbon washed over her face.

Her heart sank. He'd been in the kitchen, drinking. Heaven only knew how much. Liquor and lust made for a very bad combination.

"I'm not the kind of man to demand or force. Nothing's gonna happen tonight."

She blinked. Could she believe him?

His hands were careful with her, easy. Non-threatening. "I can't—" He broke off and ground his teeth so hard she heard them gnash. Finally, he muttered, "I know you had a rough time of it. I saw Jenny's note. You're not ready. Neither am I."

Her cheeks heated from such unfamiliar and intimate contact as they lay facing each other. The man was a contradiction she couldn't figure out, one moment a growling bear, the next a gentle giant. In a situation like this, what kind of man would put off taking advantage of a woman whose body he had every right to use?

"As my wife," he continued, in the same easy tone, "you'll eventually have to get used to my touch."

Retta's tense muscles slowly loosened. She wouldn't be able to deny her new husband forever. Inhaling, she detected a trace of lye soap and the natural musk of a man who worked hard. The mixture of scents further soothed her.

Hesitantly, she let her fingers unclench, though they remained pressed against his chest. The skin covering all those muscles felt smooth, with a hint of silky hair.

He was so warm that Retta relaxed.

"That's better." He brushed at her curls. "I'm sorry we got off to a rough start. I won't lie to you, this is hard for me. I . . . care for your sister." He exhaled roughly. "I don't much remember you, but if this is Jenny's final wish then we must abide by it."

He tipped up her chin with two fingers. "You agree with that?"

Retta searched his intense gaze for any sign of treachery and found none. Slowly, she nodded. "I— Yes, Harrison."

"All right, then." He brought her cheek back to his shoulder, and she felt a yawn shudder through him. "Tomorrow we'll sit down and talk. Figure out what we need to do to make this work." His arms kept her pinned to his side.

Too weary to worry about their intimate position, she mumbled, "Goodnight, Harrison."

"Goodnight, Retta," came his soft reply.

The faint sound of snoring awoke him, right before he became aware of the warm woman next to him, her silken arm draped across his bare stomach, her cheek resting close to his heart. But what surprised Harrison the most was to find himself holding her.

He lay perfectly still, not wanting to disturb the moment, enjoying the feel of Retta pressed against him. One of her long, slender legs, free from the constraints of the cotton gown she wore, hitched across his thigh. A smile curved his lips. The cumbersome material, meant to cover her from neck to toes, had failed in its attempt to keep him disinterested.

Inhaling her clean, fresh scent, Harrison entwined one of her soft curls around his finger. It felt right nice having a woman in his bed. Unbidden, his shaft hardened. He could no more stop his body's reaction to her, than stop breathing.

Always mindful of his innocent bride-to-be back home waiting for him, he hadn't lain with anyone, though he'd used his hand when desperate urges overtook him. As often as the girls at the saloon tried to entice him, Harrison had resisted, much to his brother's amusement. Frank wasn't under the same constraint and often partook liberally of their charms.

Tucking the pale tendril behind his wife's ear, Harrison let his thumb linger against the base of her throat, all too aware she wasn't the one he loved, but his body didn't understand the difference. It'd be too easy to tug her beneath him and enjoy his new bride. She was no virgin, and he doubted she'd deny him.

Disgusted with his train of thought, as well as his desire for her, he lifted Retta's arm off his stomach and placed it by her side, then slid from the bed, careful not to wake her.

Though she was now his wife, he knew she wasn't ready for his touch. Jenny hadn't actually spelled it out in her letters, but he'd been able to read between the lines. Retta hadn't exactly been a willing partner when her daughter was conceived.

Scowling, he raked his fingers through his hair, studying the delicate beauty asleep in his bed, determined to ignore the reaction of his body. Overcome with the sudden urge to track this Cal down and put a bullet between his eyes, Harrison figured if he ever saw the man, he might do just that.

Spinning away from temptation, Harrison quickly dressed, shoving his swollen appendage into his trousers and carefully buttoning up. He'd promised Retta patience, and he was a man of his word. Heading into the kitchen, he set kindling and wood in the stove to start heating the griddles. Three eggs, nestled in their basket and collected from yesterday, weren't enough for all of them, so he'd check his laying hens before he began anything else. Whatever he ended up collecting could be cooked up alongside slabs of the pork shoulder from Sunday dinner.

Frank planned on stopping by today to meet Jenny. *Well, this oughta be fun.* Self-restraint wasn't his brother's best quality, and who knew how he'd react to finding Retta instead? Harrison didn't want her upset. Even though she wasn't the woman he'd expected, she was now his responsibility, as well as the child. Harrison took his duties seriously and would do right by both.

Grief tightened his chest as he recalled fond memories of Jenny and their far too brief time together. It was hard to believe that only yesterday, he had awoken filled with happiness and hope for the future.

A sigh shook his chest. *Yesterday seems so far away.*

Harrison trudged outside to the chicken coop to scrounge for more eggs.

A few minutes after he returned to the kitchen, he heard the girl stirring. Certain Retta was still sleeping, no doubt worn out from her long journey, Harrison set the half-full basket down on the floor and headed into the spare bedroom. The tot had crawled from the bed and now stood in the middle of the room, one fist clutching the edge of a blanket. The rest of it dragged behind her tiny frame.

When her sleepy gaze landed on Harrison, it held no fear this time.

Harrison vowed to keep it that way. If he was going to persuade his new bride to stay with him and make this marriage work, the first step would be winning over her daughter. *Careful, all good intentions pave the road to perdition.*

Plastering on a fake smile, not ready to admit he knew nothing of how to handle a child, he said brightly, "Are you hungry, little lass?"

Addie nodded. Thrusting her thumb into her mouth, she tugged the end of the blanket to her face and mumbled, "Potty."

Harrison sniffed. From the smell of it, a diaper change was already in order. His day was just getting better and better. For one desperate moment, he considered waking up Retta, then remembered the dark circles under her pretty blue eyes and the weariness in her voice.

He rolled his shoulders back. *I run a profitable silver mine. I can handle one small child.*

The closer he got to Addie, the less certain he was of that. The babe smelled worse than a dead carcass that'd baked in the sun a good long while. Glancing around for a clean diaper, he spotted one of the newfangled things lying on the dresser, along with a change of clothes Retta must have laid out.

"Potty," the girl whined again.

"Yeah, I'm working on it. Hold your hosses." Harrison scooped up the items off the dresser, turning back to Addie. The stench of that soiled diaper grew stronger as he approached. He wrinkled his nose. "What *did* your mother feed you last night?"

It couldn't have been anything good.

At the sharpness of his tone, the girl's lower lip trembled as her eyes welled up.

Forcing another smile to his lips, Harrison squatted down in front of Addie. "Hey, sweetheart, you ready for some grub?"

The child blinked, two tears tracking down her cheeks. Then with a sniffle, she nodded. Tossing the diaper and clothing across his shoulder, Harrison tried to tug the blanket from her pudgy hands, but Addie wouldn't let go, instead looking perilously close to crying again.

"All right, you can keep it." Wrapping the blanket loosely around her, Harrison scooped Addie up and strode briskly down the hall, over to the fireplace. Laying the child on the woven rug in front of it, he noted sourly how the diaper had leaked onto the blanket. "Let me get some water to clean you up with." He pointed a finger and ordered, "You stay here."

Harrison hurried to the foyer and lifted the pitcher of water he usually kept on the spare washstand, pouring some into a bowl. When he turned around, he nearly stumbled over Addie, who was now standing right behind him, still hanging on to the end of the dirty, smelly blanket. He frowned, not used to being disobeyed.

The toddler plucked her thumb from her mouth and burbled, "Hungwy."

Harrison eyed the trail of pee Addie had left in her wake, the hem of her little nightgown damp. The overstuffed diaper had fallen off about halfway across the parlor and now lay in a stinking mess on his oak planked floor.

"Holy. Hell." Again, he thought about waking Retta, then dismissed the idea. "I can handle this."

"Hungwy," Addie repeated with a pout.

"Yeah, I heard you the first time," he muttered to himself, feeling a bit panicked. Reentering the parlor, Harrison plopped the bowl of water onto the table and collected babe and blanket, placing both on the polished surface. "Let's get you cleaned up." He refused to think about what now smeared across his former fine piece of dining furniture.

"Mama," the child wailed, twisting around and trying to crawl off the table. Her poop-covered bottom stuck out from beneath the filthy gown.

Grabbing the girl by the leg as gently as possible, Harrison slipped his hand between her birdlike shoulder blades and eased her over onto part of the blanket. "Adeline, lay still," he said sternly, hoping his usage of her full name would compel her to obey.

Addie stared accusingly, her lower lip trembling worse than a drunk gunslinger's shootin' arm.

Tension gripped him. If things had played out the way they were supposed to, he'd still be in bed, holding his exhausted and well-loved wife in his arms. How in blazes had his life come to this?

Jenny's lovely image flashed in his mind, and his heart constricted.

Because Jenny asked me to, that's how.

Addie sniffled again, but finally did as commanded, giving Harrison a chance to dampen a cloth and clean her up, before tossing the soiled rag and her gown onto the floor. Then he cursed under his breath, recalling what both contained. A puddle of pee had settled into the wood from where the child dribbled across the room. Well, he'd have to deal with it later.

Somehow, he managed to hold down the squirming Addie long enough to get the diaper on and tied in front, willing it to stay put. Her pinafore buttoned down the front and this he managed to wrestle on despite her wriggles.

He hefted the child to return her to the rug so he could clean up the mess littering his table and floor. As he swung her into his arms, Addie patted his cheeks with both hands and smiled at him sweetly. In that moment, she looked so much like her mother that Harrison found himself smiling back.

Right about then, his annoying brother charged through the door separating foyer and parlor, coming to a screeching halt within smelling distance of the soiled diaper. His rounded eyes took in everything, brows arched quizzically.

As usual, Frank resembled a wild man, his full beard unkempt and his long dark hair in knots. God only knew what he'd been doing that had torn out both knees of his pants. His shirt was equally ragged, the wool stained and badly wrinkled. He stank of cheap perfume and blood.

Something involving women, whiskey, and no doubt brawling. Then again, today *was* hog-butcherin' day. Might explain the blood stink.

Addie blinked at Harrison, then at Frank. Her tiny mouth opened and she let loose with a screeching, "Mama."

From a sound sleep, Retta shot up at the sound of her daughter's cry. "Oh my God." She unwound herself from the heavy quilt and made it to the spare bedroom before her mind had fully cleared from sleep. Her heart sank at the sight of an empty bed. Images of Harrison hitting her baby made her stomach wrench, and she doubled over for the briefest second to catch her breath before charging out of the room and running down the hallway.

Reaching the parlor, she took in the morning sun pouring in from the largest window. Her father would have beat her for sleeping so late. Then she spotted Harrison, holding her wriggling daughter, who waved her arms around like a dervish, shrieking at the top of her lungs.

By the time Retta's fuddled mind registered the intimidating man in the doorway, she was about ready to faint. With his mane of hair and full beard, the behemoth resembled a black bear she'd once seen in a painting hanging on the wall of Bolster's First Bank and Trust.

Retta quickly closed the distance between her and her child, facing a scowling Harrison.

She held out her arms, locking her shaking knees to remain upright. "P-Please give her to me." Despite her enforced bravado, there was no stopping her instinctive flinch when he made a move toward her. Eyes pinched shut, the sound of her panicked breathing roared in her ears before she managed to wrestle her emotions under control.

Opening her eyes, Retta took in Harrison's glowering expression. His flexing jaw made him appear to be chewing on a particularly tough piece of meat. Without a word, he dumped Addie into her arms. Immediately quieting, her daughter clung to Retta's neck, shuddering and damp from sobbing.

Retta glanced toward the bearded man and found a matching scowl on his face. Edging back, she reached behind her with her free arm and gripped the corner of an occasional table. What would these men do to her and Adeline? Making amends to Harrison had to be her first priority. Her husband could do whatever he wanted with her.

She licked her lips. Unable to meet Harrison's penetrating stare, she focused instead on his chest. If it was just her, she'd hold her ground, but she had her little girl to think about. "I'm sorry I overslept." She swallowed hard. "It won't happen again."

The silence in the room grew thick with tension, and Retta braced herself, shielding her daughter against the blow she feared was coming.

The deep voice of the man across the room growled out, "What the hell, Harrison?"

Retta instinctively met his stare. But instead of ire, his frown held confusion. Her gaze lowered to the floor, holding her baby closer. Everything had happened so fast she'd been running on instinct, but now her mind scrambled for a way out of this mess. What could she say to appease these two so they didn't hurt her and Addie?

"Not now, Frank." Harrison's voice sounded weary, but it didn't hold the anger she'd expected. "Retta, look at me," he said softly.

Addie had grown calm, her thumb in her mouth, her other hand playing with Retta's hair. But though her worry had receded some, Retta couldn't bring herself to look at him.

"Retta," Harrison repeated, placing a finger under her chin and forcing her head up. The gray eyes that met hers were gentle. "I would never hurt you or Adeline. You don't have to fear me. Ever."

Could she trust his words? After every brutal beating from her drunken papa, he'd promise the same thing. But that never stopped it from happening again.

Still resting his fingers under her chin, his eyes searched her face. "Would you like to meet my brother?" Before she could utter a word, Harrison nodded toward the bearded mountain man. "Frank, I'd like to present my wife, Retta Pierce Carter. And this little cutie is her daughter, Adeline. My daughter now."

The way he claimed her and Addie, the sudden, possessive gleam in his eyes, caused her emotions to churn.

Footsteps drew near them. Retta found herself meeting another set of familiar gray eyes.

When Harrison's touch fell away, she felt a moment of regret, then resolutely faced his brother.

Discover More:

You can find all our books on Amazon. Just search for CiCi Cordelia!

Visit our website: **CiCiWriter.com** – Where we are *Writing from the Heart*

Find us on Amazon and Facebook: Author CiCi Cordelia

Connect with us on Instagram: instagram.com/cicicordduet/